My Train Leaves at Three

My Train Leaves at Three

a novel

Natalie Guerrero

ONE WORLD
NEW YORK

One World
An imprint of Random House
A division of Penguin Random House LLC
1745 Broadway, New York, NY 10019
oneworldlit.com
penguinrandomhouse.com

Hardcover ISBN 978-0-593-97733-0
Ebook ISBN 978-0-593-97734-7

Printed in the United States of America on acid-free paper

2 4 6 8 9 7 5 3 1

First Edition

BOOK TEAM: Production editor: Andy Lefkowitz • Managing editor: Rebecca
Berlant • Production manager: Mark Maguire • Copy editor: Mark McCauslin
• Proofreaders: Alissa Fitzgerald, Karina Jha, and Brianna Lopez

Book design by Susan Turner

The authorized representative in the EU for product safety and compliance is
Penguin Random House Ireland, Morrison Chambers, 32 Nassau Street,
Dublin D02 YH68, Ireland. https://eu-contact.penguin.ie

For those of us who live at the shoreline

—AUDRE LORDE, "A Litany for Survival"

Mejorar la raza. It's this Dominican phrase my tía taught me when I was a kid, dark-skinned with ashy elbows and two missing front teeth. Translated to English, it means *to better the race*. That's what I'm thinking about, mostly, while Rory's inside me. That's what is replaying like a broken record in my mind while he pounds into me with the front of his hips despite how many times I've told him the Jack Rabbit™ doesn't turn me on.

When I was a kid, I thought I'd be rich and famous by now. I thought that I'd have a record deal or a poodle or a pool somewhere out in California. Enough money in my bank account to airlift my mother out of our tiny apartment in Washington Heights, and get my frizzy hair blown out twice a week, and buy my sister, Nena, the Mercedes-Benz she always wanted. But I'm still broke, and barely even singing in the shower, and my hair is a mess, and my sister is dead, so nothing I imagined has come true.

I don't want to think about my dead sister or my empty checking account, though. It's my birthday today, and those thoughts don't feel very celebratory at all.

Instead, I change positions and roll my tongue into a U shape and push it up to the roof of my mouth so that my saliva pools around it. I feel the warmth, the bubbles, the salty flavor of the platano chips I scarfed down for lunch yesterday come forward until the wet hunk of fluid smacks down onto Rory's pink sticky skin. I wrap my legs, lanky and thin now, around his body and I move my hips up and down, faster and harder, until I see the light behind his eyes turn on and he's finished.

"*Xiomara,*" Rory moans my name with wonder. Three more times then, sweetly, pronouncing every syllable like it's a dessert. To Rory, I've always been some foreign delicacy. Something to be consumed after dinner. To me, though, Rory's like a flu shot. A chore. Something that if I'm lucky, pretty soon I'm going to forget to come back to altogether.

"I have to go," I say while Rory lies on his back and slings his arm around my waist. It weighs like a ton of bricks, and I can't help but feel like he's trying to drown the little life I have left in me. "Come on." I tap Rory's arm twice with two fingers since he's still not moving. "I can't be late."

Before my shift at Alek's print shop today, I'm singing and waiting tables at Ellen's Stardust Diner. It's a kitschy '50s-themed restaurant in Times Square full of singing servers and a nauseatingly large menu of American classics. In other words, Ellen's is a place where I *and every other Broadway wannabee* congregate to show off our talents, serve pancakes to tourists, and hope to hell we get discovered.

"Saundra will kill me if I'm late again," I groan. Saundra runs the show over at Ellen's. She's one of those women I'd hate to be, full of metallic blue eye shadow and unfulfilled dreams at age fifty.

"You're not gonna go on like this forever . . . are you?" Rory says. His voice is cold like the bottom of Mami's metal ice tray. I grab his arm then and toss it off the side of me. The black hairs of his wrists are sweaty and stuck to his skin like they've been gelled down with Murray's Edgewax.

"What do you mean?" I ask. Though I know what he means—that I'm just a girl who is hanging on by a thread to a life I dream of but will never have. Still, I want him to say it. I like when my men speak plainly to me.

"I just think it's crazy that you like the sound of your own voice so much that you actually think the rest of the world should pay you to hear it." He pronounces the *P* in *pay* hard enough that spit flies out his mouth and onto my forehead.

"We should probably stop doing this," I say matter-of-factly, wiping him off. My sister always said the one good thing about me was that I'm never two ways about anything at all. That once I make a decision, it's done.

I sit up, and when I look back at Rory, he's laughing like his dick's so good he knows I'll be back for more. Behind his eyes, though, I see a hurt, and I decide it's pathetic to see him there like that, with cum on his stomach, trying to pin down his emotions through his hissing and hysteria. When he starts talking again, I can't hear anything he's saying. My toes are too loud, buzzing, screaming at me to get out of the bed and onto the refuge of the hardwood floor. When I finally do stand up and walk away, he doesn't grab for me. That's how I know for sure we've both had our fill.

I slip my jeans on, long and baggy to hide the subtlety of my hips, and jam my naked, unpedicured toes inside my Nike Dunks, the Girls Don't Cry limited edition, which feels, in a twisted way, almost too fitting for this moment, then grab my jacket from off the back of a black office chair full of clean and dirty clothes. I'm loud when I walk out of his bedroom, quiet when I'm in the hallway, where I skip down the stairs and breathe out another thing gone for good. I'm not afraid of losing anything anymore. Grief lives all over my body.

Bennett Park is cold in the winter. Like hell with a chill that never quits. It's still dark outside when I open the door and the Fort Washington air slaps me in the face. I like these small sensations—the wind and the frostbite, the tingling at my ears. They bring me back inside my body after spending so much time on Rory's wretched planet.

I cut through the grass to get to the A train. Pedro, my old neighbor, is running past me with a black JanSport backpack that he's had since we were in seventh grade and a coffee dripping down the side of a blue-and-white to-go cup. He sucks his teeth while the hot drink burns the whites under his fingernails. He's probably late for work again. We all are.

Even without the sun, the Heights has already turned on. The echoes of Aventura and my people screaming "Flaca!" at me as I pass by pinches at my shoulders. The melody of our rhythms, urgent and desperate, rings down my eardrums and into my belly.

Ice clings to the blades of grass in the park, which is otherwise brown and muddy. Everything in Washington Heights feels lived in. Sometimes I imagine that when it's all said and done, after climate change ravages the Earth and women become barren from poison and pesticides, this will be the only place that survives. The aliens will come down from their green goblin planet and say, "Yes, there were people here once—people who lived, people who loved, people who played dominoes instead of paying their water bills."

My stomach makes a sound so loud that it startles me. I haven't eaten in what feels like days, and my body is starving, screaming at me for some sort of sustenance. I double back around the park to pop into Carlos's bodega. I watch my feet as they dodge dog shit and peanuts. I find a MetroCard stuck on the ground and pray I've hit the lotto, leaning down and shoving it in my pocket. Inside the bodega, it smells like cat litter and coffee. Every type of chip or cracker or condom you could imagine hangs down the walls. When I ask Carlos for a breakfast sandwich and coffee, the Spanish clumsily rolls off my tongue. I get why Mami hated it when I answered her in English. I've lost some of it, my culture, by drilling down so hard on what I could be if only I were an American.

Carlos hands me a piece of warm bread folded with cheddar cheese toasted between it and a coffee with two sugars and a boatload of condensed milk. One day I'll drop dead from all the dairy, but today I live to fight another New York morning. I hand him my ATM card and cross my fingers. I can feel my heart racing, praying for the dollars I know aren't there to magically appear when he swipes it. When my card declines, I pull three loose dollars out of my pocket and fold them over before I place them onto the counter. Carlos puts one finger over his lips to say *shhh* and looks away so I can see only the whites in the corner of his eyes. I say thank-you three times then shove the change back into my pockets. Washington Heights is our own little planet, our own little proof of life, and here, we keep one another's secrets.

The night Nena found out I could sing she grabbed my arm so hard it almost turned blue.

"Do it," she insisted, throwing me in front of Mami, whose back was turned toward us, her hands wet and sticky and busy making pasteles at Christmastime. The lights in the apartment were red and white, and it was cold because the heater had gone out, so we wore our scarves inside while the voice of Juan Luis Guerra filled our cardboard-thin walls.

"Do what you just did for me for Mami," Nena insisted while Mami rummaged through the drawer, searching for the wooden spoon, ready to slap us both across the backside for making such a scene on a Sunday.

"Do it, coño!" Nena pleaded, shooting me daggers with her eyes and slamming the drawer, nearly ripping off one of Mami's fingers.

Mami raised her hand, but before she could make contact with my sister's skin for swearing, I was singing. When I was through, Mami's hand still hung in the air, but she had forgotten all about Nena's filthy mouth.

Nena clapped and looked at Mami and said, "Puede cantar! Flaca puede cantar!"

"Ay, otra!" Mami screamed as they both danced around the kitchen, "Otra! Otra! Otra!" I think the kitchen was still brown then, before Nena died and the super came in and broke the pipes down and renovated it so he could hike up the rent.

After Nena found out about my singing superpower, she made me audition. She'd submit me for these little commercials using the AOL email account Mami had made to communicate with God knows who in Bayamón. When Mami caught on, she canceled the account and made me try out for the church choir, which, to my disappointment, I got into. As a result, I smelled like cod liver oil and holy water for the entirety of the sixth grade.

"Project, flaca! Project!" Nena would yell while she lay flat on the couch as I sang "Amazing Grace" in our living room like I was trying to fill a 1,700-seat theater. I'd get louder and louder, doubling down on the melody until Tony, our neighbor from downstairs, started banging with the broom on his ceiling to tell me to shut the fuck up.

We used to say we were going to move to Los Angeles, Nena and me. That we were going to be big stars—me in front of the camera and her behind it: running the show, my manager, my producer, my whatever the hell would buy her that mansion in the hills.

"Don't forget me when you're famous!" Nena would shout when we got older and I was running out the house, hair in a tight bun, a pair of LaDuca soft-sole character shoes in my hand on the way to some casting office in Battery Park.

"Forget who?!" I'd shout back while she chased me with dish soap and water on the stems of her fingertips. By that point, Mami had lost control of us. Nena was gayer than she'd ever been, wearing long jean shorts and Sharpie-marked Converse to confession, and I couldn't see anything other than the promise of my name in lights.

I booked a lot that year before my sister died. There was an ensemble role in *A Chorus Line*. A guest star in some musical theater show's pilot season. A commercial for Dave & Buster's in which my voice turned on all the kooky machines and got people dancing and having fun and spending their life savings on overpriced raffle tickets.

"I've never had a client in the running for so many things!" Francesca, my agent, would call and say. Her voice was like a roller coaster, shooting up and down when I answered the phone. Every time I got closer to making her a dollar she would send me gifts—a pair of new shoes, a leotard, hair clips, tickets to the hottest concerts in New York City, flowers on days of final callbacks.

"You've nearly done it!" Francesca called to say when I made it to the final round for the *Dreamgirls* revival. "It's just you and one other girl, and I heard she's a favor, not even a *real* talent!"

Nena and I were in the kitchen and I fell to the floor with excitement and flailed my arms and legs in the air like a struggling cockroach, while Nena followed and made atrocious noises full of hope and desire. When Mami woke up to our screams, she slapped our toes with that wooden spoon for waking her and Nena put her feet over mine to protect my toes until it was all over.

When it was quiet again, all I could hear was the freezer buzzing and Nena breathing. She put her hands around my face like she was holding a water glass. Her nails were short then, and she'd just chopped off all her hair, and to this day I can almost smell her wrists, the stench of Bath & Body Works sample scents.

"This is it, mamita," she said to me, stroking my edges. "This is the part where you make it."

"Let's see," I replied, crossing my fingers and kissing her thumbs. Her face got all sour and turned upside down.

"Don't do that," she said grabbing my shoulders. "Don't train yourself to jump right out of your joy." I think she got that line from a white lady on a self-help podcast.

In the weeks before she went, she was obsessed with "living her truth." Wearing little white tees with her nipples outlined and hanging her rainbow flag out of her bedroom window. Loud-mouthing to Mami when she didn't like what she was saying and staying out until the sun came up with her girlfriend, Celeste. I don't know, when I look back at it all, add her actions up together, sometimes the sum of it seems like she knew she was running out of time.

Nena pulled me to the window and positioned me to face all the lights of Washington Heights. "Mira," she said. We looked out at our city. The dumpsters in the courtyard were center stage, under a spotlight from the light leaking out the windows of the buildings above them, and we watched in awe as silhouettes of people just like us moved behind the thin bedsheets they used as curtains to hide inside their one-bedroom apartments.

I swallowed down my saliva. "This is it," I said. A rat made its way out from under the grate and into the basement. At the corner of 167th, bus brakes rubbed together like nails on a chalkboard, the bus announcing for the whole city to hear.

"And don't forget me," Nena said, tears in her eyes.

"Forget who?" I replied, ruffling the curls of her pixie cut. But now I'm fighting a war to remember the direction of her strands, trying to conjure up the precise and sour smell of her dirty breath in the morning. I'm arm-wrestling my way back to the me she'd say she knew. Closing my eyes until they're wet to remember the tulip-shaped birthmark she had on her left or right hip.

Ellen's is on a corner, and I can hear the staff performing from down the block. I'm racing up Broadway, weaving in and out of tourists with their eyes and fingers pointed toward the sky. As I push past people, late and with the thick skull of a New Yorker, I am quietly enthralled by their fascination with Times Square. It's the way they drop their jaws like they've never seen a billboard before that gets me. This idea that bright lights and shiny things make something worth looking at permeates every corner of our city.

I slow my speed as the blue tiles and red '50s font of Ellen's awning start to come into focus. I sneak in the door, begging my heart rate to slow down and my breath to still. No matter where I go, I always seem to be catching my breath. I worry I'll never outrun myself. That after everything that's happened, I'll always have some great load of catching up to do.

As soon as I get inside, I can taste the whipped cream and maraschino cherries. Ellen's is kitschier than I would like it to be, but I stay because this is the only place I can seem to hear myself think. The last place on this earth where my voice might still have a song in it.

Becky sees me from the corner of her eye and glares at me like I've killed someone. *Sorry,* I mouth and clench my jaw while I slink into the locker room to change. Becky moved here from Nevada last year to be on Broadway. She has long red hair and lives in an apartment not too far from my own uptown. She shops at Trader Joe's and complains about how expensive New York City is. I don't think she gets it, what it would be like to not have a stash of cash coming in from Mommy and Daddy. I guess that's why she lies to her parents at the end of every month about how well she's doing out here. I caught her once when she thought I'd already left for the day, telling them that she was in final callbacks for *Mamma Mia!* I don't think they'd keep sending money if they knew she was performing "I Know It's Today" from *Shrek the Musical* on a dirty countertop while the table below her fights over French toast.

I take off my jacket and shirt like a Tasmanian devil and catch a glimpse of myself in the mirror. I'm breaking out on my chest again. I've tried every serum and potion and poison to get rid of the bumps but they keep coming back like a stray dog expecting food on garbage day.

"Happy birthday," Saundra says, bursting through the doors. She covers her eyes with her hands to avoid seeing my bare chest before asking what took me so long to get here. I notice the way her Botox is drooping now on her left cheek.

I put on my shirt and say thanks.

Saundra is looking at me with those eyes like she feels bad for me or wants to ask about my sister. I loathe being the girl with the dead sister.

"Give Becky my solo again today," I say staunchly. Saundra's face drops. I haven't sung a solo since I started here, and Saundra doesn't like that since I have a voice of gold and she's convinced that my silence is bad for business. When I was first hired here she was sympathetic, soft even, because of my dead sister, convinced I wouldn't always be this way, but now her patience is running thin and she's been coercing me into getting back on the horse, dangling the carrot of a full-time salary in front of me. No matter how hard I try, though, I just can't seem to choke out a note. There's something sick about it now when I sing, knowing that while I was belting out a show tune for a few Broadway producers, my sister's heart was giving out on 176th Street.

"We hired you for that voice," she reminds me, tapping hard on my esophagus.

I slap her hands off my neck and give her my eyes like fire.

"Next time, just let me know if you're going to be behind," Saundra sighs. "We have a tight schedule and if you can't at least sing the harmony, then everything gets thrown off."

I don't know who is meant to tell her that nothing, really, can be thrown off at Ellen's. That all of us here are the misfit toys of Broadway.

"Copy that," I say to her while I straighten out the bottom of my shirt. I've cut it down so that the patrons can see a bit of my midriff. Anything to get more tips, really. "Can I have a little privacy?" I ask as I unbutton my pants.

Saundra purses her lips together, tight, before swinging out the doors and heading back toward the floor. I slip out of my pants and look at myself in the full-body mirror. My legs are ashy, my bikini line hairy—I haven't waxed in ages. I change into a pair of tight black leggings and my character shoes. They are basically unusable now, depleted from my old life, tattered and scuffed from wearing them every day for years. I slip out of the locker room, not too far behind Saundra, and two-step into the line of servers getting ready to belt out the chorus of "Seasons of Love."

Becky is in front of me and I pinch her butt so she hiccups and starts laughing just as she's about to go on. She swings her hands behind her to shoo me away while her voice starts the song up. She's sharp, and Saundra is cupping her eardrum with her thumb and pointer finger to signal at her pitch. By the time we're all on the counters and really going at it, I can barely hear Becky because I'm focused on trying to keep up with our movements. I've never been much of a dancer, so today I'm willing my muscles into believing that I am meant to move like this. Begging my brain and my body to match up. Kicking myself to remember that there are hundreds of women in my bloodline who danced barefoot and effortlessly on islands in the Caribbean to beats much more complicated than this. Even when I falter, I know they're all alive inside my toes. When the song is through, Becky takes her bow and the rest of us follow.

Immediately, Becky's asking me if she was sharp.

"Of course not," I say. "Saundra needs a hearing aid."

Becky's body fills with air like she has just been resuscitated. As she licks her wounds in the locker room, I go out and bus down Becky's section before heading over to one of my tables, where a party of four women who've just sat down are laughing like they've heard the last joke on earth. When I arrive, they tell me what's funny but I don't get it. It's something about one of their husbands.

"I don't have one of those," I say, and they laugh harder. I can't help but laugh a bit too. Thank God I don't have a husband. Thank God I'm finally rid of Rory. The women are quadruplets, I learn, and I tell them how rare that is like they don't already know. I shut my stupid mouth and they tell me the story of when their mother learned that there were four of them growing inside her. Apparently, she asked the doctor if she could abort just three, keep one, and go on living her normal life. When he told her it was all or nothing, she cried so hard she popped a blood vessel in her left eye.

"Which one of us do you think would have survived?" the one in a blue shirt is asking. It looks like her name should be Nancy. All four of them are red in the face with emotion, keeled over and choking on their waters thinking about how three of them might be dead if it were up to their mother. I want to crawl into her womb. Kick and scream for a while in the belly of a burdened woman. When the laughter dies down, I stand over them, waiting for them to offer me a seat until I remember I'm their server and not their friend. I take their orders: two buffalo cauliflowers and four Diet Cokes, no ice.

"Are you gonna write that down?" the one in a red shirt asks.

"No, I think I got it," I say. As if I can't remember not to put ice in her drink without scribbling on a piece of paper. I feel betrayed; I long to see my sister.

By lunch, Saundra's asking me if I can work dinner. I have a hard time saying no when someone is standing in front of me, so I nod yes and sweat about ditching another shift at the print shop. I'm trying to do the math now that I'm the breadwinner of my family. It's worth it to stay for the tips, I convince myself while I flip out my phone and start texting Alek. For the next six minutes, the bubbles of his message forms and unforms over and over again, threatening to blow me to bits the next time he has the chance to lay his eyes on me. I put my phone on "Do Not Disturb" and bring the check to table 4. When I get there, nine boys are sitting with their parents, sprawled out, drunk on milkshakes, and screaming at the top of their lungs. No one tells them to pipe down.

"Boys will be boys," one father says to me, chuckling and signing the card reader while he shrugs his thick shoulders.

"Not if I have anything to do with it," I laugh without smiling, grabbing the machine from his hands and ushering them out the door. I sing soprano and do my high kicks for the rest of the afternoon until I can feel my heel pulsing at the back of my shoe. I scream my orders at the kitchen until my throat is sore and juggle dishes until my sections are cleared.

By the time my shift is through, I can't remember if I've served one or one hundred people. Time flies like this at Ellen's sometimes. If it's a good day, all I can hear is my voice. That small thing inside me scream-ing that I can still sing. If it's a bad day, I want to go home and rip my vocal cords out of my throat, exchange them fairly for my sister's life.

When the last customer leaves, we bolt the door shut and give ourselves a standing ovation. It's a tradition we have—jumping to our feet when the night is through, acknowledging one another for the real work we've just done, the laying out of ourselves for hungry tour-ists to eat right up. I'm in the locker room jamming my feet into my Nike Dunks again and checking the subway app when Becky locks the door and tells me to sit down.

The lights go dark and she brings out a cake full of bright blue and gold candles while the rest of the servers stand behind her, belting out the Stevie Wonder rendition of "Happy Birthday." I've forgotten it's my birthday already; there have been lifetimes lived since Rory's bed this morning. Becky's eyes are lit from the flame, sparkling with joy so sweet I can almost taste it. I blow out the candles and she squeezes my shoulders, jumping up and down. For Becky, this is a beginning. She has so much hope left inside her that I want to bottle it up and IV it into my veins.

When we're done, Saundra gives me an envelope with my tips for the night. I pour them out onto the counter and lick my thumb to count the dollar bills. She's shorted me. A punishment for locking my voice inside the safe of my lungs, I think. I can't fight back now, though, not after my day of frowning and rolling my eyes and grabbing the card reader nastily back from customers.

"We don't do it for the money," Becky says to me when she sees my eyes spinning. She's hugging me so close that I can smell the lemon and cake batter on her breath. Sixty dollars for all my service.

On my walk back to the A train, I am caught in a sea of people waiting outside the stage door of a Broadway show. It's my worst nightmare to be mixed up with an audience instead of an ensemble. I'm scrambling, gripping the insides of my pockets, trying to find a way around it. I want the earth to open and suck me in, protect me from having to see the way the performers will rush out into the cold city air and sign autographs and wobble arm in arm to the nearest bar to sing another ballad, but tonight, the people are packed so thick on the sidewalk that I can't avoid it.

Two women scurry out the door and have their ritual. Their skin is bright red from the cold air and the scrubbing off of their show faces, but they are still taking photos and smiling for the fans and making big hearts on the top of their *I*'s to make their signatures more memorable. I'm like a Sims character, bumping into every wall in my periphery until I find a clear path out of my torture. When I'm out of the crowd, I turn and run across Eighth Avenue, out of breath and folding in on myself. I want to shield myself from the pain of this, the jealousy I feel, but no matter how far my feet take me, I can't seem to look away. While bikers zoom around me and taxis and buses buzz by, I'm static on the corner, trying to understand why it's them out there on the other side of the world and me over here melting with a pocketful of dollar bills and a grief so heavy I might as well anchor it to my skin and sink to where I belong, dead at the bottom of the ocean.

On the subway, I check my bank account because I'm sadistic. I see some numbers, but they're all in red, so I shut my eyes and click my phone back to black. I tap my nails, short and full of rough edges, lightly onto my skin then dig them in hard until I feel something like blood or juice pour out of my veins. It's a relief, the exhalation of all my insides like this.

Last year at this time I had more money than God. Nena and I did, I mean. We had a savings account in a mason jar under the bed that we'd been keeping since I was sixteen. It was our just-in-case money. Just in case we wanted to take a chance on ourselves. Just in case we made it big. Just in case we needed to run away as far as we could from the George Washington Bridge.

We used that money to bury Nena. Mami said it was a blessing. That God was watching over us all this time. That he'd built us a boat. To me, though, it seems like a curse. To me, it seems like God giveth only to taketh away, and I'd rather not get tangled up inside his dark, twisted web.

The train is crowded tonight. It smells like bad breath, leftover alcohol, and old pennies dried up at the bottom of a well. Across from me, there are two girls on the precipice of womanhood holding each other's shoulders and wrapping their ankles together, stealing kisses and rubbing their perfectly laid edges onto each other's necks. I can't help but see Nena in their reflection, draped over her new girlfriend Celeste two summers ago, smiling so hard their mouths might've fallen off, discovering themselves in each other's eyes for

the first time. I think that love must be tender when women do it together.

I spread my legs as wide as I can until we get uptown so nobody
sits next to me. I'm selfish here on the subway. I have to be.

When I'm off the train, I hide in the crowd to avoid Juan Carlos, our
landlord, who I can spot from the corner of my eye on 176th Street.
Mami and I haven't paid our rent in two months, and Juan Carlos's
patience for our sob story is starting to wear thin. He's pacing around
the block like he's waiting for something. I'm crossing my fingers that
it isn't me. I stand still like I'm a stunned bird that's just been swiftly
hit by a bus until he spots me and starts screaming my name. "Xiomara" always seems to sound like a threat when it's slipping out the
mouth of a man.

"Hey, Juan Carlos," I say, crossing the street casually so he doesn't
smell the fear at the bottom of my blood. Juan Carlos's hands are in
the air, making a peace sign, which after a moment I realize is actually
a two.

"Two months," he breaks out.

I nod my head to show I understand.

"Two!" he says again.

I don't like being spoken to like a child. The hairs on my arms are
starting to rise.

He opens his mouth again. "Dos, coño!"

"Well, maybe you shouldn't have raised the rent on us after my
sister died, maricón!" I snap to him.

"Xiomara, mami, necesito mi dinero." He's whispering in Spanish now as if that makes his messaging any less cruel.

"I'm working on it," I say through a breath, trying to cool myself
down.

"Next week," he says while I shoulder away from him.

"Probably not."

"Next week or eviction!"

I stop walking. "You can't kick us out, Juan Carlos." I state that matter-of-factly because I know he won't. He likes watching Mami swing her ponytail and bend over the window too much.

"Next week, Xiomara!" he screams behind me.

I get inside and lock his voice out on the sidewalk where it belongs, next to the rest of the garbage in Washington Heights.

The staircase is sterile, flooded with white light and spiders while I trudge up the steps. I'm done taking the elevator up to our apartment. It keeps getting stuck, and I can't think of a less exciting death than one where I suffocate between the second and third floors. I don't know what I'm going to do about rent. I'm barely making three hundred dollars a week from the print shop combined with the tips I'm scrounging up at Ellen's and Mami refuses to go back to work. Mami hasn't worked a single day since Nena died. She's just sat back on the couch and prayed over and over again to her nonexistent heaven and let the weight of the world begin to bury me alive. Sometimes, from six feet under, Nena's scent seems to waft up next to me, as if both of us are trying the only way we know how to get out from under the dirt.

When I open the door, which is heavy and metal and black, all the lights are on and Mami is scrubbing the stove while the echoes of the Hail Mary from the television mass make their way through the kitchen. She's skinnier than before, less full than she used to be. Her hair is thick and black, and when she washes the heat out of it, it is wavy and long and smells like roses. Her skin is the light brown color that is in vogue these days. Every time I see her, my mother, I am reminded of her beauty, and I can't help but wonder if she hates me—this black little thing who won't seem to go away, stuck in this dimension together until death do us part.

The wind blows from the open window and I catch a whiff of my body. I smell the sour from the subway and the dozens of people asking me for another round of Diet Cokes and the sweat of my skin. I stand against the arch of the door and press my jacket closed so that Mami doesn't see the pink of my shirt peeking through the collar. After Nena's funeral, she made me promise I'd be done with it all—the flashing lights and the auditions and the trying to "make it." It had been dark out, almost light as we walked back into our apartment the night after we buried her. "Ya se acabó," Mami said, banging her hands twice on the crumbling counter. She meant for me to mute my music forever. She was convinced that we invited the devil inside our doors with it all. That we sold our souls, Nena and me, for a chance at a better life.

I've tried to respect her wishes—I even thought she might be right—but now without my voice I'm suffocating here, all wound up in her misery with no song to sing. I can't help but think that now, in my silence, he's definitely here. The devil. And I just can't seem to learn how to get rid of him.

"Only sixty dollars today," I say. "Not enough for rent." I lay my tips on the counter. Mami looks away from the crumpled-up cash. She still thinks that God will send us an angel like the way He did when He stole my just-in-case money. I don't know how to tell her that angel is me, and my bank account is freezing, down below zero.

"Mami, I need you to go back to work," I say. She doesn't reply. Sometimes with Mami, it's like I'm the parent. Like I'm the one who gave birth to her and has to make sure that she eats and sleeps and cries just the right amount before she withers up and dies a horrible death too. When she was still here, Nena always complained about it, about the way Mami never acted like the adult in the room, the way she put the weight of the world on Nena's shoulders, how there was never any room for her to be honest about who she was or what she wanted. I wish I had listened sooner. I wish I hadn't been so caught up in myself so I could see how bad it really was for Nena before she was gone for good.

"Mami, I need you to go back to work," I say again, loud and to the back of her head. "Mami, me oíste?!"

When I'm demanding, Mami doesn't know how to react. In her

old body, she'd slap me across the face, and Nena would come running in to save me, but in this broken one she keeps her eyes down, scrubbing harder, catching the Brillo pad on the edge of the counter, chipping some paint off the corner and cursing in the wind.

"I can only hold off Juan Carlos so long," I continue. She makes a huffing noise when she hears his name and I understand what she's thinking—that he should have never made us sign a new lease while we were grieving Nena, the only woman with a credit score or the wherewithal to run things the right way in this household. But he did. And life's not fair. And I've learned that. And now it's time for Mami to learn too.

"We're going to get evicted," I say. Mami finally looks up from the stove. Her eye is twitching on the right side.

"Evicted?" Mami seems confused by the word. She doesn't understand that people don't care how much pain we have in our hearts. That here in New York City it's only about money. Money, money, and money.

"Bueno," she says. "I clean house." That's as close as I'll ever get to an apology from her. I push the sixty dollars toward her.

"For groceries," I say. "I'll have more tomorrow."

Mami doesn't say thank you, or happy birthday, or kiss me goodnight. She just turns the lights off in the kitchen and reminds me that it's closed, that I've missed dinner, and that there's nothing left in the cabinets for me to pick on.

Mami's story goes like this. She was born in San Sebastián, Puerto Rico, in 1964 to a very light father and a very dark mother. Right away, Mami is beautiful and smart and lucky. Her skin is the perfect color, and her hair is the perfect texture, and when she walks down the beach, which she does almost every day, all the men stare at her and ask her if they can take her for a dance. But Mami is not interested. Mami is never interested. Mami wants to move to Nueva York. Mami wants to have a better life. Mami wants to take her luck and bet it all. And when Mami meets Papi, at a small bar in Santurce on a hot Saturday night, Mami finally knows she's met her match. Abuela and Abuelo tell her to stay away from that maricón. That all Dominicans have Satan somewhere in their blood. That he's only there for the drugs and the breasts and the bad things. But Mami risks it all and she moves to New York with Papi. To Washington Heights. To the land of cocaine and rat feces and buses that break down in the middle of the street on a Friday night. She dances to Elvis Crespo every Christmas Eve with the girls from around the corner and their husbands and cleans the crumbs from the inside of the stove and dreams of Puerto Rico in the nighttime. Soon, Mami gets pregnant with Nena. Her sueñito Americano. Then Mami gets pregnant with me. Her amiguita jodida. Papi cheats on Mami, but Mami stays strong. Papi has another family, but Mami stays strong. Papi takes the money and runs, but Mami stays strong. But then Nena dies and Mami has run out of all her strong. So Mami dies too. Her body is alive and well. She's here, sitting next to me all the time, but her soul? Her soul is gone.

Cassie says I'm in my Saturn Return while she slugs down an oat milk matcha and licks the foam off the sides of her lips. She moved downtown last year after she booked her first Broadway gig and hasn't had a coffee (and barely a calorie) ever since. Her blond hair floats just under her pointy chin and accentuates her fat lips for which she paid Dr. Difabio an arm and a leg last fall. I take a bite into my burger.

"It's like when you're supposed to return to yourself or something like that," Cassie continues while she rummages through her bag for her handheld mirror. "Like, you gotta go through some shit to get to the other shit." She reapplies her lip gloss.

"Well, I've definitely gone through the shit," I say, my mouth full of pickles.

"You're sooo much better than Rory anyway," Cassie says, scrolling through her Instagram. I can tell she's on autopilot by the way she drags her *O*'s like she has to think an extra beat to make it sound like it should. Also, because I haven't brought Rory up once in this entire conversation.

"Yeah, thanks, Cass," I say. We both sip on our mugs.

Back in the day, Mami used to babysit Cassie after school for extra cash since her mom was a dancer and worked what she called "the weird hours." Cassie is four years younger than me but twenty years older in spirit. That's what her psychic says, anyway. At night, we used to rewatch *West Side Story*, acting out the tragic fate of the Jets and the Sharks together with Nena, who always deemed herself Maria.

After a year or two, though, Cassie's mom found a boyfriend with a big belly and pink cheeks and cash that leaked out of his pockets like

car oil. Cassie left P.S. 187 and went to a fancy prep school in River-
dale, and he bought the building they lived in. Renovated the whole
shit like something out of *Architectural Digest*. "We're not in Kansas
anymore," Nena used to joke every time we walked in. "Beverly Hills
and shit all the way up over the George Washington Bridge."

For Cassie, experiencing the world is like a God-given right. Asking what makes herself happy is her career. Meanwhile, people like
me are scrubbing toilets and driving taxis and asking ourselves how in
the world we might pay off our debts. That's the biggest difference
between us, the thing I envy most. That I see the world like a job, and
she sees the world like a vacation. I think that's why I'm always looking for a way out. And Cassie? Well, Cassie's always looking for a way
in. I napkin out the ketchup from underneath my fingernails and suck
the seeds from the sesame bread out of my teeth.

"Shit, I'm late for rehearsal," Cassie shouts so the whole waitstaff
can hear her. The word *rehearsal* replays and replays and replays in my
head. Like it's taunting me, the way it rolls off her tongue. We both
wave down the waiter.

"It's fine," I say, "I got it." But Cassie knows me well enough to
know I don't got shit. She takes out her wallet, small and brown, then
tosses me her credit card. It's heavy. So dark blue that it almost looks
black. It says, *I have more than you have.* Cassie knows it too; that's why
she threw it at me like she couldn't care less if she ever gets it back. I
think she gets off on it, the way she's outgrown me now. I slide the
card off the edge of the table and squeeze it in between my knuckles.
I wonder if I press down hard enough I'll be able to feel it, something,
anything, that could zap me back into my body.

"Oh, by the way," Cassie says, making her voice sound breathy
like an exhale after a vocal warm-up, "there's this open call for Manny's next project in a few weeks." Manny Santos is this new hot Broadway director. He blew up a few years ago in response to that shooting
in Minneapolis, after the industry was up in arms over Black voices
being disregarded. He's overrated, if you ask me, but you know how
white people are. Once they find a light skin to do their whitewashing

for them, they glom on. "I guess they're looking for the next big thing," she goes on, "an unknown." A breath. "I don't stand a chance. You know how he is"—she points at her white skin—"but you might." She runs her hand up my arm as she stands. Cassie doesn't give me time to respond before she beelines toward the door. "I'll have my agent text you the details!" she yells over her shoulder, then pulls on the big steel doors and disappears out into the New York City snow. The word *agent* plays in my head like *rehearsal* did until I delete it altogether. I feel my coffee turning at the bottom of my stomach, the pennies on my tongue threatening to come out.

The waitress comes over and swipes Cassie's credit card into one of those white handheld machines. She examines the card like it can't possibly be mine while the machine spits out a receipt. There's ink all over it. Red lines signal to her that she's almost out of paper.

"Thanks, Cassie," she says to me, handing the card back after I tap the ungodly 20 percent tip button.

"Of course," I say, nonchalantly, throwing the metal into the bottom of my bag. I'm trying it on. The feeling I might have if I lived a life in Cassie's skin, swigging down a twelve-dollar matcha and Ubering five blocks in the winter instead of jumping a turnstile and praying that I make it home before my fingers fall off from frostbite.

When the waitress lingers, I furrow my brow and she apologizes, putting her hand on her head like she's forgotten something in the kitchen before she scurries away. I hear her shoes squeak the same way mine do at Ellen's. The older woman sitting next to me wipes the foam of her latte from her lips, raises her eyes at me, and chuckles like she can see right through me. Rich people can smell the negative numbers of my bank account. It's no fun anymore, my game. Not when I'm getting caught red-handed wearing someone else's skin.

I push my chair out, then in, and zip myself back into my body. Everything is too tight. I'm suffocating at the thought that I have to live in here for the long haul. Bursting at the seams. What I'm afraid of now, though, with Nena gone, is that when I do explode, there will be no one left to pick up my pieces.

My chest is hot from running. Like there are thousands of bees stinging my lungs while I race through Union Square to get to work on time. The pigeons flutter away from my feet and I duck for cover. I can't afford to get shit on me today. I've been late to the print shop six times this month and Alek said on the fifth that he would kill me or fire me (worse) if it happened again.

When I round the corner on 12th, I slow my steps to catch my breath. I toss off my puffer jacket so I can feel the ice of the air on my skin. I smooth out my shirt—a rough red polo that has Alek's name embroidered on the right breast. In this shirt, I'm his property, no different from the rest of the copy machines crapping out in the corner. The bells jingle as I open the door. I'm still all wrinkled.

"You're late," Joe says to me while I toss aside my jacket. As if I don't know that. Joe is beefy and greasy and always somehow on the shift right before mine. I ask him where Alek is, and he points with one stubby finger toward the back room. Alek is always in the back room. Sometimes when I'm here alone late at night I worry that he will pop out and take me alive. Men like Alek are rabid little monsters hiding in plain sight, chomping at the bit to get their claws into me.

I slowly make my way back to clock in with Alek. When he feels me in the doorway, he barely looks up over his coffee. His long gray hair hangs over his eyes, flirting with the rim of his mug, just missing the liquid sludge inside it. His beard has crumbs lining the corners, and the wrinkles on his skin sag down. His lips are bright red and chapped like the bottom of a dog's feet in the summer. He licks them every few seconds; his tongue is white in the center, bumpy around the edges. When it lines his lips, I feel a hundred snakes slither up and down my spine. Alek grunts when he sees me, then slaps down hard on the analog clock next to him twice to remind me that I'm close to ending my career here.

When I emerge from the back room, Joe is already rolling his eyes and halfway out the door. I wave him out with my hands like Mami does to me when I stick my fingers in the tray to pull out the pernil before the table's been set. Joe gives me the finger. It looks like a porky little sausage. When it's quiet, Alek walks out and stares at me for a long time like he's waiting for an apology.

"My cousin Maria calls it island time," I say, referring to my late habit and trying to break the ice now that it's just the two of us.

"Funny," Alek says, "because I call it the last straw." My big toe digs into the bottom of my shoe. Alek grabs my arm and drags me to the door.

"Alek, I promise it will never happen again." I say his name because I read once that that makes people feel more important. Oprah aired a whole segment about how telling a killer random facts about yourself (my bedsheets are turquoise, my thumb is double-jointed, my first job was at the doughnut shop under our building), and saying his name while you do, lessens the chance that he'll carry through with the murder.

I'm two seconds away from screaming out my childhood cat's name when Alek takes his hands off me and then sticks his palm up stiffly toward my face. "I don't want to hear it. He kicks the door open with his left foot. "I've already hired your replacement." I think of Mami, and how she's going to start scrubbing toilets again this week. The cold air is burning the bottoms of my arms without my jacket to shield me.

"You can't do that, Alek!" I beg. "I'll sue!" He spits out his coffee onto the sidewalk near my feet. It's hot and smelly like the inside of a rotting Dunkin' Donuts espresso machine.

"You can barely afford an MTA card, Xiomara. Give me a break."

"Alek, come on." I'm going to play the dead-sister card. "You know I've had a tough year." I step into the shop and back him into a corner with my body, putting my years of acting classes to use. Tears well in my bottom lid, and I let my sweater slide off my shoulder. I squeeze out a few more generic words and say his name a couple more times. "You know I've been . . . trying." I make my voice squeaky and my body small. I need him to see me as something he can help. Someone he can be a hero to. Right now, the only thing I want more than my sister back is to be Alek's search and rescue mission. I swing my hair over to one side, then run my fingers through it. A few of the strands get caught on a hangnail. I lean over the printer again so he can see the outline of me. I've done this long enough to know that white men like my small frame. I bury my head in my hands and wait. I'm surprised at how real these tears feel when they come. It's like I can't separate myself from the show.

"One more chance, Xiomara," he whispers to me. "I'm not kidding around." Alek comes behind me and squeezes his knuckles into my shoulders. My stomach starts to let up. When I turn around, I can see that he wants to kiss me. That he thinks I owe him that. When I don't meet his mouth with mine, he moves his hands away from me and says, "In that case, you'll train the new kid today. He'll be here any minute."

Alek speeds back to his little office and I follow him again to ask more questions, but before I can open my mouth he disappears behind the door and slams it shut. I wipe the tears from my face, just as the front door's bells ding. I walk to the front of the store to find a man leaning over the glass counter. His body is long and lean like a string bean, a broodish yet gentle nature is pouring out the meat of his skin. All my hairs stand up on their tippiest toes. I like seeing men from afar like this. Examining them before I can hear them speak. It's like a science experiment to me, clocking when my attraction turns on and off.

"Welcome in. How can I help you?" I say in my best customer-service voice.

"I'm Santi." The man wipes his hands on his jeans and sticks one out for me to shake. His glasses are crooked on his face. "Alek called me over the weekend. It's my first day today."

"Congratulations," I say, spinning around on my heels and opening the door attached to the counter to let him in. Back here the print shop is too small for the both of us. We squish past each other before he finds a comfortable distance and takes his mittens off. I can't remember the last time I saw someone wear mittens. Santi's curls stick out from under his gray wool hat, which he pulls off while he shakes his head to get rid of the cold caught under it. He moves his hands through his hair and opens his backpack to pull out an army-green-colored water bottle. He takes a big swig and chews it down. When he swallows, I can hear the liquid slush through his teeth. This boy is a paradox to me—hot and not. I want to play him like a puzzle.

"Where should I get started?" Santi's rubbing his hands together. They are tan, like he just left the beach, soft like the shore at dawn. Freckles splatter across his cheeks and nose all the way around to his hairline.

"Printer. Copy machine. Scanner." I point while I walk past each. Santi trails behind me. "Behind door one—Alek." I press the door open, and the fluorescent lights reveal Alek's lanky body slouched in a computer chair, sleeping already. I pull the door shut. Santi's face is all screwed up like he's not sure what he's gotten himself into. I keep walking. "Garbage goes out at ten. Recycling comes on Wednesdays. The customer is always right. Snitch on me, I'll snitch on you. Don't get in my way, I won't get in your way. I think that's everything. Any questions?"

Santi smiles. There's a gap in his teeth the size of my thumb. "Bathroom?"

I knock on the door to my left. "For employee use only. Shifty plumbing. Keep that in mind, for all our sake." The printer croaks behind me and I slam it twice with the back of my palm. Santi slides around me. Examines the printer. Opens the back flap and moves the needles around until I hear the printer sigh with relief and spit out paper like it's been waiting to do its entire existence.

"That should do it." Santi gives me a thumbs-up. A literal thumbs-up. The printer begins again.

"One more thing," Santi says while I try to disappear into the back room. I stare at him until he speaks again. "Your name?"

"Oh, I'm Xiomara."

"Xiomara," Santi says while he flips through a stack of pink papers. When he says my name I don't flinch like I usually do when the rest of the men in Manhattan spit it out. I wait for a beat to see if something sick will come out next. When it doesn't, I shift my weight between the balls of my feet to remind me of my balance.

"You should probably wake Alek up to let him know you're here," I say.

"I'm not so sure about that." Santi says, raising one eyebrow and talking out the opposite side of his mouth. "He looked pretty comfy." Just the left of his lip is moving up and down. It's distracting. My synapses are firing left and right.

"It's now or never."

"Okay," he says, "but for the record I'd rather stay out here with you." Santi opens the door to the back room and gives me a look with wide eyes and then jokingly opens his mouth to pretend like he's screaming before he hurries into the room and closes the door behind him. I shake my head and feel my cheeks start to bubble away from each other, my eyebrows raising too, now, and my eyes sparkling like a child.

It's quiet almost long enough for me to wipe myself clean before the bells ring and a gust of wind from outside swings into my orbit. Miss Monday walks in, the same woman who walks in every Monday. She has the same saggy jeans and stringy hair and mascara caught between her lower lashes as she did last week. The same fumbling through her bag, loose papers, and highlighted sides. The same chaos.

I've gathered that Miss Monday is an actress. Mostly commercials, though when she was absent for six weeks last summer, I was convinced she'd booked a pilot.

"More headshots?" I ask while I press the print button on her file.

Miss Monday swallows down her smile like she has something she wants to tell me. "Yes, more headshots." *Ask me what they're for,* her eyes are begging. *Just ask me. Ask me already.* I give in. Maybe it will feel nice to know what twisted TV shows women in this city are being asked to perform for.

"What are they for this time?" I say. I'm picking at my nails again. Monday's face lights up.

"*SVU: Law and Order. Law and Order: SVU.* If I book this one, I'll be playing dead girl found in freezer number two. *And* I'll be missing a finger." She's beaming. America is obsessed with dead girls. It's sickening, really, the idea that we are so much more valuable dead than alive.

I hear the paper smack together, the buzz of the printer as it spits it out, the toner jug squeak. It's going to jam. I can hear that in the machine before it even begins now, and I wonder what it says about me, that I'm psychically connected to a Xerox machine. I make my way toward the back and hit the top of the printer tray twice with the palm of my hand. The printer speeds up. I catch a glimpse of her photos. They look the same way they look every week—perfectly polished, screaming "Pick me." Nena took my first headshots on an old gray digital camera. They were out of focus, watermarked with a red date in the corner, but they had the same hope inside them. The same longing for validation. I think of Cassie and her open call.

I slip Monday's headshots into an envelope and make my way back up to the front counter, counting my steps and peeking in the back room to get a look at Santi. He's standing there with his arms crossed, entertaining Alek's bad jokes and nodding his head like he thinks they're funny. When I give the envelope to Monday, she's like me at the bodega, crossing her fingers that her card goes through, handing me loose change when it doesn't.

"Good luck," I say, my voice going up an octave while she shoves at her bag and forces the envelope in.

"Thanks," she says brightly, then spins on her heels and heads out the door like she's already been booked.

I'm grateful I don't have to do this anymore, I decide. The auditions every day and the performing and the rehearsing all the time. The sitting by the phone and scratching the skin off my arms until Francesca called with something, anything, for me to give my song and dance to. That kind of thing is overrated. Self-indulgent. Out of touch.

When she's gone my cheeks get hot and my lips start to tremble. The air is stale. I can feel the stinging of my stasis taunting me. I hope she gets that part. I really do.

At Ellen's, everyone is buzzing about Manny Santos's new show. I guess it's about a Black girl, an explorer—so a woman, I should say—who travels the world and finds a different version of herself in every place she lands. Like a multiverse set here on earth, where she meets all her possibilities in human form and ultimately has to choose if she likes herself enough to go back to her roots. Apparently, it's big and bold and a role that a Black woman like me should kill for. To me, this sounds like another show written by a man that dissects the inner workings of womanhood.

"I heard he wants someone with a whistle tone," Becky says, screeching in the locker room.

I toss my bag in a locker, kick it closed with the back of my foot. Jacey walks in and rips off her shirt while she sings the scales. Her waist is tiny and her breasts bulge out of her bra so I can almost see the light brown of her nipples. Her skin is like Mami's, smooth and light. Becky widens her eyes and drops her jaw. I slap her on the shoulder.

Becky's totally in love with Jacey. I, on the other hand, can't stand the sight of her. Jacey doesn't say a word to us, but she does brush past Becky close enough so that we can smell her perfume. It's sweet like vanilla with a hint of BO from what I'm sure is her morning audition rotation. Jacey's a straight woman who flirts with girls for fun. Nena had a laundry list of stories about women just like her: our neighbor Celia, her swim instructor Paige, and Cassie sometimes too, she said, when no one was looking.

When Jacey's done changing and out on the diner floor, Becky grabs my shoulder. Her face is red and her eyebrows are all melted into the center of her face, folded over each other and wrinkled up like she has something to be worried about.

"Breathe," I say, and then I count to four and wait until I can see the red under her cheeks start to dissipate.

"X, honestly, this part was made for you." She's back to her normal color now, talking about Manny's play. "What are you going to prepare?" There's a wild thing in her voice. Something free from disappointment. I wipe a smile off my face from the laughter I feel bubbling up. It's a response to the way she says *prepare*, like we are in eighth-grade biology class or something, about to dissect the inside of a dead frog. I take her hand off my shoulder.

"I'm not."

Becky's face drops.

"I'm not going to audition for that." My feet begin moving toward the door.

"That's the stupidest thing I've ever heard," Becky blurts out as she follows me.

"I guess my trash is your treasure then," I say, pushing past the rest of the waiters harmonizing to some Jason Robert Brown tune. "I don't know how many times I have to tell you that open calls are a waste of time. You'll never get seen and you'll spend a morning hanging on to this fallacy that maybe *today* is the day you are going to be chosen."

Becky's not moving with me anymore. When I look back, her face is twisted and teary like I've just sacrificed her first child.

On the floor, I've got a three-top and a table of eight screaming middle-school girls. I take their orders: a burger cooked extra well done, an alfredo, and a vegan burrito for my table of three—all men in black suits—and an assortment of All-Day Breakfast for my eight screaming ladies.

I punch the orders into the computer and get in line for the cabaret dance break. Becky won't look at me, and Jacey is singing the lead, nailing every high kick in the choreography. I flail behind her. I think

I'm starting to get a bad knee. Midway through the chorus, I can hear Jacey's voice start to fry. I try to give Becky a look again, but she won't meet me there. Her eyes are still all red and watery, looking down at the floor. I don't want to be that person for her. The one who takes the magic out of Broadway just because for me it's covered in soot.

The bacon is burnt when I get back to the kitchen, and Joey, our head chef, flips it on its belly to hide the black on the bottom.

"You know they'll still be able to taste it, right?" I say swinging out the double doors. Joey gives me the finger. I love him. Someone who speaks my sweet language. When I get to my table of the girls, they're all giddy, wearing pink velour.

"Enjoy!" I say while the one in the ponytail takes a bite of the bacon, crunches up her face, then gives me a thumbs-up and a smile and swallows it down. My table of three wants coffee, but we're all out so I grind up espresso and add boiling water to mimic the taste.

"This is a great *a m e r i c a n o,*" one of the gentlemen says as he slurps on it. The difference between men and women, I guess, is that we'll scarf down the burnt bacon with a smile on our faces.

It's time for *Les Mis,* so I'm standing on the counter trying to find my balance, humming the harmony of "On My Own" while Jacey sings the solo. I survey the room to make sure none of my customers skip the bill and duck out during my big number. It's true what Rory says, I think: When I'm singing like this I like the sound of my own voice. I can hear that it's the best one in the room.

When I'm done, the gentlemen in the suits stand up and whistle and clap for us. One of them points at me and gives me a thumbs-up. In front of men like this I feel like I'm naked, showing them my wounds while they applaud me for my pain.

I hop off the counter and bus table 26. The gentlemen are waving me down now for a check, and my eight girls are telling me they are going to be late for their show. A table in another section is asking me to flag down their server. At Ellen's, everyone else's problem always becomes my own.

I usher all my parties in and out the door for the rest of the evening. At the end of the night, Joey makes us ice cream sundaes with the leftover chocolate soft serve in the machine. Becky's giving me the cold shoulder, but I slide my stool next to hers.

"Okay," I say, getting ready to be the bigger person. "What about you? What are you *preparing*?" I draw out the word like she did so she knows this is my apology. I take a bite and get a brain freeze. Chocolate seeps through my teeth. Becky slaps my arms and screams with laughter then pulls out her audition book full of every soprano song ever known to man.

It doesn't take long until we are harmonizing, trying out all the different tunes in her little book, and counting the coins of our tips. I only ever knew how to fight like a sister anyway—kicking each other in the face then giggling under the covers until the morning.

"Promise me you'll think about it, X," Becky says to me before we leave. "You're too talented to keep throwing the baby out with the bathwater." *Baby* and *bathwater.* I love these sayings white people pull out of their asses.

"I'll think about it," I say, which is technically not a lie since all I have done is think about it—on the train, at the print shop, here at Ellen's, of course—since the day Cassie told me about it in the first place.

Grief is a wild animal, and today I can feel her crawling all over me. Some days I'm like this. So thick with rage and emotion that I'm covered in slime. Cassie keeps telling me it's a blanket I'm putting over my sadness. I say at least it's keeping me warm.

I'm on the subway sitting on my pins and needles when I see a man groping his penis while he stares me down. I've seen all types of dicks on the A train. Short, fat, skinny, long, curved, you name it. But this one is different, like an elephant's trunk shoved into a baby's bottle, purple and red veins bulging all around it like someone is squeezing it too tight.

The first time this happened I was barely seven years old, holding Nena's hand and swaying to the beat of the train's bumps after school. Nena slapped her little hand over my eyelids and started screaming out like Mami always told us to if a man came too close or offered us candy. I peeked out between her fingers while she flailed, letting the light in the curves of her fingers illuminate him across the way. I watched in awe as he rubbed himself, smirking toward me like he knew I could still see.

I guess that's why I'm unsurprised as I sit here on my way to the print shop, already counting the hours until I can go home and have a tantrum, making direct eye contact with Elephant Dick while he strokes himself to the sight of my fresh face. I survey his body. It's small. Square against the shoulders, round around the center. His skin is light and gray underneath, hair everywhere on his arms and his neck and the tips of all his limbs. His ears are small like mine. I have tiny ears. His mouth is open, yellow teeth and cheesy tongue hanging out. His hands start moving faster while the women around me wince and find their ways out of the train car. I can see the fire behind his eyes, the way they refuse to break contact with mine, the way they turn pink and widen and become more serious every second I stay watching. I lean forward to say *I'm not scared of you* until his entire body tightens up and his breath exhales sharply and his shoulders start to shake and a wet spot forms at the center of his blackened sweatpants. I keep my eyes on him as he wipes his hand on the sides of his fabric, moves right then left from hip to hip like he is embarrassed all of a sudden. I stay sturdy. Intensify my gaze. Let him know that he doesn't get to throw me away now just because he's finished. Look, I want to say, who is small and wet and embarrassed on the subway. And look now who is victorious. I'm the captain of this train car.

We're at Union Square right on time. I stand up and swing around the pole once to be sure he sees me, and then make my way out the train car. I tap on the window before the train roars away. He turns his head slowly while I plaster my middle finger to the plexiglass. *FUCK YOU,* I mouth to him, baring my teeth. I take a snapshot of his face—bewildered and afraid, a new look behind his eyes.

At the print shop, I'm with Santi, who always seems to have the sun around him, and we can hear Alek farting in his sleep in the back room. Santi has been here only a few weeks, but he's gotten really comfortable talking my ear off, and I'm somewhere between pretending to hate his voice and gripping on to every word of it. Today, Santi is going on about some short-story collection he's been listening to on Audible. I *mhm* and *mhm* until I can't *mhm* anymore. I'm distracted, have been all morning. My phone is vibrating. Probably Cassie calling about the audition. Or maybe Becky asking me to cover a shift for her. Or worst case, it's Juan Carlos to make good on his threat or demand that I sell him my soul or give him my first-born child. All my nerves are spiking. I hit the side button twice without looking and get back to supervising Santi and his golden fucking aura.

I look toward the printer Santi is hovering over. He's saying he "can't fix it" and that it's "making that sound again." He's calling my name and calling my name until I yell back at him, "I'm coming, coño." Santi's face falls whenever I yell like that, when I lose control of my censor and it breaks through my membrane to show the ugly me under all this skin. My head is pounding. If I'm going to be Santi's manic pixie dream girl, I think I'll have to be more delicate.

The print shop is buzzing today. The bells ring. Customers come in. They're printing their wedding invitations, their graduation photos, more headshots, their lease agreements. No funeral cards today, though I bet someone died and we'll just never know their name.

I find the hollow spot on the printer and slap my palm into it twice, like I've done for the last twelve months since the croaking started. It feels good, the blood rushing into my hand, the stinging, the control. When the croaking continues, I slam my palm in harder. Then the noise stops and the papers start to spit out, but I go again, even harder. My legs start to tingle and the space between my temples turns to cotton. I float out of my body and I lose all my senses. I think I'm addicted to this feeling. I slam my palm in over and over and over again until I hear something crack and Santi grabs my wrist to stop me from accosting the Xerox machine. I taste pennies in my mouth. I feel a sharp pain take over my wrist and knuckles.

"I'm fine," I say, ripping my hand out of Santi's grip. But my entire arm is throbbing now. "Ice," I say, "in the freezer in the back room. And don't tell Alek or I'll fucking kill you."

Santi moves like it's an emergency and I come back into my body. My hand is red and swollen. My head is pounding. All I can feel is pain. Or maybe I should say *at least* I can feel this pain. At least while my hand is on fire I can recognize that I'm alive. I'm alive, I remember. I'm alive and my sister is dead.

In the morning, I wake up at my cousin Maria's house. My wrist is blown up like a balloon and I feel like the muscles under its skin have been burning in a pot of acid all night.

"Wake up!" Maria shouts.

I can smell the coffee and the blow dryer and the sex. Maria's always having sex. Always drinking coffee and doing hair and having sex. I roll off the couch and onto the floor. Maria lives across the street from Mami and me. Her apartment is tiny, but it's rent-controlled, so she'd be crazy to give it up. Five hundred dollars for a studio in Manhattan is unheard of these days, even if it is only the size of a child's shoe. Maria is in the bathroom pressing the flat iron to her skull when I find her.

"Look who decided to roll through," she says, setting down the hot iron and kissing me on both my cheeks. She has rosacea and tatas like watermelons. Even in a turtleneck, she looks like a porn star.

Maria grabs a folding chair out of the closet and instructs me to sit before she places my head under the sink. I'm still wiping the crust out of my eyes when I feel the ice of the water hit my temple and then her nails scraping on my scalp. If there's one thing about Maria it's that she's always dying to get her hands in my hair.

"What happened there?" she asks, pointing to the bruise on my wrist with the back of her brush. I can't get anything past Maria. She's like the only person left on this planet who can see me.

"I fell off the counter at Ellen's," I say, closing my eyes and pulling the sleeve of my shirt over my injury so she won't ask more questions.

"Bueno," she says, scrubbing harder. It's my punishment for lying.

"So, me and Rory are finally finished," I say. It's easy to distract Maria with gossip. I see her smiling upside down above my head.

She doesn't ask any questions, just makes the sign of the cross and says, "He was a loser." Her accent makes it sound like *loose-her*.

I laugh. He was a loser, but at least he got the job done. Now this is the longest I've gone without fucking since I was sixteen, and my vagina is flaming up and dripping down every time I see a man who has eyes or shoulders or a part that can be stuck inside me.

It takes another hour and two thousand degrees of heat before Maria hands me a mirror, and I let a sigh out. My hair is flat and falling just above my collarbones. It has no personality left in it. She's sucked all the air out.

"Gracias, mamita," I say and slip out of the chair. "I have to get home before Mami files a missing-persons report. How much do I owe you?" As if I even have my wallet on me.

Maria puts her lips together and raises her eyebrows at me. "Ay, Xiomara, don't offend me." She kisses me twice on the cheeks and slaps my ass when I turn around to leave. While I walk to the door she's behind me, spraying hairspray and shoving a shower cap in the front pocket of my bag. I'm not going to use it. We both know that for sure.

"Flaca, you're all skin and bones!" Maria screams after me from the window when I'm outside. I give her the middle finger with my bad hand. It hurts me more than it hurts her. Then I disappear into my building.

"Dónde estabas?!" Mami shouts almost through me when I walk inside the apartment. The blue light of the television shines on her body. She's sitting up straight, eyes closed as she clings to the rosary beads in her hand. In the kitchen, I trip over a basket of prayer candles that have the face of Jesus stickered to the front. He's always with us in this house, with his hands on my throat begging me to be a good girl. I warm up the leftover yellow rice and kill a cockroach and listen to the heater as it chokes behind me.

"Mira!" Mami shouts again, demanding I answer her question. She's in the kitchen now. This tiled floor is our boxing ring.

"Don't worry about it," I reply, ducking out of the fight and turning the corner to the rest of our apartment.

"I worry!" Mami yells after me. I can hear the thick of her accent in the *R*'s, the way they roll and get caught in the back of her throat before she can finish the word in English.

"Well, don't!" I say, bracing for impact.

"You don't go there anymore." Mami's wailing and standing up now, frantic like someone's been murdered. She thinks I've been at Ellen's all night. "You don't go to that place! You don't be around those people!" By "those people," she means gay people. I feel a fire light up in my belly.

"Ay, Mami, ya, do I need to remind you that Nena *was* one of those people! Stop already!" Mami forgets that she's not so far removed from it. Not so holier-than-thou. That my sister was a lesbian and it's not a fact that she can keep sweeping under the rug and lying to her little church friends about.

I can tell she wants to hit me. I can tell she sees the disdain behind my eyes. I dare her to follow through before she sinks to her knees and starts wailing again. I follow her to the ground, placing my hands underneath her body while she drenches my shoulder in sweat and snot and a million other displaced emotions.

Mami is small in my arms. Like a flower that's been drenched in the rain. All wrinkled up, brown and muddy where she used to be pink. When I look at her these days, all the good is gone. No more dancing in the kitchen. No more Elvis Crespo on Christmas Eve. "That's okay," I whisper and start to sing her a lullaby, but before I can get a note out, her hands are over my mouth and I'm all wound up again.

Three years ago, when I was twenty-six and Nena was the age I am today, she went on a ski trip with Celeste and their friend Junior. I begged her not to. "We're Dominican," I said. "We don't ski. Plus, who wants to be in the snow like that? All cold and freezing and trying to keep your balance." Before she loaded her puffer into the car I could hear her laughing, shaking her head back and forth at me like I'd never stop being the annoying little sister. Like I really needed to live a little.

"I fell off the mountain," she said later when she called, and Mami had a conniption. "I broke both my wrists and my elbows and I was out there for almost an hour, but then a helicopter came to get me and, Xiomara, let me tell you it was SICK." She was excited, high off the adventure. I had held back the urge to say *I told you so.* My head started pounding, the way it is now in the waiting room of this doctor's office, and I started sipping on my saliva. I wish Nena hadn't lived so much life so soon.

"Xiomara Sanchez?" A nurse pops her head out the corner of the door and looks around until I stand up. It's been almost a week since my episode at the print shop and my wrist has only gotten worse. It's almost bubbling now, bruised up and tough around the edges of my skin. Not that I'm seriously considering it, but I'll never be able to audition for Manny's show like this. I'm taking it as a sign from hell.

"That's me," I say to the woman sitting next to me. I'm looking for Mami in her eyes. Someone to nod their head and tell me it's going to be okay. She doesn't speak English, so she just stares at me with pity and confusion. She has a rash on her face that I should have noticed sooner. Those types of things can be contagious. In the examination room, the nurse asks me to get naked and put on a surgical gown to cover my body.

"But it's only my wrist," I say.

The nurse laughs and walks out of the room. When I strip, I remember that I'm not wearing underwear. The air is cold on my nipples. When I look down, I notice all the hairs on my legs are standing up. I'm not wearing any lotion either. The doctor knocks twice and walks in, and I'm relieved that they are a she and not a he as I had imagined.

"So," she says while I stare at the ash between my big and second toe, "what happened here?"

"I fell at work," I say. I think I need to get a new story since she doesn't seem to be buying it either. Her eyes bat three times and wait for me to elaborate. "I work at a restaurant, you know, and the floor was slippery, and I fell."

She grabs my wrist and I wince.

"Looks pretty bad," she says, then tries to make a circle with the joint. I feel the pain all the way up and down my spine. She nods her head as though she's made a diagnosis then says, "We should take some X-rays and—"

"How much will that cost?" I cut her off before she can finish because this is what I was afraid of, and there's simply no way I can pay for an X-ray. The doctor looks at me and tilts her head. She's a blonde, I notice now, big-boned and pale in the face. On her right breast, her last name, Pataki, is on a name tag, crooked and hanging on by a safety pin.

"About three hundred dollars without insurance," she says. "But how 'bout this: I can bill you now and you can get reimbursed by your employer"—she pauses—"since they are liable . . . right?" She's challenging me, trying to force out the truth.

"I would hate to throw them under the bus like that," I say, breathing through it. "They're like my family, so really, no harm, no foul." I pause. My wrist feels like there are a thousand demons at war inside it. "Is there anything else we can do?" I'm picking my cuticles down to the quick.

"I wouldn't recommend it," she says. "We should really see what's going on in there."

"No X-rays," I insist.

The doctor looks at me for a moment and lets out a big breath, then scurries off to find me a brace.

"Can I ask you a question?" I ask, breaking the silence when she's back in the room wrapping my wrist up in a big black cast.

"Sure," she says, "go ahead."

"A girl falls off the side of a mountain skiing, breaks both of her wrists and elbows. She sits in the cold for an hour before someone hears her screaming. A helicopter comes, lifts her out of the snow, and takes her to the nearest hospital. They patch her up and send her on her way. Two years later, she crosses the sidewalk and her heart gives out. Just stops beating. I notice her wrists are a little swollen in her casket. Do you think one could have caused the other?"

The doctor's face has softened. Like she feels bad that I can't afford the basic cost of healthcare or that I'm crazy enough to say what I'm really thinking.

"No," she says, "I can be fairly sure one had nothing to do with the other. But you never know with these things. The human body is a mysterious thing."

I nod my head, and then she leaves so I can put my clothes back on.

When I'm done getting dressed, I open the door and can hear the doctor talking to the nurse about me in the lobby. I walk out of the examination room and step straight past the front desk as the doctor tries to get my attention. It's hard for me to make eye contact with her. There's a particular shame in admitting to white women that you are poor *and* pathetic. It's like telling them something they already believe, and I want to be the exception not the rule. She gives up on trying to connect and yells after me that she'll send a bill. Later, when I get it, I'll crumple it up and let it go to collections. I walk straight to the elevator, where I can start to pretend none of this ever happened.

When I pull out my phone, I see that I have two missed calls and a text from Santi: "Are you ok?" Then an emoji like he's been worried sick.

I want to say yes, I'm fine, I'm perfect and good and there's no need to worry about me, but I'm getting quite tired of not telling the truth.

Turns out that working at Ellen's is harder with a brace on.
I can barely pick up a plate without being reminded of my circumstances. Only Becky asks me what happened when I walk in; everyone else is too caught up in their own lives to notice. I tell her that my hand got caught in the subway doors and I had to rip it out before it got ripped off. She *oohs* and *aahs*. There's still something small-town enough about her to believe me, and her naivety is a welcome change.

I am coercing the host to seat my section back-to-back while she whisper-screams at me to stop being a pest. The end of the month is coming and I'm nowhere near catching up on our past-due bills. I'm dropping balls left and right today: Table 17 needs their matzo ball soup. Table 12 has been waiting for the check for more than ten minutes. Table 21 doesn't even have waters yet.

"Someone's asking for you at table forty-one," Becky says, spilling salad on my T-shirt as she passes by.

"Not my section," I bark back. "Tell Greta." I'm wiping off the dressing and making a fuss about the vinegary scent that's going to follow me around for the rest of the day.

"Don't shoot the messenger!" Becky yells back to me.

I ignore the request and stay focused on my section. I drop off the matzo ball soup. Take orders. Refill waters. Becky comes back around two or three more times. "Table forty-one is still asking."

I breeze by Greta and yell, "Handle your fucking section," before I land at the table in question and see Francesca, the agent who fired me last year after Nena died, eating a vegan burger and blinking quickly like she always did when she had bad news to tell me.

"Xiomara." I almost don't recognize my name the way she says it. It's flat in the center like someone has squished it all up and run it through an assimilation mill.

"Hi," I reply. I can feel the prickles of the sweat start to form under my arms. Neither of us talk again for a moment so I have time to notice her big hair, curly now like she's used a diffuser to get it that way. She always did have a thing for Blackness. Next to her sits a little girl, hair just like hers tucked half up in a ponytail while the rest hangs out and stops bluntly right above her collarbone. They both have big green eyes shaped like oversize ovals.

"I thought that was you," Francesca says, like she's accusing me of a crime.

"Gotta keep the lights on somehow." I hear my tone with her. It's cold, but I'm too stubborn to check it.

"So, you work here now?"

No, I don't work here. I just try on this costume and run around the diner with ketchup stains on my shirt for fun, I want to say. But instead, I nod my head. She doesn't deserve the verbal confirmation. It's silent again. Somewhere in another universe, parallel to this one, I am screaming. Stomping all over her vegan burger.

"Well, good for you."

"Is it?" I say almost involuntarily.

Francesca brushes the girl's hair behind her ear the same way she did to me last year when I sank to my knees and sobbed and begged her not to drop me after I fumbled that *Dreamgirls* callback and then missed twelve auditions in a row. It wasn't my fault I couldn't get out of bed long enough to make it downtown, Cassie keeps reminding me. My sister died.

"You always did have that fire," Francesca says, eyeing me up and down. It's a dig, but one that agents tend to get away with. Like a dagger hidden behind a string of happy words and positive affirmations.

"Do you need something here? I'm done talking to you and want to leave." I can't help but to be blunt with her after her betrayal.

"No, that's fine. Just thought I'd say hi."

The little girl waves at me.

"A bit of a delayed hello if you ask me. She should probably get that checked out."

I grab the empty plates on the table out of habit before storming off, leaving a trail of steam and shame behind me.

When I'm back in the kitchen, I tell Greta that 41 is ready for their check and she apologizes to me for missing the memo. "It's fine," I say, "just lock it up," but my eyes are glued to Francesca's table. I watch from the glass behind the double doors as Greta hands them the check and Francesca leaves.

"I guess that lady was an agent," Greta says to me and Becky after our shift. "She was here to sign Jacey." Now both my hand and my head are pounding.

"*See*, Xiomara," Becky sing songs while her eyes brighten up. "I told you real people come through here." She's dancing around the kitchen. "Ellen's is not a dead end after all."

"You're right," I say, softening, "this is just the start for us." I stroke Becky's hair between my fingertips. Today, I want to keep the lights on for her. I shove my things into my bag and make up some excuse about where I need to go so I can be out on the sidewalk when I cry, but instead, when I find myself out in the cold air of the city, I'm dialing Cassie.

"Fine, I'll go." My voice is low and matter-of-fact. "To the audition," I continue. "I'll go to the audition." Cassie screeches in my ear. I exhale. "It's just for . . . fun. I'm only going for fun, Cass."

"Yes." I can hear her nodding her head madly through the phone. "You're just going for fun."

I hang up before I can change my mind. I'm terrified that I've just unlocked the Pandora's box I've tucked away in my brain. If I'm not careful, it could let out a million little dreams that might obliterate me all over again.

Mami goes to work now every Monday, Wednesday, and half a day on Friday. When she locks the door behind her I run to the window and watch her walk toward Broadway, to the train that will take her to another train and drop her off in a place that is much greener than Washington Heights, to a home that is three times the size as ours so she can scrub it.

She is back to cleaning houses in Westchester and coming home to tell me that she was meant to *have* a home, not *clean* a home. Mami thinks she's better than all of this. I think that's where I get it from. This idea that I was born in the wrong skin and the wrong body and the wrong cross streets on the map of Manhattan.

When she's out of sight, finally, out of sight and into the depths of the subway like a shadow, I change into my leotard. It's tighter than it was before, when I would count my calories and sing my heart out and go to acting class twice a week while Nena and Francesca scoured *Backstage* for new auditions for me. My pubic hair pokes out through the tights, which are two shades too dark for me now, more like the color of my skin in the summer. My entire body trembles. If Mami saw me, she'd tie me to the cross. Tell me I've betrayed her. Judas! She'd point at me and combust.

My chest is tight and my inner thighs are tingling. I have this feeling like I'm going to puke and fall face-first into it. Maybe I'd drown there, on the ground, and Mami would find me. Then she'd know. That would do it. She'd know that I'm doing something I promised I'd never do again. She'd know that I'm a two-timing, backstabbing bitch who doesn't care one way or another whether my sister is here to see me succeed.

I turn off all the lights in the apartment and clear my throat so many times it starts to scratch. When I'm at Ellen's, I always phone it in so no one can really see me. Give all my solos away. Fade into the background. It's nothing like what I'll need to do in the audition. I point my foot and bring it back into my body, catch a glimpse of my silhouette in the dark mirror, a shadow of the person I used to be.

I breathe in deeply and watch my stomach fill with air. I remember how Nena would tell me to fill up my diaphragm first, not to breathe with my ribs, to load myself up properly. I place my hand on my belly. It rumbles with fear like it knows what I'm about to do. When I exhale, I let out a sound that pierces my ears. My eyes crinkle. My shoulders drop. I hear Nena and Mami in my head—otra, otra, otra. I fill up again. I open my mouth, the sound vibrates through my house, through my body. I'm overtaken with something familiar, something that has been dying to come out. I let myself sing like I did that night in the kitchen. I riff and I whistle and I tap my hands on the bottom of my torso and I push and I sing the melody until I hit the highest note at the top of the song and feel a relief wash over me. Like I'm underwater still but have grown fins. My body grasps for a breath and I give in. When I finally close my mouth, I know I've unraveled something that I can't tuck back in. I'm ravenous for the music, for the drama, for stories that wait to be projected to the last row of a packed theater. The chill of the blinding lights at curtain call; the heat of people screaming my name. I'm hungry for it all.

I let out another note, long and loud until I hear a thumping under me three times. It's Tony with the broom, shouting, *"Callaté, coño!"*

I stop. I just wanted to know if I still had it. I think this proves I do.

On the subway, I rehearse what I'll say to Santi when I ask him to cover my shift for me so I can go to Manny's audition on Monday. I keep tripping on my words when I play them in my head because I can't decide what should come first: my ask or my apology for the antics last week.

When I get to the print shop, it's lunchtime and Santi is chewing his food in the back room so violently that I can see his molars. Silver fillings line the back of his mouth, but at least his teeth aren't stained like mine from all the coffee. His teeth sparkle, like he's only ever drunk water. Joe's here today too. He works the front while Santi and I sit in the back, avoiding the customers and the copy machines.

"Did you know that ninety-seven percent of the sea is undiscovered or something?" Santi says to me while I open the microwave door to reheat the rest of the beans Mami made last night and pray they don't make me gassy. "It's terrifying," he continues, making a point, "how much we don't know about the Earth." The microwave smells like old tuna, so I eat the beans cold.

"Well, that's like, a metaphor for life at large, isn't it?" I say in response. I'm trying to be friendly, trying to get him to join my team. Sauce gets caught on my top lip, and Santi makes a hand movement to tell me that he can't take me seriously with this stuff on my face. I'm always amazed by people who can do this, act as though they are close with someone when they barely know their first name. I napkin off the side of my mouth.

"I guess so." He seems to be searching in the back of his head for something else to say. "Lots to discover."

I'm chewing now and nodding my head up and down. I feel his eyes make his way down to my palm. "So how's your hand?" he asks, pulling on a cheese string. I guess it will have to be my apology first, then.

"It's eh," I say, though it's actually feeling a lot better since the brace went on. I can even close my grip now without wincing, and I'm starting to get the hang of carrying my food trays at Ellen's again. But I'm afraid if I tell him that I'm almost healed he might stop asking, and I like being baby, so I rub my right hand over my left where it used to hurt and pretend that it's still sensitive to my touch.

"So, anyway, sorry about the other day," I say. "I'm . . . embarrassed." I'm not embarrassed, though. Not really. I'm angry inside, sure, and lost and maybe a little rotten in the center, but I don't think I'm embarrassed. Not by what I did, anyway. Maybe just that he saw.

"Nothing to be embarrassed about," Santi says in between bites. "I get it." I usually hate when people say that, say that they understand where I'm coming from when they really fucking don't, but there's something about the way Santi slips it out that makes me unclench my jaw. It's like he can actually see me.

"So, uh, anyway," I say, "I'm bad at beating around the bush. I'm just gonna get right to it."

"Please," he says, like he knows I've been playing a game this whole time.

"I need next Monday off. For an audition." The word *audition* almost gets stuck in the back of my throat like one of Mami's *R*'s.

"An actress!" Santi smirks, genuinely excited to get something out of me. "Go on."

"A singer, really," I correct him, "but that's neither here nor there. I was thinking that maybe I could switch with you on Wednesday." There's a beat. "And I could even pick up your Sunday." Another beat. "Only if you really need it, though."

"Two for the price of one," Joe says, storming into the room and grabbing his coat. "I'm outta here," he says to me. "Don't trust her," he says to Santi. Then he's gone and we're alone again.

"Okay, I'll play," Santi says, folding his arms across his body and leaning back in his chair. "On one condition."

"Okay, list your demands." I roll my eyes. It's always this way with men. *I give you this if you'll give me that.* But he's looking at me closer now, and I kind of like it.

"One coffee." Santi lifts his eyebrows. "One coffee . . . together."

I realize he means a date. One where I sit across from him and unpack my feelings and sip on a shitty espresso. I inhale and hold the breath in my chest. Santi sways his head forward and cups his hand around his ears to signal to me that he's waiting for a response.

"I don't appreciate your need for quid pro quo," I say, sticking my bad hand out, "but I do respect it."

We shake on it. His hand lingers on mine, strong, firm, like he might never let go. Mami always said you can judge a man by his handshake. She said Papi's was like a floppy fish, so she should have known. I feel my knees start to sink together before he pulls me closer and whispers: "You know, I would have done it either way."

With my hand still touching his, I'm waiting for sparks or fire or something to make my heart beat out my chest, but instead I get all static and my eyes are droopy. It's like he's a doctor or something, the way his eyes move around the surface area of my skin, examining and rubbing warmth into me like he can make it all better.

I can't remember the last time I've been taken care of. It's a funny feeling, surrendering myself to it. When the bells on the door ding, I shift in my hips and he lets go of my hand softly, like he's placing down a baby bird who isn't yet ready to fly out of its nest. For Santi, my hands grow feathers.

"I got it," he says, his voice like water.

When he's gone, he leaves just his scent in the room, lingering around me. I hear him helping a customer in the front who is asking for a refund. I'm thinking about how we don't do refunds here because Alek's a cheapskate and also about how my body isn't burning with heat and heartbeats. I'm confused at how grounded my feet feel, especially here in the back room of Alek's, trying to find a good reason to justify why it is that when Santi touches me, I slow down, I don't speed up.

It's the first of the month today so all the ants in my blood are congealing together. Clotting, making it hard for me to breathe.

"We give him what we have," Mami says. She's concerned and awake today like the ants have gotten to her too. "We tell Juan Carlos we give the rest in next month."

I want to shake her until she hears me say that this is not how it works. We don't have until next month. "I have to go to Ellen's tonight," I say, not caring enough about her opinion today to hide my whereabouts. I can tell Mami is holding in her anger by the way she sighs and taps her nails on the counter. "Don't open the door if he comes," I add. The ants are turning into hornets, getting ready to sting me so I go into anaphylactic shock. "Don't open the door," I double down.

She makes a hand gesture like she's zipping her mouth and throwing away the key. When I leave, I check the bolt on our door twice.

In the hallway, I'm looking over my shoulder. There's this sense that something is behind me waiting to shake me until hundred-dollar bills finally fall out of my veins. Outside, I'm doing the same, turning my head every which way to make sure that Juan Carlos isn't chasing me down the street with an eviction notice. By the time I get to Ellen's, I am exhausted, completely wound up from the roller coaster of my morning. Behind the doors of the locker room, Becky is crying.

"His name was Rupert," she says to me, completely seriously, showing me a photo of her and her parents and their (*now dead*) dog lying in bed together under tacky blue sheets, all of their bellies in the air. The dog is gray and shaggy and looks like it smells wet, like the undercurrent of sand after the shore washes away.

Saundra is showing some sort of remorse, rubbing her back, saying, "They really are like family."

I don't quite know what to do with my hands. Saundra looks at me like she pities my inability to be present in hard moments and then tells me to bus Becky's tables. I fold up my jacket and make my way out to the floor. Ellen's today is like a circus.

Becky's section is already bustling. I can see the people poking their heads out from under their menus, anticipating the show. I can't believe how badly I want to sing today. It's from the unraveling. From letting myself get a taste of the things I love again. From my stupid crush on Santi and the softness starting to reveal itself in my heart. All I can think about is getting on that counter.

Table 13 is calling me over. It's a girl and her mother and a man who seems like not her father. He's talking a lot when I arrive.

"Finally," the girl says. She's about thirteen and has an attitude, but I fall in love with her anyway. It makes me excited to see impatient young women. Young women who know exactly what they want exactly when they want it. It's just too bad when I'm on the opposite side of their anger.

"I've been waiting all day to see you too!" I joke back. She rolls her eyes while she tells me her and her mom's order, then commands the man who I now know is most certainly not her father to tell me what he wants from the menu. He sweats and laughs a hundred times before he finally lands on the cinnamon roll pancakes and a Bloody Mary.

"Gross," the girl says under her breath. The mom pinches her under the table. The girl pinches back. I grab the menus from the table and walk away completely full.

I'm not on the schedule for a solo today, but Becky's still crying so I take her song, "There's a Fine, Fine Line" from *Avenue Q*, which I'm not nasal enough for. I see Saundra run out the double doors when she hears my voice. She's nodding her head and giving me a thumbs-up, wiping the sweat off her forehead as if I've just saved her small business.

When the people clap today, I feel naked suddenly, aware of what I've done, of what I've given of myself, and I try to squirm my way out of it so I can finish my shift with my head on straight. It's okay, I'm telling myself, it's okay that I'm only ready for my sofa to hear me really sing right now. I'm like Stella. Just on my way to get back my groove.

"That was *gorgeous*," I hear someone say behind me. When I turn around, I see it's a man at table 6. I know I know him, but I can't put my finger on how. He's wearing a fedora like my great-grandfather used to and a tiny round pair of black glasses that I can tell don't have a prescription in them because from the side they are not even a little bit distorted.

"Thank you," I say. I'm out of breath, surveying his face for clues to where we've met before.

"Can I get a coffee?" he says to me under his breath, like he's waiting for me to put two and two together. I'm bad at math so I still can't place him. I nod my head and scurry off to the kitchen. Jacey and her minion Jenny are whispering in the corner and staring at me like I have five heads. I pour the coffee and swing back out the double doors. I hate them so much.

I place the coffee down and it loses its balance and spills all over the table and onto the man's red trench coat. I croak that I'm sorry and grab the rag from my apron and start moving the liquid off of him and onto me. He's laughing so loud that it's drawing attention, and I'm saying I'm sorry I'm sorry I'm sorry until I'm nearly blue in the face. His hand stops mine from moving and tells me it's okay. I can feel the calluses on his knuckles. Jonah, my favorite busboy, comes over and gets the rest of the coffee drippings while I crouch awkwardly on my ankles in the booth.

"How long you been singing?" the man asks.

"I don't know, maybe my whole life," I reply. I appreciate the way he's calming me down, even though I've just spilled scalding hot coffee onto his very expensive clothing.

"You're really good." He states it like he knows for sure. Less of a compliment, more of a fact.

"Thank you," I say. I try not to add *but there are so many people who are so much better than me.* The urge to tear myself down is detrimental to the groove I'm growing back. "You have to be more confident in yourself than they are," I hear Nena telling me in the back of my mind, "because you'll scare them away if they can see your insecurity."

Once the table is clean, I go get another cup of coffee. In the kitchen, I decide he deserves the whole pot. When I arrive back at the table, I place it down and curtsy.

"For your troubles," I say.

He winks and then hands me his credit card. It's like Cassie's but heavier, like a block of gold at the bottom of the ocean.

"It's on the house," I say, returning the card. "I'm sorry for spilling on your . . . cape."

He laughs again so loud the whole restaurant hears him.

"Shhh," I put my hand over his mouth instinctively, "don't go getting me fired!" As he quiets himself down, I take my hand off his lips and realize I've only just met him. "I'm sorry," I say again.

"That's at least your hundredth apology today," he says. His smile is like fire.

I walk away from his table red and hot and with butterflies flocking all over in my stomach. I go to the bathroom to splash water on my face and slap myself a few times to get out of my tizzy. When I come back out, he's gone and the rest of my tables are twisting their necks around for my attention.

In the kitchen, Jonah comes over to me. He's red in the face too. "I can't believe you just spilled coffee all over Manny Santos."

It's Manny. Manny, Manny. The only Manny in America who anyone even cares about. The entire waitstaff is screaming and buzzing and asking me questions. I'm too embarrassed to say I couldn't place him. Jacey and Jenny are still in the corner, giving me eyes like I've killed their baby.

When I go back to clear off table 6, I find an envelope under the pot of coffee. There's a note in it that says "For your troubles" tucked around another stack of papers that I soon realize are ten hundred-dollar bills. I taste pennies in my mouth, and suddenly my feet are moving. I run outside, sure he didn't mean to leave me this much money, and when I can't find him right away, I stop looking. I tuck the envelope into my pocket, and as I walk back inside, I'm right on time for my cue to climb on the counter. Up there, my voice is beaming like lasers, bouncing across the walls of this restaurant. I can't think. I can only sing. The whole time I'm too electrified to ask questions. Maybe Mami's right about God or something. Maybe I can get with it if He's starting to work in my favor.

"Are you fucking stupid?! Of course, she's going to keep it," Maria says to Cassie while she slugs down her Hennessy and Coke. They're arguing about Manny's money.

"There are strings with stuff like that, Xiomara, trust me." Cassie can barely look at Maria without gagging, as if she finds her entire nature filthy.

"You're both too late," I say. "I already paid our rent with it."

Cassie's face drops.

Maria is clapping her hands and twerking. "Get paid, bitch! I know that's right."

"And what are you going to do next month, Xiomara?" Cassie asks.

"Ay, Cassie, callaté with your fucking moral compass. You're one to talk!" Maria screams while she passes me the scissors. We're all spread out on her floor making pink beaded bracelets that read NO BOO JUST BITCHES and watching *Fifty Shades of Grey* for Valentine's Day.

"I just think you should be careful—"

"And I just think you should be quiet!" I slam back. I'm done with this conversation. Even with Manny's money, I'm still behind on bills. There are student loans from my year at Carnegie Mellon, and ConEd bills, and taxes that dance around me while I'm trying to dream. I don't know what I'm going to do about next month! Who knows if I'll even make it to next month! These could be my last living seconds! People die all the time!

The doorbell rings while Mr. Grey is blindfolding Anastasia with his tie.

"That's my date," Maria says. She's putting on lipstick in the mirror and cupping her tits up in her bra. "Y'all need to go."

"Wasn't the point of this that none of us had dates?" Cassie asks. My eyes are glued to the screen.

"Things change, mama. Just because you aren't getting any dick doesn't mean the rest of us have to stay celibate with you." Maria swings the door open and nearly pushes us out of the apartment while a man in a wifebeater walks in. He's licking his lips like Maria's a steak dinner.

"I didn't even get to finish my bracelet!" Cassie's yelling.

Before we're in the elevator, I can hear Maria moaning.

"Your cousin is fucking unbearable," Cassie says to me a few seconds later, as the doors open and spit us out in the lobby.

"Yeah, well, she's the only one I got," I say. I hug Cassie goodbye and run across the street back to Mami's. I turn and see Cassie, clutching her purse all the way back to the subway.

When I'm inside and getting ready for bed, I'm so horny that I'm dripping through my cotton underwear. I haven't been laid in so long, and tonight all my nerve endings are begging to be touched. I'm brushing my teeth in the bathroom and staring at my reflection in the mirror, wishing Mami weren't home and that I could call literally anyone to bend me over the sink and get me where I need to be. I spit the toothpaste out and watch the blue foam circle its way down the drain.

I drag my feet down the hallway and into my bedroom. It's like a time machine in here—old NSYNC and Aventura posters on the wall, pink stickers and marker stains lining the edges of the window. I get into bed, the same twin-size one I've been sleeping in since I was seven years old. It has a white crown of flowers on the headboard, staring down at me telling me to be a good girl. I toss and turn until I finally give in and let my right hand make its way down inside my panties. It's already warm and wet and all my nerves are on the edge of their seats. I think about Santi squeezing past me at the print shop. His shoulders—the way they are wide but not too bulky. His skin and how it feels like butter. His hands and how they rubbed on my wrist. How his mouth is always sparkling, winking at me.

I close my eyes and take a deep breath, drawing out the sounds of the merengue blaring through the window from Yvette's bar across the street. While I pull down my panties, I imagine the people are dancing in there, men's hands sweating against the waists of the women they want tonight. I start to move my fingers, up and down across my clitoris until my heart rate picks up and I'm surprised to see Alek's face against the back of my eyelids. I go with it because I'm too far in. He smells like fresh mint and cigarette smoke. Suddenly I'm transported back into the print shop. I'm trying hard not to think about why it is I'm craving to be here. I'm more busty in this print shop than I am in reality, leaning over the counter as Alek sticks his nose between my legs and Santi grabs my hair and tells me I'm beautiful. I'm speeding up with my middle finger, covering my mouth with my left hand to hold in my moans. I don't let myself be distracted by the sickness of my fantasy. The way I want four hands on my body, telling me what to do, throwing me against the wall, sticking themselves inside me one right after another.

I'm breathing so heavy and so hard that I don't hear Mami rustling around in the hallway. I just hear the insides of my skin, buzzing with excitement and buildup until I cum and Santi's staring into my eyes while Alek is choking me with two fingers in my mouth.

"Asquerosa!" Mami shouts when she flicks the light on.

I'm still panting, pretending I'm sleeping, making a show, and squinting my eyes so she'll think that maybe I've just been dreaming this whole time.

She speeds out the room and the lights blind me while I wipe the sweaty strands of hair away from my face. I rub my hands against the blanket just before she returns. She's screaming under her breath with her rosary beads in her hands. I'm scared she'll scatter rice down on the floor and make me kneel in it until I'm bleeding. Her eyes are full of fury while she makes me pray, shaking her hands against mine with the beads, demanding I give her what she wants. I recite a prayer to

Santa María over and over again until salty tears fill my lids and I'm sucked into believing that I'm good for nothing. It's like these words coming out of my mouth are meant to make me wonder why I am the way I am. Why I have this thing inside me that refuses to get better. I pray that I can change. That I can dig my own grave and bury myself in it. I pray that there's an end soon. One Hail Mary until every bead is done. When I'm through, Mami slaps me across the face and turns off the lights. Amen.

The sun has barely risen over the Hudson River as I make my way from the A train to Manny's open call. Salt is crunching under my feet and turning the snow into slush. I'm careful not to slip on black ice and break my back before the world can recognize me for my talents. When I finally make it to the audition, everyone looks just like me but better. It's like there have been six thousand cardboard cutouts of Xiomara Sanchez dropped off here on the corner of 18th Street and Tenth Avenue at six in the morning. I walk down the hall and keep my eyes to myself. It smells like cold cement and pigeon shit. The lights are fluorescent and I'm freezing. Overwhelmed by the competition. Everyone here has a dream. I wonder what exactly makes me think mine is so special.

I approach a makeshift plastic desk and tell my name to the receptionist, who is just another girl who wants the same part. She hands me a black pen and a sheet of paper and tells me to write out my name along with my height and the part I am going after.

"I'm auditioning for Dolores," I say like she might call the paparazzi to snap some early photos of me. "The lead," I add after another long breath.

The receptionist has already moved on from me. The names before mine take up nearly the entire page so *Xiomara* is squished down at the bottom so sloppily written that I'm sure I might as well be disregarded from this alone.

My bag hangs heavy on my shoulder until I can't feel my arm anymore and I have a big mark from the weight of the bag's fake leather strap carved into my muscle. I feel a throbbing through my nervous system. I slap the bag down on the ground and sit in a corner. I dream of Manny coming out, seeing me, and dismissing the rest of the girls piled up here and handing me my ticket to stardom. I pull out my water bottle, take a big gulp. The honey I put at the bottom coats my throat. Girls are being called in, some one by one to sing, others in big groups of about ten or so to learn the dance number. I hope I sing first today. My singing is an A. My dancing, on a good day, is a C+.

I fold my body over my legs, and my hamstrings tighten up like a spring. It burns between my knees as I reach for my toes. I exhale and feel my chest like a pretzel, all in knots. The floor between my thighs is dusty. I can see the lint balls and the loose hairs and the leftover salad dressing all meeting there between my legs. I wonder how many other people have sat exactly where I'm sitting today, lifting their arms above their heads, stretching their necks from side to side, dreaming they'll get their lives changed.

I yawn a hundred times in a high pitch to open up my throat. When Jacey walks in, it all closes down again. She's floating today, wearing all lavender and a silk skirt that hangs around her hips like it was painted there. When she glides by me, I can smell her scent, a potion she concocted to make everyone swoon after her. It's like amber and rosewood, serious but sweet enough to define her femininity. It works; people turn to check her out. She looks right through me when she sees me as if we don't spend every hour of every evening serving French toast and singing show tunes next to each other. My wrist is throbbing.

My daydream of calling Jacey a cunt and slapping her in with my good hand is interrupted when a white lady with a giant clipboard and big curly hair like Francesca's emerges from the room that holds all the dancers. She calls out a bunch of names—Caryn, Sabrina, Maya, Jacey—and then points at me and says, "And you too. Room for one more."

My underarms get hot and sweaty. I'm dancing first. I leave my bag in the hall and slip into my dance shoes, which are marked up and overworn. My hair is tight, gelled back into a bun on the top of my head like all the other girls next to me as we line the mirror-filled walls. We all get numbers on a slip of paper. I'm seven. I don't like that number; it feels like a curse.

Behind a fold-out table, I see the producers—Lisa, Larry, and Terry—who I recognize from my past life. Lisa was my teacher at AMDA five years ago. Larry and Terry tried to get me for *Hairspray* a month after Nena passed. I'm hoping they don't remember me. Hoping none of them know about the way I ghosted my agent and sunk into oblivion last year.

"Xiomara Sanchez at an open call!" Lisa says, looking over her stack of papers and reapplying her ChapStick. She remembers. Jacey cackles and clears her throat. I pretend like it's not getting to me, the groupthink and the pretty girls, and the dreadful knowing that I have to move my feet to a beat in what will likely be less than sixty seconds.

The door slams behind me and Manny flies in. He's in his red trench coat again. It's dragging behind him, floating on the wind. He's barefoot, moving like the Mad Hatter.

"LADIES!" he shouts and whips around to face us. I'm shrugging my shoulders up to my ears. Clenching my jaw and standing on my tiptoes like a child. When our eyes meet, I want to ask him if he remembers about the diner and the spilled coffee and the ten loose hundred-dollar bills. I want to ask him if he sees me. My problem in life is how badly I want to be seen.

The girl with the big clipboard tells us that Manny is going to teach us the choreography for the day. She wraps her hair on the top of her head to match ours while Manny moves the balls of his feet up and down, tapping to the music that is blasting through the speakers. I don't recognize the melody, but I can hear every note, all the breaths behind it, the hours that it probably took to create something so succinct and special. I'm ravenous to sing with it. The words are bubbling up in my throat and I'm struggling to keep them down so much that I miss learning half the movement.

Manny is shouting—"Right, left, right, LEGGG, left, right, left, GET THAT LEG HIGH, turn, turn, contract, AGAIN!"—and I watch the girls around me as they study his body, every micro move-ment vibrating through his muscles. I try to catch up, mimicking his big motions like a shadow.

Manny walks us through it again, slower this time, step-by-step. I thank fucking God that he's repeated himself, and I make sure not to miss the first half again, which looks more complicated than the last. My leg is tight, half as high as the rest of the girls when I kick it into the air. Manny comes behind me and whispers, "You're okay, gor-geous," before he catches my leg in the air and stretches it long above my head. Maybe he does know who I am. Maybe he is here, finally, to save me. I'm just moments away from a snap in my tendon and the whole room is watching us now. I feel that naked feeling again, and I don't have the chance to shake it off. I'm still recovering when he splits us up into groups of five and we run through the movement once more.

Manny sends two people home right away. They smile like they're unaffected, but if it had been me, I'd flush my face right down the toilet. We're soon down to four groups of four. Then three groups of three. At the end, there are just four of us women left, standing in the room, our bodies hot and sweaty and dying to look beautiful while we prance and kick and fight for our lives in here. That's a job assigned to women, I guess. To look like Sunday morning, even amid a mad and wild workweek.

Manny partners me up with Jacey, and before I can protest, he counts us in. I feel myself floating in my mediocrity. Dancing is like Spanish to me—I pretend I'm fluent when really I know only enough to smile and get by. Jacey, on the other hand, is tight like a robot next to me. It's so obvious she's been training her entire life for this mo-ment while I've been lying under the blankets with the lights off eating potato chips.

Leg, leg, leg, I think in my mind. Right, left, kick, higher. My hip flexor is threatening me. I finish like a fish washed up on the sand, desperately trying to swim while the pebbles scrape up my insides and leave me hollow. Manny dismisses us all. We file out the room. No singing today. The lady with the clipboard tells us to expect an email if we've made it to the next round, to expect silence if we haven't.

When I get back to my bag and start to unravel myself, my toes are bleeding through my shoes. I can feel them crusted over, sticking to the fabric and the sweat between my feet. Before I change into clean socks, I wipe the blood from between my toes onto my fingers. Everywhere on my body is red from pushing it so hard. I force my Dunks on too roughly and my toe starts gushing again. There's nothing I can do so I keep moving forward and beeline for the elevator before the rest of the girls can see me.

When I'm inside, I press the door-close button a hundred times but it's like the lift refuses to hear me. Jacey slides in and I thumb through my cell phone, pretending to answer emails or texts, which in reality I have none of. Somehow, she looks already showered. Refreshed. More beautiful than before.

"You sucked ass in there," she says after a long breath.

My eyes start stinging and my body is trembling more than I can manage. "I'm sorry" is all I can think to say. It's just like me to apologize during the live stream of my public stoning. On the way out, I throw my number into the garbage. I hope seven burns in hell. I knew it was a curse from the start.

Even when I sleep, Jacey's words ring in my head: *You sucked ass in there.* I wake up mumbling, searching for my contact lenses above my bed and refreshing my email's inbox repeatedly. I haven't gotten an email from casting yet, but I'm manifesting it. Putting whatever Santería there is left in my veins to good use. I'm also sneaking off to the studio every day to rehearse and using next month's rent money to cover the cost. I've evaded Juan Carlos before; I have faith that I can do it again.

It's Friday so I only have five hours until Mami gets back and starts asking questions. I watch her leave from the window and slip on my leotard and run down the steps and toward the subway. I'm meeting Cassie at Ripley-Grier to go over the choreography. She's going to be cruel about my dancing, but I know that's just what I need. I hop over a puddle of mystery liquid and swing over the turnstiles at 181st Street. The train pulls in and I sprint on and claim my space by opening my legs. I search my surroundings. No masturbating men today. No women who look like Nena and Celeste either. I forget that sometimes it can be like this, peaceful in New York City. That sometimes in between a night out and a morning after, the subway becomes a liminal space. A rocket ship zooming me downtown at the speed of light to meet my well-deserved moment.

I close my eyes, and when I open them, I'm already at 34th Street. It's more crowded here, people rubbing their eyes awake and spilling their coffees on the tips of their tongues. I walk up and out into the foggy New York City air.

I head uptown, toward 37th Street, past the bagel store and the Broadway billboards, and the Macy's that Abuela used to come to every Sunday after mass.

"Xiomara Sanchez," I say, checking into the building. The security guard is eating a slice of pizza at nine in the morning, playing Candy Crush on his Android. His face is so red it looks like the pepperoni. I clear my throat and tap my finger on the counter to get his attention.

"Back up, ma'am," he says to me, completely seriously, like I'm a threat. I want to stretch my arms out and strangle him with the gooey mozzarella caught in his beard, but I back up from the counter and wait to hear him lose his game. When he does, I hand him my ID and he takes a photo of me from a weird angle.

Cassie walks in right behind me. "Hey, Stew," she says to the guard and heads straight to the elevator. She presses the button three times and points to me. "She's good." Since Cassie's debut, the studio invites her to come here all the time. She's like a shining star with her little white body and glowing white skin.

Stew looks at me up and down and up again. "How do you say your name?" he says to me now, like all of a sudden he's interested in getting dinner.

"Back up," I say while I grab my ID out of his hand.

Cassie and I take the elevator up to the tenth floor. When the doors ding open, Cassie nearly sprints to Studio A.

"This is the best one," she's saying while I try to keep up with her. I don't have the heart to tell her I rented out Studio B. When we're inside the space, she locks the doors like she knows and I plop my bag down. No mark on my shoulder this time. Today I'm not so heavy. I slide off my sweats and stretch until I'm on another planet where gravity doesn't apply to me.

"Okay, let's see it," Cassie says. I feel the sweat from my nerves dripping out of my pores. "C'mon, let's go."

I stand up and throw off my wrist brace. It's not going to help me look like a Broadway star, and I need all the help I can get. I start moving my body, and I know it's clumsy, she doesn't have to tell me. I'm hearing in my head *right left right LEGGG*, and shooting every muscle in my memory with a dose of adrenaline. I forget the steps to the hook. It's harder without the music, harder without Manny standing in front of me or behind me whispering that I'm okay. I stop my steps and feel my heart race and the water start to drip out my eyes.

"That's it," I say, throwing my hand up like I'm tossing a piece of paper in the garbage.

"Okay, X," Cassie says after a long minute of silence and staring. "Don't get mad, but that's like really bad."

"That's why you're here to help," I say, snapping. I get defensive when people tell me the truth.

"Okay, okay, shake it off, just like, what's this play about again anyway?" Cassie's trying to do a fucking scene study.

I take a breath. "It's about an explorer," I say. "A Black woman who is traveling across the multiverse and finding different versions of herself. And her decision to come home or not. To get back to herself or to stay away."

Cassie's thinking. "Then, I think you need more longing. You need to feel that all the way down to the bone. All the way out in your fingers." Cassie shows the choreography, perfectly, like she'd been practicing all this time. Her body looks right doing it. I'm trying not to melt down. "Go again," she says to me when she's through, and I do, because I want this. I'm almost sick to my stomach now with this ginormous realization of how I want this so bad that I'll do anything. I'll be anyone.

"Okay, again," she says. Her voice is like my sister's. We go over and over until our feet are in a perfect line and even the rough parts of my palms look elegant.

"I'm at capacity," I say, out of breath, when I think I have it down. She keeps going.

"Eight shows a week, X. You gotta be able to give me more than that."

I accept the challenge and jump back in until every step of choreography is burned into my muscles.

A woman in a nude jumpsuit comes in and tells us she's booked Studio A. She's watching us like a shark, circling around the room as though she wants to eat us both alive. I feel myself holding down the spare chunks of my breakfast. I can't speak, so Cassie tells her we'll be right out and packs up our things.

"Better," she says to me on the elevator. "You're doing better."

I know what she's saying, but I'm overtaken with a feeling, like a sharp needle stuck underneath my toenail, because I wish she'd mean that about something more than just my dancing.

Out on the sidewalk, we bump into Santi. He's waving me down with a smile so big it could take up the entire Atlantic, clutching the handles of a Citi Bike and running across the street through traffic.

"Hey," I say as he approaches. I'm wearing just my leotard, leggings, and a hat. Even with the sweat, the exhaustion, I'm pleased with what I look like for once.

"Xiomara, what are you doing here?"

"Rehearsing," I say, pointing to the building behind us and then to Cassie, who waves.

"Dope," Santi says. He looks different outside of the print shop. Brighter. Like he has places to be.

"Hey, mama, I gotta hit it." Cassie has a blaccent around boys she thinks are sexy. "Nice to meet you . . ." Her voice trails off.

"Santi," he replies, filling in her sentence.

"Nice to meet you, Santi." She's sticking out her hand, giving him those doe eyes and pouting out her lips. Santi is still looking at me.

"Okay, bye, Cassie," I say, nearly pushing her out of our orbit.

When she walks away and only I can see her, she turns around and mouths, "HOT!" before disappearing into the back of a taxi.

"So . . . is this what you were so afraid of?" Santi says, locking his Citi Bike around a bus pole.

I lift my eyebrows like I don't know what he's talking about.

"Like, seeing me outside the walls of the print shop so I can actually see your face instead of just seeing you like . . ." He motions his hands over his head chaotically, pretending to be me, overtaken by grief, attempting to slam my hand off my body. His hand accidentally lands on a businessman's cashmere coat.

"Sorry, man," he says and lifts his shoulders to his chin while he laughs a little. The man scoffs, and Santi gives me a look. "White people. Coffee?"

"I guess now's as good a time as ever," I say. I'm trying to keep it cool, though I can feel the no-chill seeping outside of my pores. Somewhere between the print shop and this sidewalk I think I've developed a crush. I put on my sweater, and we walk two blocks to a coffee shop. Inside it's all sepia toned so Santi's skin looks golden. I order a hot chocolate and he orders a black coffee.

"I think I'm more addicted to sugar than I am coffee," I say. Santi laughs and throws over two packs of Stevia, and I stick my tongue out.

"So," he says to fill the silence when we finally sit, "how was your audition?"

My cheeks get hot at the mention of it. "I sucked ass."

Santi howls with his mouth wide open. "Sucked ass?!" He claps his hands together twice and throws back his head. It's charming to see a man be that free. "Come on, you did not suck ass."

I place my lips around the rim of the mug and suck up the whipped cream, so I have a mustache when I speak again. "I did, I sucked ass, even Jacey told me I did."

"Right, and obviously we believe everything Jacey says, don't we?"

"Exactly." I nod my head up and down.

"Exactly," he floats back to me, then licks his thumbs. "I think you're cool."

"You barely know me," I say.

"Yet." Santi points his finger up toward me, finishing my sentence and breathing out the steam of his coffee.

I roll my eyes. Guys like Santi think this life is some sort of romantic fucking comedy.

"So," he says, "tell me about this Jacey character anyway. How do you know her?"

"I sing with her at Ellen's," I answer, and I'm scared he's going to judge me. Find out I'm just a weird musical-theater girl who memorizes Jason Robert Brown in her spare time.

"Ellen's?" Santi's an amateur.

"Ellen's Stardust Diner," I say. "Look it up."

Santi pulls out his phone and asks Siri what Ellen's Stardust Diner is. She replies and I see him pinching his lips together, raising his eyebrows like he's discovered my dirty little secret.

"Shut up," I say.

"I didn't even say anything!" Santi's hands are in the air like he's not at fault.

"Well, shut up anyway."

His eyes are lighting up like we're kids on the playground and he's pulling at my pigtails. "This is cool," he says, his eyes not leaving mine. "I gotta stop by one of these days." I'm blushing but trying not to.

Santi doesn't make me stare at him for much longer after that. He insists on walking me to the subway, and I let him, though I do protest enough that I'm worried he thinks I'm dying for this to end. We skip down the subway stairs, and a drop of water from the ceiling lands on my forehead. Santi sticks his thumb in his mouth and wipes it off.

"Ew, you've been all around New York City. You're gonna get Ebola," I say, slapping the wet of his spit off my face. The uptown train is three minutes away. Santi stands next to me and starts making names for the rats that run down on the tracks.

"That one looks like a Teddy," I say, joining him. "That one's an Angus; he's a Sam-Marshall."

"Why are all your rats men?" he interrupts me.

"Sam-Marshall could be a woman," I reply coyly.

"Yeah, yeah, yeah." He bumps his shoulder against mine.

It's quiet again so I start counting the people on the Brooklyn-bound side of the track. There's a woman with an umbrella. A girl with a stomach that hangs outside of her shirt. A boy cracking a Rubik's Cube and thrusting his hips up and down in the air out of celebration. My eyes land on a man with two fat children tugging on his pants. He's yelling at them to stop. Slapping their little hands off him, grabbing them by the wrists. I hear his voice, one like I've heard before, threatening me with a cocotazo. I squint my eyes and lean forward, then realize that it's Papi standing there across from me with his modern family.

My breath leaves my body. I stare too hard, and he must feel me because he looks up and sees me too. I'm always fascinated by the fact that humans can feel when there are eyes on them. I convulse, make a sound loud enough that Santi steps back. Papi's spine straightens and I turn toward Santi, grab his collar, and press my mouth against his until the train comes. When I hear the wheels screech to a halt, I let go.

"Don't say anything." I put my hand over his mouth and then hop on the subway. Santi's face is like an amusement park, full of wonder. As the doors close, his eyes won't leave me. The train pulls away.

I ride the A all the way back uptown while my heart races and my mind folds in on itself. Into the tunnel I go, out at 181st Street, never to see my father again.

Papi's story goes like this: He was born in La Guajaca, República Dominicana, in 1967. Right away, he is working. Tending to the farm and praying that the land is fertile and taking a bath in the river when the sun comes up. He does this until Papa sends money for him to move to Washington Heights. When he gets there all he craves is Malta India, so he skips school and gets some at the bodega and ice skates at Rockefeller Center and learns broken English so he can sing and ask for money on the A train. He drops out of P.S. 187 and starts work as a doorman at an upscale hotel near Columbus Circle. He saves his tips in the back of his drawer for vacation. When Papi finally has three hundred dollars he goes to Puerto Rico, where Papa tells him not to go off and get anybody pregnant because Puerto Rican women are sucia. But then Papi meets Mami and he falls madly in love. They marry, he brings her to New York, and Nena is born and then so am I. But Papi has a wandering eye. He is looking everywhere but here. He is looking at the women in the church and on the corner and at the bodegita and at the casino, but Papi is never looking at Mami. So soon Papi has more children and less time. Less time for Nena. Almost no time for me. He is gone when Nena dies, and sure, Mami doesn't handle her death well, but Papi doesn't handle it at all, doesn't even show face at the funeral. Last I heard he moves upstate with a new girl, a Dominicana, a morenita, a gringa. I hear he has two kids, boys, who stand across from me on the subway platform and tug at his pants while he yells, slapping their hands away from his body.

A few days after our kiss on the subway, I've picked nearly all the skin off the side of my thumb while I wait for Santi at the print shop. I know it wasn't even anything real, our kiss, but I haven't been able to stop feeling it, his lips on mine and his eyes following me into the train car. It's starting to scare me, the way I'm beginning to care about some dude I work with while I'm in the shower and on the A train. Santi walks in thirty minutes after our shift has started. At first, I pretend not to notice him jingling the door handle while I reorganize the shelves of paper and envelopes. I want him to see me from afar. Want him to notice that I'm more appetizing than he remembers. I pout my lips a little like Cassie does and tuck my cheekbones in, giving the illusion that my face stands like this all by itself, even when no one's watching.

Santi steps behind me and my entire body lights up. He drops his bag down and punches in his code to the computer while I picture his hands on my body, ripping this stupid red Alek's Print Shop polo off me. I'm animalistic in my wanting, so wild that I have to hide it.

"Hey." Santi comes back around and puts his elbows on the counter.

"Oh, hey," I say, pretending to be lost in a thought. I'm casual like a girl in a movie. Santi takes his gloves off. "You're late."

"Yeah." Santi looks down toward my chest. My nipples are shadowing through my shirt and I "forgot" to wear a bra today. "Subway delays," he says. I can tell he's lying.

"Subway delays," I mimic.

He moves his head to the left and right like he's not enjoying my foolery. The printer croaks and I spring up to my feet. Santi puts his hands up to tell me he's got it.

"So about the other day," he says to me, staring me dead in the eyes when he's back. In this light, I can see the black specks around his pupils, like a galaxy waiting to be discovered. I'm frozen like a deer in headlights.

"Don't mention it," I say, cutting him off and shifting my weight between my feet. "It was nothing."

Santi's lips hang open, but nothing comes out. He takes a breath in and holds it, waiting for me to change the story about what's going on between us. I want to, but I don't know how.

"Yeah, that's right," he says, after I don't budge. "I guess it was nothing." He looks at me again. His wanting is here now too.

"Yup, that's what I said . . . nothing." I wish I had more room for him or that he wasn't so nice to me so I could justify the way I go hot then cold. I twirl my hair between the tips of my fingers. I want him to kiss me again, but instead we work the rest of the day in silence.

Since the masturbating incident, Mami makes me keep my bedroom door open and my lights on when I go to sleep so when I wake up in the morning it looks like it's already noon. I'm wearing the pajamas Abuela made me the night before my eighth-grade recital. They still fit since I still have the body of a middle school boy. The pajamas are thin cotton with red and white daisies stamped into them. Lace lines my waist and shoulders. I check my phone one hundred times. Still nothing from casting. I'm starting to get weary. I roll out of bed and throw on my outfit for Ellen's, then skip out the door before Mami can see me.

On the subway, I count the specs of dried-up gum under the bottom of my seat with my left hand. Each piece is caved in and crooked, like the teeth that make up this city. The people in New York are disgusting, but I can't seem to get enough of them either. Maybe that's why I'll be stuck here forever, "Until further notice" pinned to my forehead on the subway like a Post-it note.

I close my eyes and drift into a dream world until "42nd Street—Times Square" blares through the robot of the speakers and shakes me awake. I wonder why it's always a man's voice, always announcing to us where we are and where we're going. Why it's never a woman, softly caressing us out of our train cars.

Before I'm fully awake, though, my thighs pop up and my heart skips a beat because I see Nena draped over a book, feet crossed, big hips, pelo lindo swinging from her ponytail right across from me. My stomach pulses and my knees launch forward. My voice croaks out a sound before I can stop it. But when Nena looks up at me, her face is unrecognizable. In between my dreams and the startle of waking up again, I forget that she's gone.

"Sorry," I say. "I thought you were someone else." She purses her lips and shifts her eyes back down to her novel. My stomach flips backward and I shuffle off the train. Sometimes on the subway, my eyes see what they want to.

At Ellen's, Becky won't quit asking me about the audition.

"Come onnnn, tell meee, Xiomara," she says, dragging out the words. "Just tell me what it was like." Becky didn't get to audition since she got there an hour late and, really, because she's white and this is not that kind of casting for once.

"Becky, I don't know what you want me to say." I'm placing a side of syrup and two chai lattes on my tray. "I went in, I danced, I sucked, and I left. No singing. No callbacks. No nothing." Becky's face is spinning. Every little thing I say attaches itself to the inner parts of her brain.

"I got my email this morning," Jacey says. She's been listening over the counter. She pulls out her phone and shows me the note. In big bold letters I can see it, the way it reads, **JACEY GRAVES**, and lists out how much they love her and want to have her back in.

"Great for you, Jacey," I say. I picture Santi throwing his head back and hear his voice saying, "And obviously we believe everything Jacey says, don't we?"

My phone rings. I nudge it out of my pocket. It's a number I don't know, so I send it to voicemail. These damn fucking debt collectors won't quit.

I run my syrup out to table 14. My chai lattes go to two men in miniature beanies sitting at the counter. "I try not to judge people on superficial things, you know?" the one in the black turtleneck is saying to the other. "That said," he continues, "I'm not sure I have interest in spending time with a friend who wears a yellow tank top every day." The man in the yellow tank top is trying not to twist his face around too much. "It's not because it's out of style, dude, it's because I'm just getting tired of seeing a yellow tank top, you know?" I go to grab their check and place it down in front of them.

"Down the middle?" I ask when I return and both their cards are peering out the leather envelope.

"I got regular milk, and he got oat," the guy in the black turtle-neck says. "So I think his is like a dollar more." At the pay station, I charge his card twice.

"Thanks for coming in," I say when I drop the check back off, then I run into the locker room so he can't correct me.

The rest of the day drags by. I have Jacey and Santi and Juan Carlos in my head. Cassie asking, "What are you going to do about next month?!" and Maria scraping at my scalp to get my hair to calm down. I don't sing today because we're busy. Saundra is staring me down like I better get on that table or she'll drag me out on the side-walk and behead me. I point to my wrist. It's fully healed now, I think, and has nothing to do with the singing, but I still have my brace on so I can hide behind it.

The guy in the black turtleneck comes back in and wants to talk to my manager. I point at Becky and he takes it up with her, slamming into me for stealing two more of his precious dollars. Becky puts on a good show like she'll fire me, and then he leaves, satisfied, staring me up and down like he's really had his way with me. Men just loooove to have their way.

At the end of my shift, I drown out the sounds of Jacey bragging about her callback and change into my warm socks for the walk to the subway. I pack my bag, and Becky asks me to go for a drink, but I'm too tired and I only have six dollars in my bank account, so I pass.

"Next time," she says with a smile on her face. It's impossible to break this girl's spirit.

Outside, I have a voicemail on my phone from the undisclosed number:

Gorgeous, this is Manny Santos. I got your number from . . . well, who cares? I want to talk to you about . . . you. And my play, of course. Meet me for dinner. Friday night. The Gramercy Tavern. No need to return my call. Just be there if you want to be anywhere ever again.

"Gorgeous," I say, mimicking his own voice and spinning on my heels. There's a foul ring to it, even when it's coming out of my mouth. I don't care, though, because my cells are tingling in every part of my body. Even my toenails are dancing.

Cassie tells me I'm a slut for making dinner plans with Manny, but I'm immune to women slapping me with their projections.

"I'm rubber, you're glue," I say. We are lying face down on her California king–size mattress downtown while I paint my nails a bright pink color before dinner. Cassie makes an L with her finger and her thumb and sticks it on her forehead.

"Plus, who cares if I'm a slut if it's taking me places," I say, polishing my ring finger with a heavy bit of top coat.

"Yeah, places like urgent care for your fucking STDs," Cassie says. I stick out my tongue and blow on my nail beds before I get up and walk to the bathroom.

"Stop. It's not like I'm going to fuck him. It's just dinner," I say. Cassie coats my eyelids with silver glitter. I look in the mirror. "Too much." She wipes it off.

"What do you think he wants to talk to you about?" I can tell she's asking because she's jealous, not because she cares. Cassie's never been happy for me. Not really, anyway. Not when I got the lead in our middle school musical, not when I lost my virginity before she did in high school, and certainly not now, when I'm on my way to dinner with the buzziest Broadway director on this side of the century and up for a part that her whiteness has automatically ejected her from. The phone rings. It's Santi. I don't pick up.

"Your lover's calling," Cassie says, looking at my phone. It's just like her to change the subject before I've even squeezed a good word out.

"He is so *not* my lover," I say. "He's just . . . my friend."

"Yeah, tooootally. A friend. A friend you want inside of you."

I throw a stray tub of gel eyeliner at Cassie's head and call her a bitch. It hits her right where I want it to. I'm laughing, but her face looks like she might call the police.

"Sorry," I say. I forget I can't let myself all the way loose around here.

"Okay, I think you're ready," she says. She wants me to go. Cassie does this when she's done with me, pushes me out the door before we're really through.

"I agree, I'm good!" I grab my bag. "Wish me luck!" I say, rubbing her nose in where I'm going.

"Break a leg, slut!" she yells after me.

"I prefer 'whore,' by the way!" I scream back, then I let the door slam behind me.

On my walk to the subway that will carry me to the restaurant, I dial Santi back. I'm surprised that I'm willing to talk to him like this tonight, out of the blue, for no reason. When he answers, he sounds as if he's moving. I can hear people behind him like he's at a party or a function or something that involves socializing and alcohol.

"Hey, what's up," he says, his words a little slurred.

"What is this, a drunk dial?" I ask. I hope it is. When you're drunk you always call the people you wish you had the courage to call while sober.

"Maybe," Santi says. It's quiet in the background now.

"Okay, hey." I stop outside the West 4th Street subway station before I have to go underground and lose service.

"So my friend's playing at the Rockwood tonight and I think you should come," Santi says. I imagine what his friends are like, hip and listening to music that sounds like Pharrell in his early days, talking about philosophy and smoking cigarettes on the sidewalk. I want to say yes, but Manny's too important, waiting for me at a table with a candle lit on it.

I make up an excuse about my uncle and a family party and then blackout while I pile on detail after detail for another thirty seconds. "Next time, though," I hear myself saying at the end of it.

"Well, we'll be out for a while," Santi says, pressing. "So call me when you're done . . . with your family party." He knows I'm lying.

"Sounds like a plan," I say. I hear the train barreling toward me underground.

"My best to the happy couple," Santi says. The screaming starts back up again in the background.

"Yeah, thanks." I hang up and run down the stairs, then stick my foot between the closing train doors until they open up again and swallow me in.

When I arrive, I find that the Gramercy Tavern is not meant for people like me. They might as well have a NO BLACKS sign hanging out front. I walk in and it smells like baby powder and sandalwood. The restaurants I'm used to smell like palo santo and sofrito. White people's palates tend to confuse me.

I look around the room until I see him—Manny, I mean. He's sitting in a dimly lit corner, and I step out of his line of vision so he doesn't notice me. I'm not ready to be seen. I ask the host, whose skin is darker than mine, if my party has checked in yet, and she asks me who my party is, exactly. I'm embarrassed that I still notice these things—the shade of other women's skin and what their hair looks like on any given day.

"Manny Santos," I say, unbothered. A light twinkles in her eye. She's probably just like me, a wannabe actress washed up on the shores of Midtown Manhattan.

"Fancy," she laughs, trying to level with me. I give her a side smile. We are not the same, I convince myself. She purses her lips. "Right this way."

We walk past a plethora of heirloom tomatoes and vodka cocktails and steaks the size of my skull. When we arrive at the table, the host raises her eyebrows. I wonder what she's thinking about me, this little naive thing on a date with Manny Santos. But it's not a date, I want to tell her. It's a business meeting. The launching pad for the rest of my life.

Manny looks me up and down like he's never seen a body before.

"Smaller than I remember," he says out loud, like I can't hear him, then he takes a sip of his water. I sit down. Manny's hands are bigger than I remember. Maybe because they aren't drowning under a trench coat tonight or maybe because it's the first time I've really had the chance to see them. They are full of meat and look like they could wring my neck. He is hotter than I remember too. A bit taller and more muscular. His skin is not as pale in the warm light of the tavern. It is golden. Gentle even.

When the server arrives, Manny orders another bourbon and I say I'm good with water.

"Have a drink," he says to me, then says to our server, "She'll have a martini."

"I hate olives," I say. "Really, I'm good with water."

Manny looks disappointed and I regret it, so I look at the waitress and take back all the words I said before, and order a tequila, on the rocks, with a lot of lime juice to make up for it. It's wild how quickly I'll shape-shift for my dreams to come true.

After a few sips of his drink, he moves his hand and gurgles, "So tell me about yourself."

"Well, I'm Xiomara," I say. He moves his entire head around like I'm stupid.

"More than that." He's somewhere between demanding and genuinely interested. I don't know where to start first—the dead sister, or the self-loathing, or how badly I want to be in his musical.

"Well, as you know, I'm a singer—"

"But not a dancer," he interrupts. It hurts but I hide it.

"Neither are you," I say. I know men like this. Papi's one of them. You just have to show them you can bite back.

Manny claps his hands in the air. "Touché." I'm pleased I've won this battle.

Before I arrived it seems he's ordered everything on the menu. There's bread and cheese and meats all over the table. Fruit and honey too. Leftover caviar and tuna tartare in the center. Manny grabs a tortilla and scoops a big chunk of the bits onto it, then puts it on my plate before asking if I've ever had something like this before. I'm embarrassed to say I haven't, so I nod my head yes and stick the whole thing in my mouth. I don't like the texture. It's gooey and tastes like the salt at the bottom of the ocean. Still, I slug it down and have two more scoopfuls. We're laughing at how long I've been chewing when a giant piece of steak comes. The blood is pouring out so red that I think the cow might start mooing again. He cuts it up into small pieces and puts some on my plate.

"You *have* to try this," he says. Everything with Manny seems to be in italics, underscored by the drama of his life. For Manny, even meat is high stakes. I take a bite and my mouth is full of flavor. It's peppery and spicy and buttery all at once. We are both closing our eyes and making sounds like sex before snickering and taking more bites until it's all gone and there's just sauce left on the plate.

"Speechless," I'm saying. "Actually fucking speechless."

"I told you," Manny says before dipping his fork in the liquid left over and licking the remnants up.

"So what was that, the other day," I ask, finally, about the money that he threw on my table at Ellen's. By this point, I've had two tequilas and I'm feeling brave.

"What, can't a man be nice?" he asks.

"I haven't seen it," I say. For some reason, though, a portrait of Santi pops up behind my eyelids.

Manny gets kind of serious and shifts a few times in his seat. "I used to work at a restaurant when I was your age." Manny probably thinks I'm twenty-two or something. "Those were the hardest years of my life. Running out pizza slices like that and praying to God I'd make it someday." My lip twitches with familiarity. "I think I just saw myself in you and thought, I don't know, that maybe you needed it."

"I did," I say. "I needed it so badly and I wanted to thank you."

"Don't do that," Manny says. "Let's never mention it again." There's some silence. "So, let's talk about the part then, shall we?"

"Yes, let's," I say.

"Why do you want it?" he asks. "The part in my musical."

I can't think of a single reason that feels appropriate or nonchalant so I go ahead and say what's ugly and true. "Honestly?"

He nods his head yes.

"I think that it will save my life." I say it matter-of-factly and without any shame. If Manny could lean in any farther, I think he would. I guess that means he likes my answer.

"Go on," he says.

"Look, frankly"—my voice gets quieter—"I don't know if you know my . . . history." He nods his head again like he does, but I go ahead and tell him anyway, about the way I used to book shows and sing at nightclubs and how Francesca dumped me after I ghosted that *Dreamgirls* offer. I leave the part about Nena out, though. There are some scars not worth sharing.

"Look, kid," he says, and it bothers me because I'm not a child. "You're fantastic. But—"

"I know I have two left feet." I name the elephant in the room before he can say it on his own. "But I bet you'll never meet someone who will work harder than I do." I wave down the server for another tequila.

"Well, now I'm nervous," Manny says to me. "Are you nervous?"

"What are you nervous about?" I'm genuinely confused.

"Well, I don't know, it's a big deal, having you sit across from me like this, then. You're the next big thing." I can't tell if he's serious or making fun of me.

"I'm barely the next big thing," I say, "but you're very kind."

"Confidence," he says, cutting me off again. "If we're going to do this, you need to have more confidence in yourself than I do."

"What does confidence mean to you?" I ask, spinning his lesson of becoming self-assured on its head.

"Ah, a philosopher," Manny says, swigging down his cocktail. He doesn't answer my question, but he does move an inch closer to me. "What does it mean to you, Xiomara Sanchez?"

"Well, to me, it means being vulnerable enough to say when you're not sure. Not pretending you're always at the top of the mountain." I signal to the grandeur of this restaurant and the thousand-dollar poison he's drinking. Then I take the glass out of his hand and finish it for him. Now it's Manny who is speechless. I can tell he likes a challenge.

When the bill comes, I go to take out my wallet and offer to pay, though I know the total probably costs more than my rent and I can't come close to affording it.

"Don't be silly, gorgeous," he says to me. The server swipes his card and I see the machine light up in all green colors. What I'd give for that machine to give me a go signal. When it's just the two of us again, Manny puts his feet on top of mine then takes out his wallet and hands me five hundred dollars.

"I can't take this," I whisper, though I'm already gripping it so tight I know I'll never find a way to give it back.

"Just keep working hard and think of me as Mr. Nice Guy, Xiomara," he says.

Manny gets up from the table and walks out of the restaurant like our business is through. I fold up the money and place it in my bag. I can barely look at my reflection when I catch it staring back at me in the silverware. I sit alone at the table for a minute longer until the host comes over and tells me that she's given up my table and it's time for me to go.

"I'm already fucking going." I walk out of the restaurant with my hands shaking like there's an earthquake within my bloodstream.

In the morning, I check my email. Nothing. I pull down on my notifications and let my heart do what it does when it wants something. With these damn callbacks, I'm like a dog waiting at the door. The gray circle spins clockwise, taunting me, until I see a name pop up across my screen and a subject line that says: CALLBACK INFORMATION.

My stomach jumps out of my skin and into the sweaty palms of my hands as I click and click and let my eyes run across the screen to salivate at the details. There are dates and times and songs to choose from that might be acceptable to sing. Some instructions and formalities and thoughts have been forged here in this virtual note sent to a screen meant just for me. I'm trembling all over. My brain turns on and starts running like a good engine trying to make its way out of a lemon. I feel Manny's money burning a hole in my jacket pocket across the room.

I dial Nena's number and let it ring halfway before I remember she's dead and my skin starts to eat itself. I still forget sometimes that I don't have her here anymore. I still I poke my head out of the shower sometimes to say something to her—she should be flossing at the sink—until the silence is firm enough to make me sick. Out of everything I could do today, all I want is to talk to my sister.

My fingers keep scrolling and typing and my heart keeps beating until Santi's name is front and center in my messages and I'm sending him a screenshot of the email. I add, "Sorry I didn't hit you last night," along with an emoji of a monkey covering up a few parts of her eyes. I need him to take the bait. I need to talk to someone who is willing to see me.

I notice dots appearing and disappearing from my view until a heart surrounds the photo and a black text pops up that reads, "I'm in your hood. Meet me at Floridita in five."

I get dressed so fast that when I get to the restaurant and look down I realize I've put on two different socks.

"Hi," he says when he walks up to the table and stops abruptly. The pastelitos I've ordered are hot so I'm skipping them from my right hand to my left to distract myself from the discomfort.

"Hi," I say. I wipe my hands of the grease and crumbs, then stand up so he can see me. We hug from the side. He's not yet someone I can wrap both my arms around. I can feel the muscles in his hands tighten around my rib cage. It makes me want to curl up inside them.

"You're wearing a skirt." Santi isn't asking a question as much as he is making an observation.

"I'm wearing a skirt," I reply. All my words are gone. I hope that I can find them before lunch is over.

He slides into the booth. I can smell his cologne from here. He's wearing a gray sweatshirt and saggy black nylon pants and his skin has clearly just been lathered up with some cheap skincare serum that he probably bought right before this at CVS. When the waiter comes over, I'm extra nice. For some reason, I think Santi will like me more if I'm not one of those horrible people who can't say please and thank-you when the waiter comes to the table.

"Mangú con los tres golpes," Santi says to the waiter. His Spanish is seamless, not so much because he's learned it from his family as much as he studied abroad in Barcelona, but still I think about how proud Papi would be of me if he saw me with a man like this. I cringe when I remember he already did.

"Yo tambien," I say, trying my best to hide my American accent.

"I speak English too," the waiter says to me, and I'm embarrassed. Santi gives me a look like he's on my team and it washes away.

"Okay," he says after the waiter leaves. "So callbacks."

"Next week." I pull out my phone and hand it to him so he can see the email. His eyes dart around the screen. He's genuinely excited for me. I can see it in the way he mouths the words on the note and blinks like he can't believe what he's seeing. When he's done reading, his jaw drops open and he gives me a high five. I miss his hand completely, and we do it again and then again until it makes the exact sound we want it to. Then he's pressing me for more information—what I'll wear (my leotard, duh), which song I'll sing (I'm not really sure yet), if that bitch Jacey is going too (unfortunately yes and fuck her).

"What else?" Santi asks me as our orders arrive.

I remember about last night's dinner and a chill runs cold through my body. "Nothing else!" I roll my eyes before he tells me that one day they're gonna get stuck there in the back of my head like that. There's so much else, though, and I wish I would just say that. That there's always going to be so much under the hood with me.

"Are you good?" He's taunting me with his words, and I am starting to sense my feet getting ready to bolt out the door, my hands locking it behind me, burning the whole restaurant down so I don't have to face all the things I'm suddenly feeling.

"I'm good," I say, but my shoulders are to the ceiling.

"Are you sure, because you're kind of acting like you've never had a meal with a human being before."

My face gets electrocuted when I'm angry. I can't hide it. "You're kind of an asshole." I grab my phone back from his fingers.

"No, I didn't mean it like that. Sorry." Santi lowers his voice. "I just mean it's okay. You can relax."

"I can't relax. My sister is dead and everything's ruined," I blurt out before I realize what I am saying. I put my head on the table. I haven't gotten into the swing of it yet, haven't cracked the code on how to tell people that I *had* a sister once and not that I *have* a sister. Underneath the table, his feet find mine. They feel different than Manny's did yesterday. Like they are protecting me, not holding me underwater while I drown and beg for clean air.

"Yeah, I can see that." He takes another bite. "My mom died when I was fourteen." It rolls off his tongue like nothing. Gentle, like he's had practice saying it and now it's his native tongue. It doesn't sound like a wound the way my confession did. His is more just like a gnarly scar, not spraying blood on everyone every time he walks into the room.

"That does not make us the same," I say. My body hardens up and I unravel our feet from each other. I've learned that I am bitter when I'm close to the shore. Even when I think whatever is coming my way might be my life raft, it's like I don't want to be saved.

Santi moves his shoulders like he's shaking off my dagger and keeps on. "When I was a kid, you know, when she was really sick, I always thought death was like this horrible, magical thing. Like a black hole that would eventually suck her up while we were happily eating lasagna at dinner." Santi opens his mouth in the shape of an *O* and fans the heat of his food out through his lips. "After she died, though, I started thinking about it more like"—he pauses to make his words match—"I dunno, more like going to the grocery store. Like death is something anyone can do anytime they want. Like it's not this lurking black hole but instead like that thing on the bottom of your to-do list that you never want to cross off, but eventually you know you will have to. It's a chore. And I guess we should all hope it's not as bad as we make it out to be because, I dunno, none of us are getting out of here alive."

My stomach flips over at his messy metaphor. My thumb rubs around the rim of my coffee cup. I place my feet back between his. It's as close to an apology as he'll ever get from me. I'm like my mother that way. "Do you mean, like, there's not that much to be scared of?"

"I mean whatever you make of it," he says, like a philosopher sitting on top of the galaxy somewhere.

"I mean whatever you make of it," I repeat in his same tone, bobbing my head and pushing my imaginary glasses up the spine of my nose. Santi crinkles up his napkin and throws it at me. It lands between my tiny breasts. I take it out and swing it in front of his face while it turns red.

"How'd she go?" he asks. "Your sister."

"That's the weird part," I say. "I don't really know. She was just walking across the street, back home, and her heart stopped. Cardiac arrest."

"No real ending," Santi says. "Just a place where you stop the story." He's quoting Frank Herbert to me.

"My sister's not part of your book report," I joke, but I'm serious too. I don't want her to be a lesson as much as I want her to be a human.

"It's okay to be scared," he says to me, "but I don't think you really are. Not of this audition or anything anyway."

"How would you know what I'm feeling?" I ask.

"I wouldn't."

I keep shooting him down like a navy jet and it makes me queasy to see the way he dodges all my bullets.

Santi asks the waiter for the check, with his thumb and his pointer finger, then pays the entire bill in ones and kisses me on the cheek after he slides out of the booth. I grab his hand before he leaves because I'm tired of controlling myself. I don't want him to go.

"It's refreshing," I say, serious now, done with my frigid sensibilities. "Your thing about the grocery store and the stopped story."

Santi smiles at me like he hasn't before. Even the one side of his lip that usually curves down bends upward on his face. "It's only up from here, X," he says. "You're at ground zero." My feet get hot before he pulls the door open and is gone.

When the waiter returns, I order another pastelito and a hot coffee with cream and sugar in English. "My sister died last year," I say out loud to her with a straight face. I am practicing my new native language. It doesn't roll off my tongue just yet, though. It still feels like I'm burying a bone that was once inside my body.

The last time I talked to Nena, we were in a stupid fight. She'd fallen down a flight of subway stairs near the 6 train, and I laughed too soon after, she said, even before checking to see if she was okay.

"Falling is inherently funny," I kept saying while she shook with anger on the ground. She could never tell when to flip the switch with me. When to decide whether I was laughing at her or laughing with her. We were downtown on the east side, and the white women around us were gawking while they walked by, moving their bags to the shoulder farthest away from my hands while I kept assuring them that she was fine.

"You're a fucking bitch," Nena spit at me through her teeth. Still lying on the platform, she grabbed her heel and rubbed it with the back of her palm.

"Don't call me a fucking bitch," I spit back, laughing and pulling out my cell phone to take a photo.

"I'm serious, X," she said, lying on the floor while her ankle started to blow up.

I couldn't stop smiling. My lips were zipping closed, but my teeth kept slipping out. I put my hands over my mouth to stop them from showing. The flash flipped on when I tried to take a second photo, and it lit up her body, awkwardly splayed out on the platform floor. I could see it clearly then, that it was not the body I remembered from our childhood bedroom. That it was more masculine, starting to be built differently by design.

"You're so fucking selfish!" Nena started screaming. She covered her face and her body and squirmed around. I kept thinking *Get up already* because I was embarrassed and I didn't want anyone to see her like this. "It's always about you."

Nena began crying. Now I can see that it wasn't because of her ankle.

"How is it about me?!" I said. I didn't understand why she always got so angry. She had a fuse so short, I could barely see it sometimes. "You're fine," I said, trying to convince her that it was true. She was still on the floor and I was starting to judge her, lying there like an injured animal.

"*YOU'RE* fine, Xiomara." Her voice was cutting my name up like a prisoner hanging over some hidden barbed wire. "Just because YOU don't have any problems doesn't mean there are none."

She stood up and slapped her hands together like a gymnast does before a big competition. She didn't look at me as she hobbled up the staircase. I think I called out for her to come back, but I can't be sure with the way my memory works. I had an audition and the subway train was only a minute away, so I didn't even try to follow her. Now it feels like a sick joke, a revenge tale, the way I go over that day in my head every morning. The way she has taken my life and made it all about her.

I've heard envy is just a sign pointing you toward what you want in life. If that's the case, then it seems what I want most in the world is to *Freaky Friday* into Jacey's body.

"It's not polite to stare," she says to me with a hard face as she bends over, her tiny legs crowding my vision.

It's not polite to be impolite either, I think to myself in a kindergarten voice.

The sun is hot today, piercing its way through the studio windows, shining its light on my acne scars and dry skin while I wait here with seventeen other women at this callback, rotating between stretching and singing while we wait for Manny. It's been weeks since our dinner and I haven't heard a peep from him since he bought me at the restaurant. I'm a little off-center, wondering how he'll see me now that I've been inside his wallet. It was nothing, I convince myself. A random act of kindness.

In the waiting room, everyone has their groups—two girls who went to college together, three who have the same agent, and a few here and there who know each other through knowing each other. Jacey and I stand alone. Our isolation makes her inherently mine.

When Manny walks in, our spines straighten and beg him to see us. He's in a green trench coat today, the same style as the red. He swings it back and forth like he's in some trench coat cult or like he knows he's the sun and we're all just here to revolve around his gravitational pull.

Manny's sunglasses make it so that we can't see most of his face, but I know deep down that he's looking at me. I feel his gaze up-and-downing my body, looking at my old shoes like I'm some poor charity case. His eyes are like an infrared light burning against my cheeks.

He calls us in, two at a time. Jacey goes first with a girl who has light skin and a big curly red fro. They are in and out. I have barely gotten up to go and come back from the bathroom before they are wrapping themselves back up in their sweatshirts, packing their bags with their water bottles and ballet slippers. Everyone else has their turn while I chew the skin on my thumb. My habit's gotten so bad now that the appendage is losing its color, the only part on my body that will ever get the chance to know whiteness.

I go last, me and number 18, a woman with darker skin than mine and a shaved head and muscles that make mine look close to invisible. The room is cold. Manny likes to keep it this way. He tells us that the audition today shouldn't take too long. He'd like to see the dance number again, for us to "really visualize it." I hear him in my head— *but not a dancer.*

He turns on the music and we take it from the top, both at the same time. Manny's eyes are glued to me, watching the way the skin on my stomach wrinkles when I kick my leg high. It's as if we are the only two people in the room, like number 18 doesn't even exist. "Again," he says without blinking, coming behind me, straightening my spine, spotting my waist, dancing next to us both now, in a line.

"Good," he says after we're through. He makes a hand gesture to dismiss us and then, without looking up from the ground he says, "Xiomara, stay."

Number 18 makes a face like someone has gone into her chest and squeezed her heart until it's turned black-and-blue. She bows her head and says thank-you while she sucks back her tears. Then she's gone.

"It's because I can't dance, isn't it?"

Manny folds his arms and cocks his neck. It's like our dinner never happened. "No, it's because I want to hear you sing." He disarms me with his smile, which is spreading across his face like a deadly disease. "What have you prepared?"

Prepared. I think of Becky.

"Right." I pull out my sheet music and place it on the piano in silence. He moves to it, floating almost without his feet, and begins to play the tune until sound slips out of my lips. I've chosen "I'm Not Afraid of Anything" from the Off-Broadway musical *Songs for a New World*. "The song is about how being fearless sometimes makes you the monster," I say. "The first time I heard this song I felt it all the way down in the depths of my soul. It reminds me of myself and that scares me."

I've said too much already and I want to swallow my words so I stop talking and begin singing. Every other vocalist tends to sing this song delicately, but I make it my own, belting the high notes instead of fluttering above them in my head voice.

I'm not afraid of anyone

I press where others usually pull.
I get loud where they get soft.

'Cause after all I'm not afraid

I can tell Manny likes this choice because he's speeding up the tempo and tapping his foot against the pedal hard enough that I can feel it on the floor.

My voice is touching the ceiling, filling the entire room with vibration. Manny's eyes close, and I can feel his contentment in my belly. I follow him, shutting my eyes now, pushing out every last vowel.

When I'm through, I am breathless. He walks over to me and kisses both my cheeks and grabs both my hands.

"Gorgeous," he's saying to me, "just like I remembered. Absolutely gorgeous."

I get that feeling I get in the backs of my calves when I think I've pleased someone other than myself. Whether it's right or wrong, when a man tells me what I'm worth, I believe him.

When I'm in the elevator, I'm wishing Jacey could see me now. Have her nose all pressed up to the glass to watch me win. I put my hands around my stomach and thank God that I am here living in my own body, not out there on the street living in hers.

Santi's surprised me at Ellen's today, so he's sitting at the counter and I'm turning my face away from my customers like I don't work here at all when they call me over or have a question.

"You realize you have an entire section to tend to, right?" Saundra shouts behind me as I make my way out the double doors of the kitchen and onto the floor.

"I do?" I shout back like I don't notice. It seems I'll never turn off my smart mouth.

While I walk to Santi I feel like a kid on a playground folding origami or playing MASH or something. I have a fat crush, and it's bringing me air to start to think that I could find joy in someone again.

"Hi," I say, sneaking up behind him. A few of my tables have given up and cleared out so I have a few minutes to talk, finally. Santi and I haven't kissed since the subway and I'm not sure you can consider that a kiss anyway, but I'm convinced that the way he's been putting his arms around me when we hug is different these days. It's closer, like we've known each other for years. We're in a rhythm now, Santi and me. Somewhere between friendship and the indefinable. I've been jonesing for him in the mornings.

"Hi!" Santi seems surprised to see me, though he's the one who's showed up unannounced and has been sitting here watching me run around for half an hour.

"Welcome to my other life," I say, gesturing like I'm Vanna White and spinning on my heels.

"Pretty glamorous." Santi runs his hand up my shirt to follow the line of a chocolate stain.

"I know, all the cool kids are doing it." I cover up the stain with my hands and stick out my tongue, then pour him a hot cup of coffee. "Do you want to order something to eat?"

"No, I'm just here for the show."

"Ick," I say, motioning like I'm gagging myself. "So are you ready for this?" I can't wait to tell him about my callback. About how I'm moving my life forward. I'm ignoring the small dumb things I've had to sacrifice, like my dignity, to do so.

"Lay it on me," Santi says.

"Okay, so Manny held me back and had me sing for him, and"—I slap my hands against the counter to make a drumroll—"he said it was GORGEOUS." My jaw drops like it's the first time I've heard that story too. "I think I should hear back soon."

Santi's raising the roof with his shoulders and palms.

"You're such a dad," I say with my vocal fry and shake my head. I hear my cue and have to go but would much rather stay here. "I'll be right back," I groan, and burst into song as I walk away from Santi. I have secondhand embarrassment for myself, belting Broadway show tunes at a diner while my crush slurps down a coffee and my customers give me dirty looks for ignoring them all morning.

When we're done, Santi stands up and whistles and claps so loud and screams, "Wepa!"

I bury my head under my T-shirt and wave my arms to tell him to stop. When I'm back at the counter, Santi is staring.

"I want to talk to you about something," he says. It seems like he's serious, so I'm searching his face for a sign.

"Uh-oh," I say. "Who died?" We both get a laugh, knowing they're already gone, the people we cared about most. "I'll be off in half an hour," I say, "can you wait?"

Santi nods his head yes and stays until the end of my shift, then waits out on the floor while I grab my things from the lockers.

"Xiomara and Santi sitting in a tree," Becky's singing in the locker room. "K-I-S-S-I-N-G."

I slam the doors in her face when I leave and give her the middle finger while we both cackle. When I'm outside and I look back she's in the window, wrapping her arms around herself and pretending she's making out with someone.

"Okay, so you're amazing?" Santi says with his arms around me while we walk toward Eighth Avenue.

"Yeah," I say.

"You mean 'thank you'?"

"No, actually, I don't," I reply, giggling like a schoolgirl. With my singing, it's hard for me to act shy.

"Humble. I like it." Then he says, "You're like a turtle right now." He's alluding to my pace. The entire time we've been walking I've been measuring my steps and silently begging him to kiss me. "Didn't you tell me you were from New York?" He grabs my hand and pulls me forward.

"Slow and steady wins the race," I say, but he doesn't respond and something deep inside me is screaming that something is wrong, that there's too much quiet in all the space between us. "So what did you want to talk to me about?" I ask, trying to break the ice, get him to spit out all the sour parts so I can suck them right back up.

"Never mind," Santi says. His eyes are moving quickly left and right like I've never seen them go before. "I was just in my head a little."

"Let me in too, then," I say. "It's cold out here." I'm stalling, but it feels like Santi is rushing to something. He's shaking his head and zipping his lips shut. "What, do you have somewhere to be?" I ask, stopping on the sidewalk, expecting him to cool down.

"What, do you not?" I'm surprised by the way his words cut. We get to the subway entrance and head down the stairs.

"Okay, well, I'm going downtown," he says, tapping his foot and gesturing to the staircase for the Brooklyn-bound trains.

"Okay. Well . . ." I say, and I can't think of anything to say after that.

"Keep me posted on the callbacks." Santi gives me a hug.

I stay in his arms, but I notice that it's not as close as it was yesterday. I feel like a weight between his arms. Something dragging him down. When he pulls away, I stop him halfway and wait for him to meet his lips with mine. It's scary, but I know that we both want this. I know we are both two seconds away from something good. But then he lets me go completely and sprints across the station to the stairs that shoot him down to his train and I'm left there like discarded trash, then scurrying to the uptown train like a subway rat. There's no K-I-S-S-I-N-G like Becky said there would be.

The entire way home I trace it over and over, our interaction stuck in my mind, like a toddler trying to solve a jigsaw puzzle.

My cousin Maria is too rough, but she gives a mean blowout, so I put up with her hard hands. She makes my hair look silky, like it grew out of my scalp stick straight and doesn't frizz up at the drop of a hat. I haven't had my hair in rollers in ages and I'm itchy. Maria slaps my hand away from my head with the back of her comb every time I go to scratch it.

"Sooo, tell me about this Santi," she says casually, like she's not fishing for information. I've barely mentioned his name this week but Maria knows me.

"It's nothing," I say. Though I don't think it's nothing. I think it's something enough for me to be blowing my curls out before my shift at the print shop and overthinking the hug he gave me last Saturday. I'm going to talk to him about it today if he'll let me. I think it's time for me to thaw out a bit.

"Nothing ni nothing," she says in her broken English, grabbing down on my scalp even harder.

"You better not have put relaxer in this, Maria," I warn. "I swear to God my head feels like it's in a fucking oven."

"Ay, Xiomara, shut up," she barks back. When Maria is red in the face I get scared. Memories from our childhood of her slapping me up against the wall and choking me until I gave her what she wanted— the extra candy, the password to Mama's safe, the remote control so she could watch her novelita—rush into my head.

"Okay, maybe it is something," I say, rubbing my scalp with the inside of my wrist.

"I fucking knew it," Maria says, pointing the back of the comb at my forehead. "This is good for you, chica. You need to get out of your head. Move on a little. Get laid or something." Maria is trying to rush me out of my grief. As if some crush is going to make me forget my sister.

"Yeah, yeah," I say. "Whatever. We'll see."

"Exacto, mami, we'll see. Just stay open," Maria says.

I'm done with her Dr. Phil special, but something tugs at me. I do wonder if she could be right. If my frozen heart is thawing out or something, if maybe this is a first step to recovery.

"I'm on fire, diablo!" I shout when I can't take it anymore. Maria blows on my head skin to lessen the burn then pats on my head hard enough to remind me she's in control.

"Ya!" she says when she's done and spins the chair around so I face the mirror. "Te ves bella." Maria only tells me I'm pretty when my hair's straight. I hide my satisfaction, barely looking at my smile in the mirror.

"Gracias, mami," I say to her, but I don't take out my wallet this time. I just pack up my things and wink at her before I walk out.

"Bueno," she says, sucking her teeth and yelling, "It's on the house!" sarcastically before the door slams behind me.

While I walk to the subway, the strands of my hair blow in the wind. I hold them down in place with the palms of my hands to save them from the mess of Manhattan. I feel pretty and I don't want to be all ruined before Santi can see me.

My hands are tapping the glass counter at the print shop when Alek tells me that Santi's gone for the next few weeks. "His girlfriend is sick or something like that."

Girlfriend. All the beetles crawl up my skin. My jigsaw puzzle is solved.

"Just me and you today," Alek says, leaning over, pressing his forearms into the glass. "Just . . . me . . . and . . . you." I can tell by the way he drags out his sentence that he's noticed me. The only thing is that today I don't want to be noticed. I inhale and feel Alek's cigarette-soaked scent make its way up my nostrils and down into my gut while I try to wrap my mind around all the reasons why Santi would lie to me.

"You coming in today?" I text him, and immediately regret it. For the next five minutes I check my phone a hundred times for a smoke signal from Santi, who I thought would be waiting at the door for me today with flowers.

A few minutes later it's still quiet and Alek won't stop moving. He's folding papers and changing toner tins and dusting the printers. He can smell it on me, the hurt of something. He rubs his way around me a few times and I let him get too close because I want to feel beautiful. I hear Manny in my head. *Gorgeous.* My throat closes up a little bit. I'm trying to remember what I am.

The shop is full of pastel colors and dirty white machines. A white girl in a burnt-orange minidress and black-rimmed thick glasses comes in and asks me to print out her manuscript. "It's a romance novel," she tells me. "Both the protagonist and her love interest are of color.

I'm sure you agree there really are not enough stories about Black love."

"Maybe that's because it doesn't exist," I say. She's caught me at the wrong moment. I can see the confusion in her eyes. When I open the file, her draft is 468 pages. I tell her what it'll cost to use that much paper single-sided and ask if the story *really* calls to be that lengthy. She scoffs and tells me not to be so angry.

"We can probably close early today," Alek says when she's gone. His eyes are scanning the ceiling for cobwebs.

"No rush," I say. "Nowhere for me to go." I stare at the back of Alek's neck until he looks me in the eye. I wait for him to speak and think about the way he was in my dream the other night, with his hands on me.

"You thought that boy had a crush on you, huh?" He says it like I'm funny. Some kind of punch line or clown at a kid's birthday party.

"None of your fucking business, Alek," I say.

"You can do better, X," he says. "Don't stress it."

I'm definitely stressing it.

Alek unlocks the cabinet under the counter and slides out a bottle of supermarket pink champagne. It's like he planned it this way, to get me alone on my worst day and make the most of the moment.

"Might as well pop a bottle," he says, shrugging his shoulders.

"Might as well," I say firmly, sliding my butt up onto the counter and letting my legs swing. Alek doesn't like it when I sit here, but right now I know he won't correct me. The bottle makes a sad popping sound when he pulls out the cork.

"Anticlimactic," I say, rolling up my sleeves. He sweats a little and I smile like an angel while he looks for the red cups we used at last year's holiday party—just me, him, and Joe.

"I don't need a glass," I say. I grab the bottle and swig it down. I can feel myself heating up. I'll do anything to be desired. The bubbles get caught at the back of my tongue and I cough a little, dramatically really, so that he'll move closer. I'm the predator, I tell myself. He is the prey. The closer we get to taking our clothes off, the more power I have.

"You sure you're okay?" he says as he moves toward me, putting his hands up and around my shoulders to keep me steady. I wish that men would stop asking me that, if I'm okay, like they are qualified to help me recover.

When Alek is this close to me, I notice he has yellow teeth. I hand him the bottle. He takes a long sip, and when he pulls it away, I can see a few droplets of alcohol in his beard.

I lean into him, looking down into his eyes from the counter, and whisper, "I think you should lock the door."

He moves faster than I've ever seen him, locking the door and pulling down the blinds. Grabbing my hand, he leads me to the back room and pushes me onto his ketchup-stained couch to fuck me. I pull off my pants and close my eyes. I bet Santi would be so mad if he saw this. I wish we could live stream it straight to his cell. Make it all worthwhile.

"Okay, stop," I say through bated breath when he licks my face and his beard scrapes the skin on my neck. I know he hears me, but he doesn't listen. Instead, he slaps me and turns me around and holds my arms behind my back while he pushes into me. I'm not here when he's inside me. I'm outside the door. On the ceiling watching down. It's such a relief, finally, to have that superpower.

When he's done he rolls over onto the couch and puts his hands over his eyes like he can't believe what he's done. As if he wasn't here for what just happened either.

"I need to take the rest of the week off," I say, unhooking myself from his hands and jumping back into my jeans. His eyes are still closed as he holds up both of his thumbs. I wipe myself off and leave him there in the back room to atone for his sins.

I'm waiting in line at CVS and deciding what voice I should use when I ask the nice man at the counter for Plan B. He's tall and white and has black hair and a beard. His voice sounds just like Vince Vaughn's, and his top half is heavier than his bottom.

"May I please have a pack of Plan B?" I say when it's my turn. I think it's funny that I chose to use words like *may* and *please*. As if being proper makes this more palatable.

The cashier raises his eyebrows at me. He wipes some spit off his chin and slaps the cardboard case of emergency contraception over to me. His motions are violent, like he wants to tear the nonexistent fetus out of my stomach with his bare hands and watch me bleed to death while he puts it up for adoption.

"Thank you," I say, though *For absolutely fucking nothing* is what I mean.

When I get outside, I run straight toward the subway, and as soon as I hop on the train, I rip the box open. I shove the small white pill into the back of my throat and chase it down with my own saliva. There's a woman next to me who has no teeth. A girl across from me with a backpack the weight of ten bricks. An old man pushing past me to find a seat.

At 59th Street, a woman gets on with a stroller and a baby and a belly the size of five basketballs all stacked up horizontally on one another. She looks down and strokes her stomach while my uterus turns, surprising me with its wanting. My body is screaming at me that I will eventually run out of time. That if I can't be a sister, then maybe I am meant to be a mother. Or at least something that takes care of another thing. I close my eyes and pretend that when I get off this train I will walk out onto an earth where Nena never died and Mami didn't have to clean houses and I did something, anything right for once. When the train stops, the woman gets off and so do I. I grab my belly and waddle all the way home.

In the morning at the apartment, I'm bleeding. I lock the door of the bathroom and bite into the palm of my wrist so I can feel a pulse inside me beating. When I've been in here for ten minutes, Mami bangs on the door and yells, "Open, coño!" while she wrestles with the handle. She hasn't left for work yet because she probably thinks I'm filming a POV porn scene. I'm nearly thirty, God damn it. I bang back until she's quiet. When I finally open the door, she has a look in her eyes like fire. I know she was out there wishing that her other daughter would appear from the doorway instead of me. My stomach hurts like hell and I have a wad of toilet paper in between my vagina and my underwear, but I've rented out studio space again and I can't miss it, even if I'm bleeding out another body. I push past her and then make my way into my bedroom, where I start to shove my rehearsal clothes into the pocket of my backpack.

"Dónde vas?" she says, scaring me with her precision and slamming the door in my face before I can sneak out of it. I don't have the energy today to fight with Mami.

"I'm going to work." When she knows I'm lying she stalks me like a lion. Here we are in the jungle. Dancing around each other to decide who is predator and who is prey.

"Juan Carlos came by yesterday," she says, staring at my skull, waiting for me to flinch. I hold my breath in.

I've paid rent where I could, but we are still so behind and Mami wants to know where the money went. With her cleaning job and my jobs at Ellen's and the print shop, we should be covered, but I've had to use so much of it to pay for rehearsal space that at the end of the month I'm still scrounging for loose change under my mattress.

"I don't know what to tell you, Mami. Things are expensive." I'm trying to work my way around her, but she's gripping the doorknob.

"Math is the same in every language," she says to me. She can barely say the word *language* with her accent. It's cutting up her tongue to try it.

"Please move. I have to go to work."

"Work ni work," Mami says, stuffing her greasy hands into my bag. My hand quickly follows, grabbing at hers to get them out. "Mentirosa!" she screams. Mami has me. She pulls out my old dance shoes and waves them in the air like they're a sin. "What are you doing, Xiomara?!" Mami cries out. "Why don't you want to get better?" She talks about my dreams like they are a disease.

"That's what I'm doing, Mami! I'm getting better! I'm moving forward instead of staying stuck like you!" I grab for my shoes, but she moves out of the way, so my fingers slam against the door and start throbbing.

"You go back to school and get a real job, Xiomara!" Mami wants me to be a doctor or something. I've tried to tell her a thousand times that that ship has already sailed and sunk to the bottom of the ocean.

"I'm never going to be Nena!" I burst out, grabbing my shoes and shoving them back into my bag. "Nena's dead, Mami! All you have is me!" I'm surprised by my mouth. I throw all the ingredients of my bag onto the ground and hold up my hands, surrendering to her judgment. My eyes are big and red, gushing salty water all over my hands. Mami slaps me across the face so hard I can feel the blood pooling between my cheeks and my gums. I bare my teeth.

"I'm done," I shout at her. "I'm fucking leaving. Good luck making it on your own."

When she lunges at me again, she is screaming, demanding an answer, crying for Nena and her soul to come into this house and replace me. Asking God to take back her bad one, her Black daughter, and replace her with the other. I move Mami out of the way like a linebacker. When I hear her talk like this, I don't feel bad for what's to come. I grab for the door and pull it open to escape to the other side. When I'm there, in the heat of the hallway, I can hear her behind me, begging me now to stay.

When I was nine years old, I ran away from home for the first time. Papi caught me out on Broadway hailing a taxi by myself in the snow and picked me up by my armpits and dragged me back inside while I screamed for help. "She was going to die out there," he told Mami. But I don't think I would have died. I like to think I would have made it through.

The night I decided to go, "for real this time, Nena," I was mad at Mami for her rules and her rosaries and her never-ending insistence that I be a good girl. Good is something I never learned how to be. Nena brushed my hair into two pigtails, scraping at the back of my head until the blue bolitas of my hair ties hung off each strand perfectly. Nena always did a good job of that, covering up the nastiness of my insides with some spruced-up version of my outsides.

In my bag, I had two peanut butter sandwiches, a Thomas' English muffin, and black beans in a Ziploc bag that later leaked all over the bottom of my backpack. When Mami asked me where I was going, I zipped up my yellow jacket and told her that my elementary school teacher had a big house in Harlem and would be a better mother for me.

"Ah, okay, bete then, Xiomara," she said, shoving me out the door. "Tell Miss Carla I say hello." I heard the chain lock slide behind me and my heart started to race, knowing that I was onward and upward to a more peaceful life in a brownstone. I pressed the elevator button and waited for it to buzz up to the fourth floor while I tinkered with the straps on my backpack.

"Don't go!" Nena yelled down to me from the window when I got outside. From the sidewalk, I could see the specks of liquid glittering in her eyes. "Really, X, don't go."

I yelled back that I had to, and then she asked me how she would be able to find herself if I wasn't there to find it for her. "I don't know," I screamed back before I bumped into Papi. "But you'll have to learn."

And now it's me, walking around New York City at midnight, searching for my soul, scared of what will happen if I never find it.

Mami could die.
Papi could be charged with murder.
Or rape.
There's gonorrhea.
And AIDS.
And Alek's bastard baby.
Manny could lose my number.
And I could never be famous
or leave this godforsaken city.
A rat could make its way up my pants.
Bite me and give me rabies.
There are bed bugs,
and black mold,
and the IRS.
Santi could drown in the Hudson River (with his stupid fucking girl-
friend, hands tied behind her back, next to him).
I could get hit by a subway train tomorrow.

Sometimes I make these lists to remember that the world won't likely give me the ending that I want. After Nena, I don't like surprises.

Cassie lives on West 4th Street with her new money now. It's a big brownstone full of pink trinkets and mood lighting and a backyard that I thought was only possible in the suburbs. She slinks around the place like she deserves it. Like there is nowhere else in the world she could possibly be, while I rub the nail polish off my fingernails and suck my thumb clean from the alcohol leaking into the open cuts on the sides of my skin.

"Maybe she just wanted you to tell her, you know?" Cassie always takes Mami's side. "Maybe she just wanted to be a part of your decision to get back into the game."

"I don't think now is the time to play devil's advocate, Cassandra."

She rolls her eyes at me and throws over a pair of pajamas. I'm small, but Cassie is even smaller. These will never fit. I lie on her bed and try to get the thorns of the day out of my chest.

Cassie curls up next to me and strokes my hair. Her hands are cold and I want them to be warm. I close my eyes. I thought I'd be all torn up over Mami or Nena before bed tonight, but surprisingly, while I shift under the covers I mourn for Santi. The tears pool up in my eyes and I flush them down, poke them out with the tips of my fingers before Cassie can notice and start telling me about my Saturn return again.

"He ghosted me," I say. She doesn't have to ask to know I'm talking about Santi. "After all that bullshit, he just threw me away." Cassie doesn't say a word, just strokes my forehead and sings a soft melody to me. "Can I stay here for a while?" I hate asking her for help. It's like asking a kindergartner to tie your shoe, but tonight I'm in a bind. I can hardly reach my toes anymore.

"I thought you'd never ask," she says. It's like she's been waiting for me to hit rock bottom so she can swim down and save me. But it doesn't feel good, being pulled out from the depths of the waters like this. There's still liquid in my chest and the CPR isn't working.

I'm pouring out a perfectly good glass of orange juice at Ellen's when Maria texts me about going over to Cassie's tonight.

"We want to take you out," Maria types, and I know she's full of shit because when it comes to Maria and Cassie, there is no "we." They are different species, two strange types of animals running around the world with their heels dug in, insisting it's either their way or the highway.

I give Maria a thumbs-up because I know in my bones that I don't have another option. When I see the delivered message, I open my texts with Santi. It's like picking at a scab, the way my mind insists on obsessing over my last "You coming in today?" text. I'm horrified by the way it still sits there in the cloud, stale and unresponded to. One day I'm sure I'm going to combust from it all, the pent-up emotions sitting inside my head like this.

"You're singing today," Saundra says to me like it's an order. I imagine her brains, blown to bits and landing all over my crusty apron. Before I can think of any more dark thoughts, though, I'm on in my chest voice on the counter.

After hours of singing and serving, when my shift is through, I don't feel any better. Not even my singing could save me today, and I wonder if it's me, not Mami, whose veins are full of rot and mold.

On the walk back to Cassie's, which is long and wet from the April rain, every man I see looks like Alek. He's following me, with his facial hair like razors and his sour smell. I cross my arms tight across my body. Between him and Santi and Mami and this fucking roller-coaster ride of an audition, I think my Saturn return is attempting to eat me alive. I want to tell someone about all of this stuff living in the shadows of my aura, but I don't. I just keep walking so I can get away from it and get on with my life already.

When I get to Cassie's, Maria's already there waiting. I can hear them arguing about the volume of the music before I walk in the door.

"Hey," I say, warning them I'm here and making my way through the pink beads that hang down from Cassie's ceiling.

"Your cousin's a fucking bitch," I hear Cassie yell.

I'm tired of their fucking feud, but I let it slide. Maria's not my sister or anything. There's no secret code that insists I punch Cassie in the jaw for talking shit. When I turn the corner, I see Maria standing in the living room. Her face is red, and I feel like a traitor. I'm always leaving my people behind, turning my back when they need me the most.

"Whose dick did Cassie suck to deserve this place?" Maria says loud enough so Cassie can hear her. Maria's never been to Cassie's brownstone before. I was just as confused when I came here the first time. Maria is holding up a small golden statue of a woman with her head in her hands that was on display at the Whitney last winter. Cassie got it gifted to her by the curator after she read his tarot.

I throw down my jacket and take off my shoes before lying down on Cassie's couch. Maria doesn't sit. She's walking around the entire place and picking things up and putting them down. Below 96th Street, Maria's like Christopher Columbus, an explorer proved wrong, because she was convinced that Manhattan ended just after Harlem.

"I couldn't let my girl go that easy," Maria says to justify why she's down here.

Cassie comes out of the bathroom. She's wearing her blond hair pulled back into a tight ponytail with a middle part and gold hoop earrings that are larger than my hand. The sleek-backed look is "in style," chic even, now that white women are trying it.

"Ay, no," Maria says when she sees her. "We're not going out with you like that."

Cassie's wearing shorts at nine p.m. in April. White people like to be cold, I've learned. I don't want to go anywhere, really, but Maria's come all this way so I pop up from the couch, pour myself a tequila, and raise my glass to the sky.

"What are we cheersing to?!" Cassie screeches, running to the kitchen, ass cheeks out, so she can pour herself something too.

"Another fucking loser!" I say. I'm talking about Santi. Or deep down, maybe Alek too. Shame sits in my stomach, pulsing like a fucking parasite. I wait to hear Nena laugh the way she usually does when I'm being melodramatic. When she doesn't, I chug my drink down and pour another. It never gets old, feeling the depth of her absence in quiet, unexpected moments.

"Here's to that," Cassie says. It doesn't take much to get Cassie on the man-hating train. She's convinced she's a feminist because she's just finished a three-month dating sabbatical.

"Y'all are depressing as shit," Maria says. She's looking for Hennessey in Cassie's bar and I'm waiting for her to be disappointed when she doesn't find it. "Just fucking call him, Xiomara. We're adults."

I throw my phone onto her lap. "If you like him so much, why don't you go ahead and take his number? It's all yours."

Maria sticks her tongue out at me and chucks my phone back at me hard enough that I think it might crack my collarbone in two. "I'm just saying, why don't you get a straight answer before you rule McDreamy out altogether."

"If he wanted to, he would," Cassie says.

I tie my Jordans and beg them both to follow me out the door.

At the bar, which Cassie's chosen in SoHo, there are velvet chairs everywhere and a disco ball in the center of the dance floor. The DJ is playing ABBA, and under these lights even Maria looks like a Black girl. She makes a gun with her fingers and lifts it up to her temples before she pulls the imaginary trigger. Cassie's on the dance floor already making out with some promoter. He's wearing black jeans and a black polo with a red moose on the right breast so I can tell it's a knockoff. His hair has so much gel that I can still see it glistening when Maria and I walk across the room to the bar. Their tongues are moving so hard against each other's mouths that I think one of them will have to fall off.

"Let's get outta here," Maria says before we can even get a drink. I pretend I don't hear her, though, and find a white boy to flirt with. It feels good, fetishizing myself like this. I'm free when I remind myself that to a certain breed of boy I'm something spectacular, something they'll be on the floor begging to touch while my heel is pressed up against their neck.

When I'm done playing this game, I look for Maria and find her twerking on some fat white dude to Billy Joel while he grabs her ass. "When in Rome, mamita!" she's yelling. I'm dumbfounded by how fast she's succumbed to the madness.

I can barely feel my tongue inside my mouth anymore, so I walk outside and call Santi. Maybe Maria has a point. Maybe I need to get my answer. No response, so I call again. This time I hear a breath at the other end of the line and what I think is a woman's laugh in the background, and then a dial tone and then just my own breath and I'm alone on the sidewalk with my phone in my hand and egg on my face. Alek was right about the girlfriend, then.

Cassie walks out of the bar with a different dude from the dance floor, and before she gets in her cab, she yells, "Don't come back to the apartment tonight," because she's so so sooooo fucking selfish. I sit outside on the sidewalk and nod my head at Cassie before watching her get in an Uber with her mystery man. My knees are all wobbled together and my hands are in my mouth, teeth gnawing at the skin on my cuticles until I feel a sharp sting and they are throbbing enough to bring me back down to reality.

I go inside and grab Maria, who says, "FINALLY!" and then follows me out.

"I'm sleeping at your place," I say. She doesn't ask me any questions because that's family.

On the subway home, I decide I'm done with men who spill their hearts out one day and stab you in the back the next. At least with Alek, or even Manny, I can recognize the devil hiding inside them, like looking in a goddamn mirror. With Santi, I don't know, it's a trick fucking candle.

I smell hair burning before I even wake up. Maria is at it again, smoking out her curls until they are bone straight, hanging like curtains on her head. My head is pounding. My body isn't made for this anymore. When I was eighteen I could drink until the sun came up and forget it even happened the next day. Now, at the ripe age of twenty-nine, my body is slower. I'm using all the strength in my body to lift my arm and hold my pillow over my head to save myself from the smell of the straightener and the light burning through the window and onto my eyelids. My breath is bad. I can taste it, and my hair is like hay, crunching while it's piled on top of my head.

Maria must sense I'm awake, because she comes into the room and slams on the light. It's bright white, buzzing overhead, swearing at me until I finally lift my head and look over at her.

"Diablo," Maria says, blinking at me a few times, "you look like shit."

I give her a thumbs-up and then a middle finger. "Coffee."

Maria already has it in her hands. She gives it to me gently so I know she has something to say. Maria is never gentle. She is a bull in a china shop with her mouth and opinions.

"What?" I close my eyes while I take a sip. "What are you going to say?"

Maria takes a breath. "I think you should go home."

I spit the coffee back into my cup. "Ay, Maria, stop. No te metas in things you have no idea about."

Maria looks at me sternly, less like she's angry and more like she's sorry. Not sorry in an apologetic way. She's sorry *for* me. Her eyes are filled with pity.

"Tía called me. She's not mad. She just wants you home. And what are you going to do, X? Keep running around with that pendeja Cassie for the rest of your life? Pretend you're a gringa until the day you die?"

"A gringa!" My mouth is pulling out the words. "Maria, you've spent every hour for the last week and a half straightening your hair and watching videos of tummy tucks. Last night you were twerking on a ginger until he had cum on his pants. Ya already with the accusations."

Maria twirls her strands around her fingers. It's how I know my words have become wounds. "Yeah, well, that's outside shit, Xiomara." Her voice is harder. "You know what I'm talking about. Because what *you* try to make yourself? What *you* try to be? That's inside shit."

"Oh, fuck you, Maria," I say, while I tear out of the bed and throw on my shoes. I barely remember that my head hurts as my rage takes over. I'm gone before she can respond. I think I should be worried, though, about getting used to slamming the door behind me.

A week later, I'm at the print shop cleaning toner off the side of my hands with a wet wipe while Alek and Joe avoid me in the back room. The ink won't come off my skin. My wrist is looking better, I notice. I decided I was done healing and took the brace off a week or two ago. I was too scared to go back to the doctor, too scared of the money and my mouth.

I go to the bathroom and leave the floor unattended. Inside, the walls are light blue. Chipped at every corner. The sink is leaking, so there's always water on the floor. When I close the door, I can hear the men laughing through the wall. I wonder if Alek's revealed to Joe what we did yet. Or maybe I should say I wonder if he's revealed to Joe what he did to me. I wonder if that's why they're laughing, Alek and Joe behind that wall. I wonder if it's because of the way I smell or the way I said *okay, stop* while my pants were already down or if it's something else completely that I do not know but Alek now knows about my body.

When I come out, my phone is ringing on the counter. I rush over. It's Manny. When I answer I'm already out of breath and my voice is flittering on the line.

Manny laughs and immediately tells me to calm down. "It's just me," he says. "You don't have to be nervous when it's just me."

I hold my breath so he can't hear me huffing and puffing like an ogre. I count to three and let out an exhale. "Hi, just you, it's just me."

"That's more like it," Manny says. I think about the money he gave me and the way it burned a hole in my pocket and about Mami and what she's doing right now and about how next month is already approaching. "Can you meet me at the studio in an hour?" Manny's asking but it sounds like a command. Like if I don't go he'll flush me down the toilet.

"Yes," I say, again without breathing. I look at the back room. The door is still locked and Alek and Joe are still behind it. "Yes, I'll be there."

"Good," Manny says. "I'm dying to hear your voice today." Then he hangs up the phone.

I punch my code into the computer and I put my sweater on over my polo, grab my bag from under the counter, and slip out the door. I hear the bells ding behind me and imagine Alek and Joe left there while a masked criminal ransacks the place for everything valuable they have to their names.

At the studio, there's a woman at the front desk who doesn't look at me when I walk in. It's like she's been told not to, instructed to avert her eyes or something. When I ask her what studio Manny's booked, she points to one at the end of the hallway that I've never been in before. It's big and has floor-to-ceiling windows and hardwood floors that look like they've just been redone and waxed that morning. There's a piano in the center and new leggings and a black leotard with cutouts in the waist hanging on the bars for me. I know they are mine because there's a Post-it note stuck on them with my name in nice, neat handwriting that the front desk lady must have been forced to write. My hands are shaking from the sick feeling that comes with him knowing what I already have on wouldn't be good enough, but I don't let myself go down that path too long. In the center of the studio, I slip out of my clothes quickly and examine myself in the mirror; I look like a doll. My waist is cinched in, my hair is pulled tight back, and my ankles are the biggest thing on my body.

Twenty-five minutes pass, so by the time Manny walks in, I'm shaking and every part of me is trying to convince itself that this is just how these things go.

Manny's all business. "Let's get right to it," he says like we are clocking into our first day of rehearsal. "I've written something new and I want to hear it the right way."

I think that means my voice is the right way. Manny doesn't mention the new clothes. My face and hands are hot. I'm picking my cuticles again, and I'm afraid that I'm running out of fingers.

"Let's hear it," I say. I put my hands in my leggings pockets, so he doesn't spot the blood dripping down. There's an art to pretending that I'm trying to master around Manny. A way of saying *I'm your equal* that both of us are having trouble buying. When he starts playing, I'm stunned at how he builds the chords together. He's stringing together melody and harmony and chords and lyrics while he bops his head on the two and smiles at me on the four. I'm so lost in his music that when there's silence in between beats, I don't think of anything other than begging for him to keep playing. Manny's music is my compass now. The only thing that can show me the way back to myself.

After he's played the song three times through, I join him while he sings. His voice is low and bold. Not classically beautiful, which makes it even more so. The lyrics are a bit broken, so we're trying to figure them out now. I'm inserting riffs and harmonies alongside him. We're tripping over our words, playing the same chords over and over again until we get it right and we're both in perfect line, landing on the same idea, the same melody, the same hook.

When we're finally quiet and we can feel the buzzing in the room, Manny stands up from his piano and gives me a round of applause. He looks at me for what feels like the first time today, and I want to go again. I feel like an addict, itching for another hit. I want to sing on the floor until I'm finally breathing.

"You're my muse, Xiomara Sanchez," Manny says. He moves closer to me and my heart is pounding. I notice his shoes, the gold in them and the red on the bottom. His long and slouching trench sways near the edges of my toes. My nerves are dancing. My cheeks are trying not to tear out of my skin from grinning.

"I guess that means I'm nothing without you," I say.

"Say it again," he whispers in my ear.

"I'm nothing without you," I say, and I'm sure this time that it's true.

Manny holds my waist and we stare at each other for a long time, lost in the magic of the space between us.

On the walk back to Cassie's, I'm all wobbly because I meant it—I meant that without Manny, and his music, and his show, and his money, I might never feel whole again.

All morning at Ellen's I've been moseying along to my tables and singing my songs on the counter and running my food without chasing my tail. I am wearing the leggings Manny gave me, and Saundra's angry. She likes me in jeans, black and loose so I can still kick my legs but look professional, like I still have a care. I cut the tip of my index finger on a knife Greta's left face up on a table and start bleeding. My hands are a fucking war zone. I'm looking for a bandage under the host stand when I hear my name, familiar and perfectly accented above me. It's Celeste. Nena's girlfriend. Or maybe it's her ex-girlfriend. I don't know what she is now that my sister's dead and she had no say in their ending. I haven't spoken to Celeste since we left Ortiz's funeral home last year. It was raining and, before even saying bye to her, I sprinted to the black car that Mami had splurged on to drive us back the few blocks we were too weak to walk. I watched her, on the corner as we drove away, searching for my sister in the crowd, trying like hell to find her. Since then, I've thought about calling, but it's been too daunting. I haven't wanted to stomach it, talking with the only other person on the planet who might be hurting harder than I am.

"Celeste, hi." My words are all jumbled and I don't know what to say.

She gives me a bear hug and rubs my curls in her hands. "I heard you worked down here now."

"You heard right," I say, making a mental note that I really have to stop that rumor from spreading. My head is on her shoulders. She smells like coconut butter. When I pull away to look at her, I notice how much smaller her shoulders are. How her long straight black hair is now chopped off in all sorts of directions and how she has a nose ring. My sister wouldn't have liked that. "It's like a booger," she would have said, I'm just sure of it. My hands touch the tip of Celeste's nose and she moves her head away.

"I had to see you *today*." She lingers on the word *today* like there's some big special reason.

"I'm about to go on break," I say, even though I have three hungry tables waiting for their pancakes now and am hours away from breaking.

"Perfect," Celeste says, but she's pointed, like there's something else she wants to say, and I am trying to read her expression. I tell her to wait there, on the rug at the restaurant, so I can wrap things up in the back before my lunch, and she nods her head, places her palm on her elbow, and ducks out of the way for the rest of the customers coming in for their meal.

When I get to the kitchen, Becky says she'll take over my tables, and I kiss her twice on the cheeks. "You're a godsend, Becky!" I shout all the way out the double doors.

"Okay, tell me EVERYTHING," I say to Celeste when we sit down. It's already been a year or maybe closer to two now, and I really can't believe how different the both of us are, sitting across from each other here. How much shrinking and how much growing we've both done. I can feel the way she's still trying to claw her way out of it too. The grief and the mourning.

"Okay." She leans forward, and I notice how black the bags under her eyes have become. "Let's see, well, you know I'm good but not *good*."

"Same, but that's boring," I say. "What else?"

"Well, I made partner, finally." I always forget Celeste is a lawyer. She has done so much stupid illegal shit that I never associate her in that way.

"Holy fuck! Yeah, you did!" I clap my hands in a circle and we both say "A round of applause" with thick Spanish accents so that it sounds more like *a-blouse* than *applause*. It reminds me that for a time we lived parallel lives. That there's another world beyond this one where my sister is still alive, and she and Celeste and I are all sitting on the couch clapping our hands together again.

"And I moved to New Jersey," Celeste says.

"Ick, New Jersey smells like cheese." We both hold our noses and laugh.

"What about you, flaca?" I miss hearing people call me that. Ever since I left the Heights it's like no one knows what to do with me. They're all "Xiomara this, Xiomara that," like they're running my name through a paper shredder.

"Well, you know, Mami kicked me out." It feels better to make myself the victim than to tell her the truth about how I left.

"That's not what Maria told me," Celeste says, staring at me from over her mug.

"Well, Maria's a fucking liar."

Celeste gives me a thumbs-up and doesn't press me anymore. "How are you taking care of yourself *today*?" she asks. I hear the *today* again and it starts to annoy me.

"I don't know," I say. "I showered and ate half a poppy seed bagel?"

"I get that," she says. There's a heaviness to it, like she's upset I didn't ask her the same. Then, "Birthdays are hard."

My stomach flips over six times like it's in the circus. My underarms get hot and start stinging. I can feel the sweat and the way it pools up over my skin, pouring out of me like a confession. I look out the window and I can sense that the air is warm like the change of a season, the way it usually is at the beginning of May on my sister's birthday. When I look back at Celeste, I nod my head and drink my water. I feel the cool of the liquid first in my throat and then thrashing like an ocean in my gut. For the rest of the time we are together, we stare at each other like children that have never spoken, her begging me for playtime, me turning my back like I'm too good for it. When she leaves, we hug and it's distant. As I watch her walk out the door and out onto the street, I'd like a master class on how to pretend with every bone in my body that I haven't forgotten my dead sister's birthday.

* * *

When I get home, I'm tired and my eyes are heavy. Cassie wants to go out again, and I don't take too much convincing. I'm like a handbag to her now, a fancy accessory she can dangle in front of the ugly friends of whatever guy she's fucking.

"Can I pick out your outfit?" she says. Case in point: I'm her Black Barbie.

I nod and she squeals off into her closet. I march into the bathroom with my arms straight out like the zombie that I am and lock the door behind me. In the mirror, my face is like a tomato, red and splotchy and discolored with hyperpigmentation bruises. I turn and sit on the toilet. I start clipping my toenails, pushing the phrase *birthdays are hard* out of my head, when my phone pings and I see that it's Santi. I swipe to read his message:

Hi.

Just hi. Nothing more.

I wipe my hands on one of the off-white towels Cassie keeps around the bathroom. In my message chain with Santi, I see bubbles popping up and disappearing while he thinks of something more important to say. The reality is I'm not so surprised he's reached out today. Men can smell when someone else has entered the equation. Nena always told me that. That men are like maggots; where there's one, there's a hundred.

I find Cassie in the living room and throw my phone on her lap. "Look who decided to pop in."

Cassie reads the message. Her eyes get wide and her hands, manicured with a rosewater pink, cover her mouth as if she's just seen a ghost. "Men are fucking psycho," she says.

"PSYCHOOOO!" I repeat. My pointer finger is spinning clockwise around my temple.

"You're not gonna respond, are you?" Cassie asks. She's checking to see how far I've fallen.

"No fucking way," I say to her.

"Good," she says. "Don't fucking answer."

I nod and pick my phone out of her hands. Later, when I'm alone in my bedroom I'll probably type out a hundred responses I'll never send.

"Here," she says as she shoves some clothes my way. "Let's get fucking drunk." Cassie's picked out a red crop top to "show off my tiny waist" and a pair of big baggy black jeans that extend my hips a hundred sizes.

"I'd do your makeup too," she jokes, "but I don't think I have the right color."

"If you're gonna make a Black joke," I say, "at least make it original."

"Sorry," Cassie says like she's embarrassed. But I know she's not. Just a little angry I've talked back.

When we're done getting ready I look like a bootleg Kelly Rowland. The foundation on my face is like cake, so thick you could slice it, and my eyes are so raccooned that I might as well be back in seventh grade. I wonder what Santi'd say if he saw me. If he'd even look at me the same. If he'd even think about kissing me or wrapping his arm around me like he did that day at Ellen's.

"Hottie!" Cassie shouts at me when I'm out of the bathroom. A few boys she went to college with are out in the living room, and she rounds the corner to dangle a plastic bag with white powder in front of my face. "Want some candy?" White people and their fucking drugs.

"Sure," I say, though I've never done cocaine before. The boys have eyes like villains, red veins popping out their heads and lips so chapped they could slit my throat. When the coke is inside my nose it tastes like salt and nickels. I pretend not to care while I have a panic attack and wait to drop dead like Mami always said I would if I ever experimented with las drogas.

Instead, though, I begin to feel like I'm on the moon, screaming and dancing all night in Manhattan with Cassie. Celebrating what would have been my sister's thirty-second birthday with a bunch of white boys who say *Latina* with a hard *A* in the middle.

The next day, I get to the print shop forty-four minutes late.
My head is throbbing, and I can still taste the salt and mucus of last
night's bad decisions. The printer is buzzing again, and I don't have
the care to stop it. Today Alek smells like sugarcane and tobacco. It's
different from his usual cigarette scent. This one is more full. Fills the
space with something like cologne and bad habits. Alek and I haven't
spoken much since our last interaction. He doesn't even make a com-
ment anymore when I stroll in like this, remarkably behind schedule.
He just stays in his back room and I work up front, and when we do
pass each other, for one to five seconds a day, he looks at me with a
frown on his face like I have defiled him. I think if Alek had the chance
to stone me, he would. It's like now that he's had his way with me, he's
all good and ready to bring me to the town center and behead me
while he and all his disgusting friends point and shout "Whore!" before executing me for his sins while he stands on his high horse full of
fucking lies.

I'm sorting the blue paper on the wall and wondering why we
keep stocking it since no one ever seems to want to buy it when Santi
walks in. This is unexpected, and I hate being blindsided. I can't move
my eyes anywhere to avoid him. They keep finding their way back to
his body, tall and lanky and sharp. Tan like he's been lying out in the
sun with some girl wrapped around his body all summer.

"Xiomara." Santi's face is full of something I don't want to look
at. Boys always say my name when they want something from me.
Today I am not willing to give up anything.

I turn back and keep mining through the walls of print supplies. I can hear Santi breathing, but I'm too good at giving the silent treatment. My breath doesn't even hitch. I work my way through the wall, cataloging the supplies. When we were younger, Mami would go days without talking to us if we swore or if we wore lipstick to school or if she caught us eating the leftovers with our hands in the middle of the night. Nena held the record. When Mami caught her looking at Sofia, her tenth-grade English teacher with big tits, for too long, she didn't speak to her for twelve days. I've been trained for this. Santi can't break me. This is a game that I know how to win. From the corner of my eye I can see him shift back and forth on the sides of his heels.

"Hey, X, can we talk?"

I like to hear him ask me, but I remind myself that it's a courtesy. That while I was peeling back my layers, kissing him on the subway, and telling him about my dead sister, he was going home at night and calling some other girl. That his smile and his charm and the way he held my hand in his was all a big game to him. A challenge or a dare or something to laugh about while he cuddled up on the couch with another fucking woman.

I pack up my belongings and keep my eyes down, away from his. I am like a wall. My cheeks are hot and I pray my stomach doesn't betray me with its rumbling. I am violent in my anger. I imagine using his head as my palm the next time the printer fusses, smacking it back and forth on the machine until he bleeds out. His head in my hands with a wild applause from one million women.

"Xiomara, I'm so sorry for the silence. I had to go home for a while, but I want to explain."

"No," I say. I'm not going to let him finish. "I already got all the information I needed." But I don't fully believe it as I say it, and I wonder if I did. I want to ask him if he means back to Providence, with his sister and his aunt. Or maybe he went to Boston to be with his father. I'm acutely aware of the fact that I haven't asked that many questions, that I barely even know where he means when he says the word *home*. I'm salivating to hear what Santi has to say. My heart is beating so fast I can hear it like drums in the background of my ears, but I'm too far down the road already. There's nothing left to do but double down. I stuff everything in my bag while Santi keeps saying my name in the background like it might change something.

Alek walks out of the back room when he hears the ruckus.

"X, please," I hear Santi say again. Under his eyes, I see dark circles. Black and blue like there's something wicked hiding behind them. I have a million questions for him, about what's real and what's not, and what if anything, I made up in my head about what was happening between us, but I can't speak, can't even stay. Everything in my body is screaming *Go*.

Boys don't like to close doors, I hear Nena telling me. *They always want to come back around to see if the latch is still open.* Santi's simply circling around for the keys.

"There's nothing left for us to talk about, Santi," I say when I'm almost out in the wild of the city. "I've met someone else."

The first time Manny asks me to take the trip to Williamsburg to see his apartment, he says it's because he's tired of the paparazzi following him around in Manhattan. At first, our relationship started slow. It was just that wad of money at Ellen's and then a bit more at dinner, and then the clothes on the bars at the studio, but lately, it's been a lot more. We've been talking nonstop and meeting up for rehearsals, and when I need it, which is almost always, he gives me some money. Manny's somewhere between my dad and my friend. Apparently he'll do anything for me as long as I lend him my voice.

"I didn't realize you were famous enough for paparazzi," I say, before remembering that a man is only as strong as his ego.

"Do you want to continue the conversation or not?" Manny says to me, and I do, so I walk it back and ask him for his address.

Manny lives in Williamsburg with all the other artists who make too much money to still wear tattered sweatpants and collect unemployment. I take the L train from Union Square and get off at Bedford Avenue. Under the summer sun, I'm in a crowd of an assortment of hipsters. Some have blue hair. Some have no hair at all. There's a sweet smell in the air, like chocolate chip cookies and last night's beer brewing. It's different from what I'm used to in the Heights, or even in the West Village, where it still smells like vinegar and dirty laundry sometimes. Brooklyn might as well be in another galaxy. Here, it's like the people even walk on different legs or something.

I follow the instructions Manny gave me and cross over Driggs Avenue to get to North 5th Street. I count three buildings into the block and ring the buzzer. From the outside, the building looks plain, like it could be torn down at any moment and not affect a single human life, but when Manny buzzes me in, it's like Oz, completely full of magic, expansive, and glowing in every corner.

Manny lives in the penthouse suite, and in the elevator up, I check my breath to make sure that it smells decent enough to hold a conversation with. I think it's okay, so I put it out of my mind. What does it matter anyway, I think, since there's no solution for a stench in sight.

The elevator opens up directly into his living room, where the windows rise from the floor to the ceiling. He forgot to tell me that his home is not so much an apartment as it is a museum, full of Kehinde Wiley and Bisa Butler pieces. I walk off the elevator, and I try not to look impressed, try not to give away that I've never seen luxury like this in my entire lifetime.

"Gorgeous!" I hear Manny's voice echo through the apartment. "Come in come in come in."

As I make my way in, I'm nearly blinded by the stark white of his walls in between sculptures and collectibles. I've worn a leotard under my sweatshirt and jeans and immediately feel the weight of my delusional decision. Manny is in Balenciaga sweatpants and doesn't have a shirt on. His abs are like stone, each one perfectly sculpted into the image of himself. He kisses me twice on the cheeks and grabs my waist. My hands land on his back, and I can feel his muscles move while he twists around to offer me a lemon water.

"Sure," I say, "I'll take one."

Manny disappears into what I imagine is a kitchen, probably designed by Jake Arnold or someone fancy like that. I set my purse down on a side table that is likely worth more than a human life and take a seat on the sofa. *Take a seat* and *sofa*. I have to say sophisticated things like that when I'm in this space.

Manny hands me a glass of water with a thinly cut lemon slice floating on top. I take a gulp. I've never tasted water so fresh in my entire life.

Manny sits on the couch opposite me and stares me up and down again. I'm acutely aware of my body right now. The way it feels insignificant against the backdrop of the rest of his belongings and the way I blend right in like I'm a piece of art that he owns. Like I, too, should be hanging on the wall.

"Ride okay?" Manny asks.

"Yeah, just a little congestion on the L, but that's to be expected."

Manny sucks his teeth "The L? I would have sent a car if I'd known you were going to take the subway."

"That's okay," I say back. "I don't mind the subway much and—"

"But I do," he says, interrupting me. "Next time you'll have to call." There's a pause. "Say it, that next time you'll call."

"Next time I'll call." I can't help but notice, even this early on, that he is projecting a next time. I cross my legs and my arms.

"Very well," Manny says, "that's a promise."

I nod my head, though I don't believe in promises. They are just a shortcut for commitments.

Manny stands up and goes to the record player. He's had his score copied to vinyl and plays it for me. I'm listening to the original music and it's full of color. I can see it floating around in here, the pinks and yellows of the piano as it plays out.

"Sing for me," Manny says to me. His voice is lower. He's not asking as much as telling. There's something different in his skin today. Something hungry. Something that makes me know I'm not here so innocently anymore. I start singing along, making words up as I go to the melody of the music. While I'm sitting there, carrying out the tune, I realize that Manny is going to fuck me today.

"Gorgeous," he keeps saying, until my legs are spread and he's down on his knees, buckled in between mine.

While he's down there, I'm enjoying his tongue against my body, disgusted at myself for the way I make these fucked-up things okay. After it's all said and done, and we are lying on the couch not speaking words, all I want to do is tell my sister. Hear her assure me I'm absolved of it, absolved of my sins. But I'm overwhelmed by a feeling, a feeling that she'd instead tell me nothing good can be just that any-more. That now, if all my wildest dreams start to come true, it won't be that simple.

Men are like dogs, Mami once said to me. They'll sit in your lap as long as you have a treat in your hand. The second you give it up, though, it's on to the next.

A week later, Manny sends me four hundred dollars to buy a new pair of LaDucas.

"Thank GOD!" Cassie says, with an extra emphasis on the G, when I tell her I'm on my way to the store. I don't tell her where I got the money, and she doesn't ask. Cassie has her suspicions but is too polite to say so, so she shrugs her shoulders and pops another strawberry into her mouth. She's on some crazy fruit-sugar-only diet. I doubt it will work, and I've been trying to tell her that if she gets any thinner, she might disappear.

"That's what I want!" she says to me. She has a lunch date with some guy named Matt, who she met on a celebrity dating app. He makes short-form content on some new video app and has something like two million followers.

"He just started his page three months ago!" Cassie says as if I should be impressed. When she leaves, in her little booty shorts and stilettos, I look him up online. His head is beefy and he asks his audience of completely white males important questions like "Would you rather fight a shark or a lion?" Cassie really does know how to pick 'em.

My phone is buzzing. I can feel it, but I can't find it. It's under the covers somewhere and I'm fingering for it. I'm wanting for it to be Santi, trying again. Texting and calling and not taking my "I met someone else" statement for a good answer. When I finally do find it, I have a missed call from Mami. I pace around the room and call her back because I have PTSD from screening her calls and also because I've been waiting for her to apologize so that I can finally come home.

"Alo," she says when she answers.

"Hi, Mami." My voice is already apologizing. It's quiet on the other end. "Did you call me?"

"Ay, sí," she says to me. "Mira, it's the first of the month and we need to pay rent. Send money. Maria can pick it up and—"

"I'm not sending money," I say, cutting her off. The temperature in my blood is rising.

"Yes, you are," she says back to me. "Goodbye." But she doesn't hang up right away. We both breathe on the line until she decides she's through and the dial tone finally kicks in.

I bang my fist into the couch so hard I feel the metal springs poke at my knuckles. I scream into a pillow and chew at it between my teeth and imagine that my eyeballs might bulge out and flop all over the floor and Cassie will come home with her Joe Rogan boyfriend and find me here disintegrating in this fucking bubbly pink apartment.

"I'm not doing that," I keep saying to myself out loud. "I'm not fucking doing that!"

When I get up off the couch, though, I text Manny and tell him I want to see him again soon. Then I call Alek and tell him I need more shifts for the next four weeks just to make sure I cover all my bases. I tell him to schedule me, any day, anytime, but not when Santi is working. And not when Joe is in either. Alek only says okay to me now. And that's a good thing because sometimes I get off on blowing his cover, renting a billboard in Times Square to tell the entire city what a jerk-off creep he really is.

I walk all the way up Tenth Avenue to 48th Street to the LaDuca Shoes. In my pocket, I feel the $375 I've withdrawn from my checking account pulsing like a drum. I can't keep cash in my account for too long or the bank will take it. As soon as they see positive numbers, all the credit card companies will come for me. I have enough for the shoes and a coffee and maybe even a taxi home depending on how much a ride is. The air smells like fresh piss and leftover pizza. New York City in the summer.

The store is tucked into a tiny building that looks like it was built a thousand years ago. Brown awnings and an old air conditioner stick out the window, perpendicular to the sidewalk like it could fall and squish me down à la the Wicked Witch of the East at any moment. The LaDuca letters are pronounced when I walk by them. Big and white, etched perfectly into the window.

When I walk in, there's a man there to greet me. His hairline is clipped to perfection. Straight strands of blond tips stick up to the ceiling. He's all gelled to the nines. He welcomes me in and I tell him that I'm looking for a classic shoe. He asks me what size I am. When I tell him he scoffs and I shrug.

"I have my father's feet," I say like I'm sorry. The words escape my mouth before I can swallow them.

The man with the blond tips shuffles into the back room, and I remind myself that he works for me, not the other way around. On the wall, while I wait for him to return, I see posters of nearly every Broadway show that's been on since I was born. There's *The Lion King* and *Wicked* and *Kinky Boots*. There's *Mamma Mia!* and *The Phantom of the Opera* and *Rent*, which is one of my favorites. It smells like fresh leather in here. I want to press my nose into every shoe on display. Ask them whose feet they've been on. Magically take on their powers. I hum a show tune under my breath until he appears again with a box of shoes and a big purple piece of fabric that he drapes over the floor to protect the sole of the shoe from chafing against the wood.

"Try these on," he says. I do. He looks at them funny. Pulls another pair out of a box. "Now these." He makes me spin around. Give me a thumbs-down. "Okay, how about these?" He puts his hands on his hips. "I think you need something darker to match those ankles." The word *darker* twists a knife in my stomach. It slithers out his mouth like a snake bite. I know he wants me to feel it.

When he's gone, I take the money out of my pocket to remind myself that it's just as green as the next girl's. I have it placed inside a rubber band, all folded up like Papi once told me to do when I have large amounts of cash on me. Like the shoes on the walls, I wonder how many hands this money has been in, how many people counted these same dollars, what their hopes were for them, what their dreams held.

"These are the ones," the sales associate says and drops the box in front of my feet. I try them on and I hate that he's right. They match me perfectly. They let me breathe in all the right places. With these shoes on, I can barely tell where my skin stops and the sole starts.

"I'll take them," I say, stepping out of the shoes and returning to my Nikes.

"These are a bit pricier than our classics, though," he says, like it's an obstacle. "Three hundred and sixty dollars." The room fills with a pregnant pause. My dollar bills are still beating. "And we don't offer payment plans."

"That's great," I say. My voice raises ten octaves. "That's perfect."

But it's not perfect. I think about that old wives' tale with Goldilocks and the three bears. How she moved around the table before she slurped down the porridge and said it was just right when, really, we have just absolutely no way of knowing whether or not she was actually burning her tongue with a smile on her face.

When I get to the counter, I take out my rubber band again and count out all three hundred and sixty dollars. I can feel my anger boiling up inside me. I'm like a lobster in a pot.

"My hooker money," I say, cold, making eye contact with him while I slide the cash across the counter. "I don't need a fucking payment plan."

When Manny calls now, I answer on the first ring. Today it seems I'm already on the subway before he can even say, "Come over." I'm in my Nike Dunks and wearing short shorts and big gold hoops and a tiny white tank top that I know he likes with no bra on. It's not just that he's Manny and his money that keeps me running back and forth to Brooklyn, I tell myself. It's that he sees me for all that I have the potential to be.

I buzz the door three times and am immediately embarrassed at my familiarity. Manny comes on the intercom and I can hear the cocaine in his voice, the alcohol on his breath already. "Come up," he says. It's more like an order than a happy-to-see-me.

When the elevator doors open, Manny has only a robe on. He's growing his hair out, so it's sleek and back in a tight bun. I can see the evidence of the night before in his eyes.

"Hi, my little bird." He falls back on the couch. "Sing to me." I can't tell what's part of the audition anymore. I haven't heard anything about the show in weeks, and seeing as Manny's inside me now every other day, I'm starting to feel like I deserve some answers.

"My mom needs money," I say.

"So does mine," he says.

"No, really," I respond. "She needs some help." I rub my hand over him. I don't feel great about my tactics, but I'm desperate.

"Then ask," Manny says. "Learn how to ask for what you want."

"Can I please have some money for my mother?" I want to get in the shower, wash all of this off me, drown down the drain.

Manny takes a big breath and then slumps into his bedroom.

When he's back, he throws some cash at me, and I put it in my pocket, then I get on my knees and start to untie his belt while I hum something that sounds like it's from the '60s. He squeezes my shoulders while I go down on him. I'm wanting for it to end before it has barely begun today. He stops me before I can feel him finish.

"Okay, spit it out," he says to me with a little more fire than I'm used to. "You obviously have something else to get off your chest, so say what it is so we can get it over with already."

"When do you think I'll hear back?" I ask. I'm blinking and holding in my tears while my knees are burning from the friction of his floors.

I see his eyes glaze over. He puts his hands on his face before rubbing them back into his hair like he's annoyed. Like I'm a begging toddler asking for extra ice cream and not an adult woman giving him blow jobs for rent money and the empty promise of a Broadway role.

"That's really just the most uninteresting thing you could say to me right now, Xiomara." He's sucking his teeth and lying back on the couch as though I'm a disappointment.

"I don't care if I'm uninteresting, Manny," I say back, standing on my feet. "That's what you're missing." I'm surprised at my gusto, but I keep pressing. "I'm on my knees on a hot red carpet with your dick in my mouth hoping that it will move my career forward. I feel disgusting already. Uninteresting doesn't add any insult to injury."

"Watch it," he says to me and grabs my jaw so I know he means it. "Watch it or I'll tell everyone that you're not just a lackadaisical singer who falls off the face of the earth after a last round of auditions. You're a whore and a beggar too."

I can't process what he's said to me before he beats himself off and I have cum on my face.

At Ellen's later, Jacey asks if I've heard back from casting. We are in the locker room and she's starting to look desperate. "Yeah," I say nonchalantly, the lie coming easily. "Yeah, actually, I have." Jacey's eyes are full of water. I guess we're not so different after all now.

The Village sounds like gringos. So at night, when I tuck myself under the covers, I mourn for the sounds of Washington Heights. I haven't been home since Mami slapped me across the face, and the lack of flavor in Cassie's house and the way Manny has snaked his way into every fiber of my being—it's all slowly chipping away. I think of a book Nena gave me for my birthday once, by a girl named Marina Keegan. "We don't have a word for the opposite of loneliness," she'd written, "but if we did, I could say that's what I want in life." That's how I feel all the time now. Longing for a sign that there are people out there who speak my language. "We're so young. We're so young," she wrote. "We're twenty-two years old. We have so much time." She died in a car crash two weeks later.

Too early in the morning, I walk to the subway and get on the A train. I stay on and don't get off until I hear *Fort Washington, 181st Street* on the speaker above me. I walk outside and smell and see everything I long for. The platanitos and the piraguas and the ten-dollar Jordans falling out the back of an unlabeled truck. When I get to Mami's building, which I am trying to call "Mami's building" and not ours to remind myself that I no longer belong here, all the insects in my stomach rumble. I walk inside and everything is exactly how I left it, except it sounds a little different. No baby crying in 1A. And a new white woman in 2R who locks the door fast behind her when she sees me coming.

I grab my key from the bottom of my bag and grasp it between my fingers. I pray it works. It's funny how, when I slip the key in, I am already saying amen. The lock clicks. Today is Monday; Mami is already in Westchester, probably on her hands and knees somewhere scrubbing toothpaste grime from the bottom of Martha Stewart's toilet.

The apartment is sparkling clean. A home like nothing is missing. There's leftover rice still out on the stove. I uncover the lid and dig my hand into it, fitting the sticky grains into my palms, then into my mouth, exactly where they belong. It tastes like relief, and as my teeth smash the rice, saliva drops from the sides of my lips. I close my eyes and let myself feel it—the familiar comfort of being home again.

In my bedroom, I find all my things. Our just-in-case jar and my extra red polo shirts and a few leggings that Mami has folded up and put on my night table. I ravage my drawers for underwear. Run the hot shower and get naked, letting the water burn my skin. I use Mami's good conditioner, the one she buys from Celia down the street, who has a big dream of becoming a celebrity stylist. I towel myself off and relish in the risk of it. Think about Mami's face when she walks in and realizes that I've outdone her again. That I've been here and she hasn't been able to stop me from doing whatever dirty thing she'll convince herself I've done. But the feeling's empty, and my eyes sting thinking about her. Her plump hips and her peach skin, the way she always smells like San Juan in the summer.

My breath is shallow, and I know I have to go. No time to dwell. What's done is done is done, and I can't stay and get myself all worked up about it. I've already proven to myself once that if I stay, I'll never leave. I stuff all the things I need into my bag. My extra leotards, socks, tights, bras, and panties. I leave cash on the counter for Mami. She'll thank God when she sees it, even though it's from the devil that I've already sold my soul to.

When I get back to Cassie's, she's in the shower with her new boyfriend, Matt, who only looks at me when she's not there. There's not as much talking as there is moaning when they are together. I have to pee so badly that my bladder might burst, so I knock, and knock again, and knock again, until Cassie swings open the door and rolls her eyes at me.

"I was almost done," she says. I know she means it in more ways than one.

"Sorry," I say, dancing around like I'm auditioning all over again. "I really have to pee."

Cassie lets me fidget while she puts on her clothes and leaves the bathroom. Matt wipes his mouth and follows her out. He looks at me; I can feel his eyes like X-rays, surveying every inch of my Black body. I lock the door and I sit down. Peeing feels like liberation. My eyes are closed, and I am in nirvana when my phone starts buzzing and I see that it's Santi. I let it go to voicemail, though I desperately want to answer it.

"Ummmmm hey, X, it's Santi. Which you, well, you know that by now. Um, I talked to Alek. And I wanted to talk to you to see if you're okay. I think there's been a miscommunication. I really want to see you . . . properly, I mean. I know you're seeing someone else, or you said you were at the print shop at least, but I don't know. Is that all true?" There's a pause long enough for me to wonder if he's off the line for good, but then he continues. "I don't want to overstep, though, so I guess this is my last attempt. Uhhh, the . . . last . . . message I'm gonna leave you. Okay. Well . . ." He's stalling. "Bye."

On the toilet, I play the voicemail a dozen times over, wanting for every ounce of breath he left on my phone line.

"Hi, papi." I make my voice raspy when Manny calls me now because I think that's what he likes—for me to be somebody different than who I am.

"Xiomara, this is Manny." His voice is cold. Like he hasn't been inside me every night this week. I think that maybe this is his new game. Like a role-play.

"Nice to meet you, Manny," I say back.

"Xiomara, this is Manny," he says again, like I haven't heard him. "Manny from the Broadway League. You have me and my colleague Justice on the line."

All the hairs on my body stand up in a straight line. I pull the phone away from my ear so I can reset my character.

"Oh. Oh my God, Manny, wow, so sorry. I thought you were someone else. Hi. Hi, Manny. From the Broadway League. Hi, Justice. It's so great to hear from you both."

Manny laughs in his fake voice. The one that he only shows to people he wants to respect him. He doesn't use that voice with me anymore. He doesn't want me to respect him. He wants me to spit on his cock and moan while I finger myself on the carpet of his floor.

"It's great to talk to you, Xiomara." Justice is talking now. Her voice is perky, and they seem to be in the same room. I'm bitter with jealousy, wondering if he's going to take her clothes off after this too.

"Listen, we'll get straight to it." Manny doesn't like to waste any time. "We love you. We think you're fantastic. We want to see you for one last round before we make our decision. We're down to the last two."

I mute myself and scream and scream and scream.

"Xiomara, are you still there?" Justice says through the phone.

"Sorry, yes, wow, hi, sorry bad reception and I am just . . . I'm speechless. Thank you so much. I can't wait. I'm thrilled. I can't believe it. Thank you."

"Don't thank us." Manny sounds disgusted by my naivety. "This was all you." I can hear his voice at the Gramercy Tavern spitting the word *confidence* out into my face to prove a point.

When they hang up, the good is clouded by the bad. I can only think about the golden handcuffs. The prospect that maybe I don't actually deserve this. The reality that in this moment, when I should feel like I'm standing at the top of the world, instead I feel like I'm hanging off the side of a long and pointy cliff. There's no one around to share it with, I'm realizing and swallowing. Worse, somewhere out there in this skyscraper city I know another woman is getting the same phone call, except that woman hasn't let Manny cum on her face ten times this month.

That Friday, Manny tells me to come over. He's demanding on the phone with me, ordering me to stop by, disappointed when he opens the door. He looks at me twice from my ankles to the top of my head, and then tells me he hates the way I don't feel deserving when good things happen to me. "It's like you're in disbelief that anything good is ever coming your way," he says. I feel it like a truth rock rotting in the pit of my stomach. "I can't have you around if you're going to keep moping like that. It's contagious, you know, your dark and stormy energy."

I apologize.

"Come in."

I do, and before I can say anything else, I am standing in the middle of his museum with my pants off. We're going then almost immediately, and I think he's forgotten about my disgusting disease.

Manny has gotten more rough, more comfortable choking me during sex. But tonight, it's like now that he's given me what I want, he owns me more than he did before. Like I should be wrapped up and put in a box like the toy that I am for him. Tonight, it's particularly bad.

My hair is rocking up against his cotton black pillowcase while I turn blue. I'm tapping his arm and begging him to stop, but he doesn't. *Don't thank us,* I hear him saying over and over again in my head, and then the smacking of the dollar bills against his thick thumbs. Now when I see him, it's like this is the punishment for my crime. I'm trying to place it, the moment it went from good to bad, when I feel all the nerves in my body lighten up before they go limp.

Once, when I was three, I fell down the stairs so hard I blacked out just like this. I was chasing Papi out the house, Mami says, trying to convince him to stay there with us instead of going out and sleeping with one of his whores. We were playing hide-and-seek, Papi says. Either way, he sprinted out the front door, grabbing his keys and shoving the door closed behind him. I weaseled my way out before Mami could lock it and took a left down the hallway and leaped down the marble stairs in our building to catch up with him and then blacked out.

When I woke up, my front teeth were black and my eyes were bloody and the cold of the ice filled up my entire head. The doctor asked me questions like "What happens when Mami gets angry at home?" and "Are you afraid of Papi?" and "Do people ever hit in the house? And what happens if they do? And how often do they do it?"

Even then, I knew when to lie, so I shook my head yes and no and said it was a mistake, because it was, I think, and then I went home with Mami while she cried and punched at Papi's shoulders. Nena stayed up all night long, looking over me, counting the seconds between my inhales, making sure I was still breathing.

Maybe that's why I can feel her breath on me now too, while I'm floating here above my body watching as Manny continues to press into me. It's the safest I've felt in a long time, having a bird's-eye view like this. Maybe I was meant to be outside myself.

I can almost even see Nena coming into focus when Manny lets me go and I sink back down into my convulsing body. He's slapping me on the face, panic setting into his eyes while I heave and gag. On the way down, I'm grabbing for her, begging for my sister not to go.

"Don't stop," I hear myself say to him. The inside of my skin is freezing. "Please don't stop."

"You're sick," he says, running his hands through my hair. But I know that he likes it. I can tell because he gets hard again and licks his lips and starts kissing my face like he loves me even though we both know he's incapable of loving anything outside of himself.

I place his hands back on me, slowly, and the engine starts back up again. I don't know what to make of myself. What to make of this small detail that I actually might like it here, inside this punished place.

In the morning, which comes as soon as my next breath, my underwear is full of blood from the pounding of sex, and I have eleven dollars in my bank account. I slip out of bed and Manny lets me. It's almost like he's been waiting for me to leave all night long. In the bathroom before I go, I catch myself in the mirror. I don't feel the pain until I see it. My neck is swollen with Manny's handprints around it. I'm black and blue where I should be brown. Searing, hot with welts and blood vessels fighting for air. I touch my hands to the marks to make sure they are real, not makeup caked on me for some horror show I might be starring in. I try to croak out a note, but I can't. Nothing is coming. My voice is nearly swollen shut. I'm melting down here in Manny's bathroom, coughing with my hand over my mouth, hoping that he doesn't come in and finish the job he started, hoping that inside my throat my vocal cords aren't bleeding.

Near the door on my way out, Manny's saggy parachute pants are hanging over the chair. I scrounge for dollars in his pockets like I'm looking for cans in a dumpster. I find enough money in there to fill my bank account back up and slide some extra cash to Mami, then I grab a long cashmere scarf off the coat hanger and wrap it around my neck. I don't have any guilt about it, these things I'm taking. He's already stolen more from me than he could ever make up for.

When I get on the L train, it is full of young white women who have thirty thousand followers on Instagram and write about their pussy like it's a magic mushroom. They have long nails and big hoops and clean faces. I squeeze myself into a corner. They look at me like I am the colonizer here, so I observe their every move, wait for them to show me how to survive. I see how they pout their lips and wisp their hair behind their ears and I mimic their movements. I bat my eyes the same doe-eyed way they do at every man who steps onto the subway car and smile like I don't mean it when someone says excuse me.

When the train dings at Union Square, I can't seem to get myself up to go back to Cassie's. I'm not in the mood for one of her big life chats. Not in the mood for deep breathing or a tarot card reading. I want to go home. Home-home. Not pink-stardust-West-Village-home. I stay on the subway, transfer to go uptown, and a few minutes later I land in front of Ellen's as if my body flew me there on autopilot.

I bolt straight through the doors toward the locker room and hear Saundra behind me like Scooby-Doo, confused about why I'm here, saying, "Xiomara? Huh? You're not on the schedule today."

"Just let me," I'm saying back to her.

She knows better than to push me when my eyes are like this, spinning, hypnotized by the madness. Saundra gives me a section and tells me I'll be here till closing now, since Greta called out to go to her nephew's soccer game today. In my first hour I'm dropping dishes left and right, and Saundra says she's empathetic to "whatever the hell is going on this time," but that she's taking it out my paycheck if I break something else. I remind her that I barely have one, a paycheck, and she smacks on the front of my apron pockets where I keep my tips.

"Aren't you hot?" Becky says to me, tugging at the scarf choking my neck while we're on the floor.

"Not really," I say. "I think I might be getting sick." I tighten the cloth back around me.

I run the hot soup du jour in my hands to table 37, and they want some hot sauce. I pull it out of my back left pocket and smack it down on the table so hard it spills down my hands. I'm too fast today, moving too quickly with all my rage. Every one of my movements is full of hostility.

When Jacey walks in for her shift, she's still in her studio clothes, tight spandex straps stuck to her body. I wonder if she was rehearsing with Manny, if she's just gotten back from a private lesson, if she's already beat me to the depths of my dreams.

"Jacey looks soooo good today," Becky says when we're back in the kitchen, banging her head against the freezer.

"You're hopeless," I say back, physically moving her body with my hands and opening the door to find the vanilla ice cream. My twelve-top at table 19 has a birthday and expects me to sing Stevie Wonder. I chug down a green tea with extra honey and hope it coats my throat long enough to last me through the song.

The ice cream is dripping down my hands while Jacey claps behind me and harmonizes while I try my hardest to belt "Happy birthday to YUH." My voice is fried. Completely fried and I'm struggling to finish the melody. I feel my throat stinging, the dryness of my despair creeping up into my mouth, bouncing off the edges of my teeth. The tears are coming now and I'm wiping them, holding in my sobs until I can't anymore, and Jacey raises her volume to make up for me while I stand there, crying over a ten-year-old's birthday candle. When we're through with our little jig I can feel her following me like a lost puppy, questions ready to fall out of her unusually tight lips. I don't want her to approach me here, in this diner, where we're expected to break out into song every five minutes, though, so I'm dodging her like a bullet, ducking left and right so she doesn't have the opportunity to stop me.

"Xiomara, wait," she says just as I'm rounding the corner back into the locker room, where I would very much so like some privacy. She puts her hand on my arm and I smack it away. I don't like being touched, apparently, by a woman. Jacey looks at me like I owe her something.

"What?" I say to her, wiping my nose and daring her to bring it up. She twiddles with her fingers and then suddenly reaches out and unties my scarf until it drapes off my neck. My bruises shine like fool's gold under the bright white lights of the diner. She looks at me with these eyes like I'm a fragile little bee who's crawling around the earth with its wings ripped off.

"I've heard," she says, "about the way he is with some women." She's talking about Manny, and I'm scared to know what she'll say next. Terrified that I haven't heard the same rumors she has. "Whatever this is," she continues, "you don't have to go through with it."

My eyes are hot and full of salt again. There's a pause. I let us settle in the silence, and then I tell Jacey that she has no fucking idea what she's talking about.

"You're jealous," I hear myself saying to her, my voice muffled in my head by the blood beating through my body. "You're soooo fucking jealous."

Jacey tilts her head a little and lets us both sit in the muddy black water I've made of her peace offering.

"Anyway, I heard you're in the final round," she says after a minute, surveying the bruises lining the veins between my shoulders and my head. I tie my scarf back on. "I wanted you to know that I am too."

So there she is. I pinch the skin on the back of my arm. There is the other woman walking around New York City completely unmarred by Manny's claws.

The next evening, Alek calls to tell me I'm finally fired. I've slept through my shift, almost the entire thing, and he says he just "can't *justify* it anymore." I look at the clock: 6:00 p.m. He whispers *justify* aggressively, as though he's given me every chance in the world.

"It's not like this is a presidential internship, Alek. Relax."

Alek scoffs, and I want to tell him he doesn't have to do that, pretend to be disappointed in me when we both know I'm giving him exactly what he wanted—an easy out. His breath lingers on the phone and then he spits it out. "Look," he says, breathing heavily, "I would really appreciate it if you didn't tell anyone what happened . . . between us." He lets what he just said sit in the air.

"Wait, sorry, did I miss something?" I say, shrugging him off. "What happened between us?"

"Okay, okay, I get it," he says, and I can hear the relief in his voice before I chime back in.

"*Oh,* you mean when you fucked me on the back couch even though that's totally inappropriate and you're a perv?" I can practically hear his body tighten up. "That?! Yeah, no worries, Alek. I won't tell a soul." The phone clicks while the scent of his fear makes its way into my bedroom and under my nose.

When Cassie gets home I tell her about the firing, and she says to me that this is the puree of life. The feeling like I'm being shredded alive that I can't seem to escape these days. She says that it means I'm doing something right, then looks up my astrological chart on her Co-Star app.

"Yep, see," she says, tossing me her phone, which has my chart pulled up. "Your Saturn's almost completely returned." She talks about the stars like Mami talks about the Bible.

"Well, it better hurry up," I say. "I'm in urgent need of getting to the other side."

"This is good. You hated Alek's. Don't be so negative, Xiomara," she says like she's my schoolteacher. Lately, Cassie's had a good-vibes-only policy in the apartment and it's stressing me out because I don't have any (which is probably why she instituted it in the first place, because I'm all doom and gloom and it's wrecking her perfect pink little bubble).

"I'm going to pick up more shifts at Ellen's. Don't worry, I won't be here more or anything."

Cassie doesn't answer. I say good night and head to my room. Still no response. I'm sure she's already inside her phone texting the guy she's been seeing that it's finally clear for him to come over.

Under my covers with my phone in hand, I get lost in a rabbit hole searching for more answers from Saturn. I learn about its 146 moons and about its giant size—ninety-five times the size of our own Earth—and about how if you listen closely, you can hear the sounds of its rings crackling and whirring with high-pitched echoes, calling out for someone to hear them. I can't help but think that those noises might be me. That I'm not really here at all. That somewhere on Saturn I'm screaming, waiting for Nena to come get me.

At Ellen's, I have the entire upstairs section. All my customers seem to have been bussed here from Maryland or Detroit or Albany, which to me is the worst. Just like me, they are the rejects, the people who didn't get to the TKTS line early enough to score leftover seats for the matinee shows.

There's a Black family at table 62, so I go there first. After all these years of us being shoved into the corners of restaurants, I like to show my preference up top.

"Welcome to Ellen's Stardust Diner," I say when I land at their table. "Have you guys been here before?"

The kids at the table, three dark-skinned girls all with their hair in two buns, nod their heads frantically.

"Yes," their mom laughs and gives me the eye, "and we love it, as you can see." Her hair is an auburn color and her nose is flat on her face. She's wearing a yellow jumpsuit and big cool sneakers and a blazer that fits oversize like a fashion model.

"Awesome," I say, handing out the menus. "Well, then, you know the drill. There will be some singing, and some eating, and if you're really, really good"—I lean down to the tiny ladies and whisper—"there might even be some ice cream." Before I can finish my words, they are screeching and clapping. Nothing like the promise of a sundae to get the kids on board. They order almost everything I could think of on the menu: burgers and breakfast and individual soda floats with the most unappetizing mix of flavors.

"Can't wait for that sugar rush!" their mom says to me as I scribble their orders into my notepad.

I sloppily take the rest of my tables' orders, and then it's time for my song. Today it's "I'm Not That Girl" from *Wicked*. Fuck Saundra for making me do this. It's like she's playing a game with me, narrating my life to music like this. I want to remind her that we're not *actually* living inside a Broadway musical. That there are stakes to my misery. I do sound like butter, though, and so I feel better when I'm done because the music has given me the thing I actually needed. A release. Not a big part just yet or even a standing ovation, but a big feeling that I can keep tucked inside myself to enjoy for the rest of the day.

"You're *really* good," the mom at table 62 says when I bring them their order.

"Thank you," I say, and I wish Manny were here to witness her compliment. "Do you want any ketchup?"

All the girls nod their heads madly again. I love them. They aren't muted down like the rest of us women yet. I fetch the ketchup, but by the time I get back, the girls are nearly done with their meals.

"That was fast!" I say. "No time for ketchup!" They giggle and I put it down on the table anyway. "For your scraps."

"Thanks," their mom says. "We'll just take the check when you're ready."

The girls boo like they don't want to leave, and their mom reminds them they have a train to catch at Grand Central or something. I print the receipt quickly, comp the floats, and bring over the sundaes in to-go cases.

"Sorry," I say. "I promised."

In a heartbeat, they are gone, across the street, the mother shoving her girls into a taxi while they lick the whipped cream dripping out of their doggy bags. I like her, the way she manages them. I wish Mami could have been that way with me, and I miss her too, the way she wasn't.

When I get home, Cassie's fucking Matt again in the bathroom. I'm tired and my armpits are sweaty and I need a shower. A good long one where I sit on the floor and count the tiles and ask myself big questions like: If I don't get this part, then what exactly am I going to do next? And do I even want to be alive anymore? There's a leftover box of pizza from Joe's on the counter. Pepperoni. I eat all three slices to pass the time and don't throw away the crusts.

When I'm done, I pace outside the bathroom door. I hear all sorts of sounds that I don't want to. Finally, I let myself smack into the handle. I do it three times so that she can hear me. The water stops slapping up against the wall suddenly. I know this because I can hear its cadence change, going from violent beads of water spraying up against the glass to soft drops sliding down Cassandra's back.

It's officially time for me to leave this place. When I'm interrupting a friend's shower orgasm because I'm contemplating the very fabric of my existence, I know I've overstayed my welcome. I walk into my bedroom, the one Cassie's made for me anyway, and pack my things. There's not too much I've brought, so it only takes three minutes.

When she comes out, in a towel and wet hair, Cassie's immediately mad about the pizza.

"You're so fucking inconsiderate," she starts to say before she sees me with my shoes and jacket and backpack on, all ready to go. Her face washes over with something that looks a lot like relief.

"The keys are on the table," I say, stoic in my stance. "Thank you for letting me stay here, Cass." I don't have any more room for the theatrics or the screaming or the doors slamming behind me in the faces of people I love. This time, I just want to say goodbye and go.

"Okay," she says, swallowing the rest of her words down. I leave just like that while Matt stands awkwardly in the corner and whispers, "Fuuuuuck," like he's sorry to see me go.

On the other side of the door, I have no idea what the fuck I'm doing, but I'm lighter, and I wonder if everything in life should be this easy.

I pace the block at least twenty times before I work up the courage to finally buzz the door. Mami lets me in without asking who it is. I run up the steps, so when I reach the top, I'm out of breath. Mami swings the door open and takes three steps back. From the hallway, I can see that she is just in from church. I can tell by what she's wearing—a long white dress in silk with velvet gloves and a mesh hat. I've never understood how she mixes texture so successfully. Corduroy and linens, silks and velvet.

It's been ten seconds since Mami's laid eyes on me and she has yet to slap me across the face. I guess Jesus must have made his mark today. I guess she doesn't want to become a sinner so soon.

Before I'm even inside I can smell the scent of the house like a bottle of fresh Fabuloso. That cleanser is like a second religion to Mami, something else she says we were born to pray to. I let my pause linger, take a deep breath, and then burst through the door and smack my bag down on the floor. Mami folds her arms and sucks her teeth so hard I think she might be saving her saliva in a secret compartment to spit at me later.

"I'm coming home," I say firmly, bending my knees slightly to ground myself so she can't put up a fight. I'm fucking terrified of the tone I'm taking with my mother, but I have to be a firecracker right now so that she knows she's done putting out my flame.

Mami unfolds her arms and tries to chime in, but I don't let her. Instead, I put my finger up and keep going toward the living room. When I arrive, I turn around and send for her with my hands. *Come here,* they say. Mami listens. She sits on the couch and crosses all the parts of her body. She can barely look at me, shifting back and forth in her seat so often I think the back of her legs might chafe. Her silence now is like a dagger or a dare. A daunting, soundless thing, dangling danger in front of me.

"I'm coming home," I say again, more definitively so I know she's heard me, and so I know I'm serious too. These words are like my launching pad. My rocket ship to the soliloquy I know I need to give next. "But things are going to be different now," I say. I'm bouncing on my knees like I'm in a theater school warm-up. Mami finally looks up at me with those eyes full of rage and something else I can't seem to place. I'm distracted, only for a moment because I've forgotten that she's so gorgeous. God, is Mami gorgeous. I kick myself back into gear to not lose the steam of the moment. "I can only stay if you agree to listen now," I say, hoping she wants me here as badly as I want to return. "Can you listen?"

Mami remains silent.

"Mami!" I'm begging now. "Mami, please, can you listen?"

She nods, so I know I've already won.

"Okay," I continue. "First, I want to say that I love you so much." I haven't heard myself say those words in forever so I say them again. "I love you so much, Mami." Mami's expression starts to soften. "But"—I take a pause to really think about it—"I have to start to love myself too." God, I sound like Cassie. Mami is shifting in her seat again as I go on talking. "And I love singing, Mami. I love performing. I love seeing the lights on the stage right before the curtain goes down and I need to be able to do it all—love you and love me and love my voice. Love all three, I guess. And you need to let me." I'm looking past Mami now, at a spot right above her head on the cracking wall so that I don't stop just when it's getting good. "I need you to let me. Because I'm suffocating here, inside this home and this skin and this outside world that just won't seem to fucking quit, so here's what it's going to be," I say. "I'm going to get a job, a normal one that you like and can tell your friends about and that has health insurance so that we can go see a doctor once or twice a year. I got fired from Alek's, and that's a long story, but you're not going to ask me about it, and I can't speak to Cassie anymore, so you were right about at least one thing, but she did teach me about this thing called boundaries. And you and I need them. For this to work, we need boundaries. And beyond that, I'm going to audition again. In fact, I *am* auditioning again, for this play about a girl and some multiverse and I'm not even sure how good the idea is, really, but I want it. I want it so bad and I've done so many things I'm not proud of to get it. But when I do, when I do get this part"—I'm speaking it into existence—"you're going to be happy for me." I take a breath because now all my cards are on the table. "And I'm going to sing. Mami, I am going to sing in the shower, and in the kitchen, and at nightclubs sometimes too. I'm going to sing like I did when Nena was alive." *When Nena was alive.* We both feel the spiders of our life crawling through our veins. "I'm close, Mami, I'm *really* close. I can feel it. And you're going to be there for me. And I get to lock doors, and talk to boys, and *sometimes* swear on the phone with Maria. I'm all you have left, Mami. And I think you might be all I have left too. But if you want me, then you have to take all of me. Not just the parts you can boast about at dinner."

"Ay, Xiomara, ya," Mami says when she's had enough of me. Then she picks up my bags and puts them inside my bedroom. "Bueno."

When I lie down to sleep that night, Mami crawls in next to me. I can feel her chest rising and falling slowly in rhythm with mine. In the dark, she holds me and it's warm, like I'm in her womb again. This is my mother, and I think if I stay right here, nothing can hurt me.

A few days later, I wake up and I'm pacing around the living room floor. I have exactly seven days until final callbacks and I'm losing my mind, singing every note I can remember from Manny's show and sliding my feet across the hardwood of the apartment to check in on my coordination. It's still shit. I still have two left feet. I'm still the girl who can sing her heart out but can't seem to stop tripping over her toes. Mami mops around me and I feel a splash of water on my ankles.

"Bete," Mami says to me like I have somewhere to go. She's been dying for me to do something other than sit here and sing since I came home. But I have with no money to take me away and no place else to practice for my auditions.

"Bete, bete, bete," Mami's saying again.

I pretend I don't hear her and spin on my heel with my hands in the air to mimic some of the choreography Manny showed me from act two. I get a splinter and fall on my back like I'm fainting. It's in these moments I remember that I'm a thespian, hungry for drama. On the floor, I'm convincing myself that my entire body is a lemon, sour and ready to be returned to sender.

Mami shakes her head twice and tells me I'm fine. Then she disappears into the bathroom and comes back out with a tweezer.

"Ven," she says, grabbing my foot while I'm sprawled out like a dead fish. I sit up, and Mami is hiding a smile while she tries to pull out the sharp edge from my heel. I'm squealing. "Ay, Xiomara," she says while I continue to kick my feet. We're both laughing because I'm such a baby. She tells me to count to three and I do, then she squeezes my skin and extracts the shard of wood from the bottom of my foot. The last time we were on the floor like this together I was six years old and my sister was eight or nine. Nena was sobbing and counting down the numbers while Mami made me pin her hands down to the floor so she could pull out one of her loose teeth. These memories are like bullets when they hit me.

Mami grabs a cotton swab and cleans my foot with alcohol. I can't feel it, the sting of the liquid against the inside of my flesh, but I pretend that I can and I wince and I toss myself back down on the ground so I can close my eyes and catch my breath.

"You need to go for a walk," Mami says. Apparently, while I was away Mami picked up the sport of putting one foot in front of the other. It clears her mind, she says, and I need to try it too. But clearing my mind feels impossible. When I turn inward, my mind is anything but crystal. Instead, it's cloudy with gray nightmares of men lurking in the back of print shops or ramming their bodies against mine in Brooklyn.

"Five minutes," I say to Mami, referring to her clarity walk. She nods her head then sets an alarm to keep me honest while she continues to mop around me, leaving a dry imprint of my body on the floor until my time is up. When the bell of the phone goes off, I keep my promise and jam my toes into my shoes before I walk out the door.

"I'll be back," I say to Mami.

"Si Dios quiere," Mami replies.

I nod, but while I skip down the stairs, I'm asking myself what God really wants for me anyway. What His plan is. What He's going to do about me after all.

My feet take me to Floridita first. Before I can even check my bank account to make sure I have enough to cover it, I've ordered three pastelitos and a coffee full of sugar and milk that will probably make me shit my pants later. I blink my eyes because I can't stop seeing Santi at the table there across from me a few months ago, saying *My mom died* with a smile on his face. I think about calling him. Then I think about trying it again, telling the cashier about Nena, but I bet she already knows. In the Heights I have this mark on me. Here, in my neighborhood, my nickname might as well be Pobrecita. When the cashier looks at me and tells me it's ten dollars, I don't use my debit card to pay because I don't want to be embarrassed. Instead, I reach into my pocket and use two fives I've collected from Ellen's this week. She eyes the tip jar, and I grab my food and move to the doorway. I eat everything at once and I'm in heaven, chewing this meat and cheese and gooey bread.

When I walk outside again, my mind is back on fire. I walk and walk and walk while I mull over both sides of the same coin. On side A, Manny calls me and tells me that I've gotten this part and that my life is changed and that I can finally sleep soundly at night. On side B, well, that's something I can't get myself to say out loud. I have to get into a studio before I walk back into that room with Manny. This week is either my casket or my Hail Mary.

I make a sudden turn onto Audobon Avenue and walk up to the door at Doña Carmen's, a dance center I've been avoiding since I was thirteen. The glass of the door has been sprayed with graffiti and there's a hole in the awning the size of a basketball. I feel my shoulders start to slouch. I miss Cassie and her golden key to Ripley-Grier Studios. I'm itching for it, her proximity to perfection. I think of what Maria said that night about me at the club. About my inside shit. About how I want to be something I'm not. About how I try to denounce myself and the people around me even when what's in front of me is all I'll ever have left. I swallow my breath and swing open the doors. Side B is not an option.

When I walk in, the first thing I notice is that the floors here are unpolished and the bars have lost their color. The walls are olive green and the mirrors are foggy like they need to be wiped down with Windex. On the wall, there's a big sign that says BAILE! and pictures a woman like the emoji with a red dress fanning out and her hands in the air. The lady working the front is wearing a hairnet holding her doobie tight together and red rubber chanclas that show the outline of her bunions.

"Buena," she says to me without looking up from her computer.

"Hi," I say back to her. I want her to see me for who I am—the girl who makes it to the top and not just another lost cause who likes a good rhythm. "Hi," I say again when she still doesn't look up at me.

The woman takes a deep breath and raises her eyebrow toward me. "Buena," she says again, like I didn't hear her the first time. She has a long and lean face. Her lips are covered in red gloss like Gorilla Glue.

"I'm here to sign up for classes."

"New student?" she asks, finally looking at me now. She opens the drawer next to her hip and slaps down a packet of paper. "Fill out these forms," she says, pushing them toward me and chomping down on her gum.

I sit down and tap my foot while I go through page by page. I list out how many years of dance I've taken—fifteen on and off at different levels and different studios because I always seem to get too frustrated and quit. I list my emergency contacts—Mami and Maria. I give them my sizes, begrudgingly, and sign a waiver that says if I drop dead like my sister, they are not responsible. I slide the papers back across the counter when I'm done.

"I need to book a private studio," I say, "and then, let's see . . . can you sign me up for this week's advanced ballet, hip-hop, and intermediate modern?"

The front desk lady laughs a little. I fucking hate when people laugh a little like that. Like they are in on some secret and about to spew it all over your face. "Evaluations are Sunday at four," she says. "You'll have to come then before we can book you or place you in any of our classes."

I feel my skin begin to simmer. "I don't have until Sunday at four," I say back to her. I'm trying to keep my cool, but I feel my devil clawing its way outside of my body.

"No exceptions," she says, folding her arms across her chest. "Sorry." She's not fucking sorry.

"No, you don't get it," I say. "I'm about to book a show. I need access to your studio space. There must be something we can work out." I take the tips I have left from Ellen's out of my pockets and put them on the counter. "How much do I need to pay you?"

"No exceptions," she says again, waving her finger in my face like she wants to ruin my life.

"Come on," I'm begging, "what's your price?"

"Mira, hot shit, I don't have a fucking price," she snaps back at me.

"Everyone has a price!" I scream. "Everyone has a fucking price!" I bang my hand on the counter and shove the dollars at her until they fall on the floor. "Forget it," I say when she looks at me like I'm losing it. "I don't need this fucking piece of shit studio anyway, if you can even call it that." I rip a piece of peeling paint from the wall next to me. "Stupid fucking falling-apart ass studio." There's a silence. I pick up my dollars and shove them back into my pockets.

On my walk home, my heart is beating so fast I think it will fly right out of my chest. Between the blood rushing through my body and the sweat dripping off my forehead, I hear a soft voice inside me that says maybe I'm wrong. Maybe it's not *everyone* who is willing to take money from people who treat them like dirt. Maybe it's just me.

When I get to my last callback, I try to forget that there are a million people just like me walking around in this concrete jungle, hoping that their lives are on the brink of change. *Relax*, I think. Mami made me a big breakfast, and I didn't dare protest. I'm bloated beyond belief and the air is blasting in the studio and I can't seem to get out of the wind's way. My fingers are bleeding again from the picking.

I hear Cassie's voice in my head saying, "The audition starts the minute you walk into the waiting room." I raspberry my lips out of habit and look for a corner to disappear into. I don't want to be judged a second before I'm ready.

I set my things down near a dusty radiator that is crackling with strange noises. I wonder who is in charge of heating up New York City, and why they can't seem to figure out a silent way to do it. When I bend down to try to prove to myself that I am flexible enough to touch my toes today, I feel a hand firm around my behind.

"What are you doing?!" I'm whisper-screaming before I can even turn around. I don't have to see his face to know that it's Manny groping me in the hallway. Broad daylight and he's still decided that I'm just his piece of ass. I pull his hand away from my body and face him as he puts his hands above his head, palms to the sky like he's not guilty.

"Are you ready for this?" He's making a voice like a baby. Looking down at me with those eyes the way I first saw them in the diner that day. He's acting like he's going to coddle me once I'm in there, even though we both know he is going to blow me to bits.

"I'm ready," I say back to him, trying to exude the confidence he's already choked out of me. "I'm ready." I say it again to take the question mark out of my answer. The whiskers on his face are falling into his mouth like the rat that he is.

"Good," he says, "because everyone's here to see my little bird sing." He should know I'd sound better if he let me out of my cage for once.

We both hear the door open before Jacey walks in. All the blood in my body rushes up to the center of my scalp, where it pools and forms a whirlwind. Jacey looks at us like she's collecting evidence to bring back to her lab or something. To her, we're like fingerprints at a crime scene.

Today she is godly. Tall and skinny and innocent, unlike me. I see Manny see it, the way she moves without begging him to notice. The way she has permitted herself to walk freely through the streets of this city. The tears in my eyes are welling up so fast that I don't have time to wipe them away before they pour over my lids and drip down my cheek onto my chin.

"See you in there, Xiomara," he says, ignoring my tears and putting on a mask as though this is the only interaction we've ever shared together. I wish I had a projector so I could play our secret little lives out on tape for everyone to see. Take questions from the audience when the truth of our ugly colors fills their screens.

Inside the audition room, my LaDucas are cutting up my heels. I haven't had time to break them in and didn't listen when Cassie told me I should walk around the house in them for a week before I showed up here. Every time I bounce, especially on my right foot, I can feel a sting. Like someone's pouring alcohol into an open wound and waiting for me to be cleansed of the demons running through my blood. Manny makes me do the dance number only once, and I know that's a bad thing. I've seen him when he falls in love with something. He beats it and beats it over the head until it's blue in the face. It's a bad sign in here, I think, that I'm not a dead horse.

When I sing, though, it shakes the building. I can see their jaws drop when I hit the whistle. I can practically see the hair stand up from the center of their bones. When I'm through, there is nothing left inside me. I'm hollow again. Bottomed out. I don't look at Manny's face before I leave the room, but I can hear him clapping, slowly, and making a bird whistle to remind me that I am his. For a moment I wonder if it's worth it, to leave it all out here like this on the studio floor. What if they don't deserve it, the innermost parts of me? What if I don't actually want to be made for consumption?

In the hallway, Jacey is getting ready. I try to squeeze past her, but she stops me in the doorframe of the restroom where I'm just about to have a meltdown.

"Hey." She's squaring me off. "Good luck." Her eyes are big and bold and full of something that I long for. "I mean it."

"Thanks," I say back, moving her arms off me. "You too."

I want to like Jacey now that she's putting her best foot forward, but I'm having a hard time finding my way to it. I've always had a thing, I guess, about the women who are getting too close to the things I think are mine.

After a few days of holding my breath and banging my head against the wall, Mami says she appreciates that I'm trying to live the "American Dream" but that I need to hold up my end of the bargain, get a real job, and "not to come home until I do." I roll my shoulders because if I roll my eyes she'll claw them out of my body and I can't afford that. I can't afford anything, really.

After I walk into Rasuelo's, my favorite little shoe store, and he tells me to get out because he doesn't hire girls like me, my feet carry me to Maria's salon. I don't realize I'm there until I arrive.

"Sientate," she barks at me when she spots me in the doorway. I guess it's too late to turn around. On the bright side, I'm happy she spoke first. I can't keep being the first to wave my white flag around this town. I only have so much good left in me. I listen to her and plant my butt in a salon chair.

Maria is blowing out a little girl's hair. She is crying while Maria waves cold air onto her scalp with her breath and tells her not to be a drama queen.

"Say thank you," the mother says when Maria's done, but I want to tell the girl that she doesn't have to do that. It's a crime, I think, that we make girls say they're grateful for the things that gut them. When the mother and daughter are gone, Maria points to the washing station. I move toward it because I'm a bit afraid of what will happen if I don't.

"Your hair is a mess," she says firmly. I know Maria well enough to acknowledge that this is her peace offering. The only way she knows how to extend an olive branch is through a roller set.

I lean my head back in the chair and I feel the heat of the water. It's scalding, but I don't say so. Her shampoo smells like peppermint and palm trees. She makes it like that from scratch. Swears that it will make even the worst case of pelo malo shine like silk.

"I'm sorry," I finally say when she gets to the conditioner. I feel like an alcoholic on their apology tour. "I shouldn't have said the things I did. I love you and—"

"Ay, ya." Maria says, cutting me off in the middle of my soliloquy. "We're good. I shouldn't have said that shit either." Then she takes a towel and wraps it around my head, moves me to the chair, and then to the dryer. I tell her everything—about Manny and the show, and Cassie and Santi, and how Mami says I can't sleep at home tonight unless I come back with a job she approves of, so I might need to crash on her couch.

"You're not working here," she says before I finish my sentence, "but a friend of mine is the principal at this fancy charter school up in New Rochelle and told me they're looking for a new musical theater teacher. I fucked him to help him get over his divorce last year, so he owes me."

Long pause.

"I'm kidding."

Long pause.

"You'll work there."

On the way back home, I stop to get a pack of tampons and a can of beans from Carlos's bodega. The neighborhood smells like it always does at the tail end of summer, thick with the scent of piragua syrup in the air.

"Where you been, Nena?" Carlos asks as he hands me a scratch-off lottery ticket.

I look over my shoulder. The memory of my sister behind me at the bodega, deciding between Doritos or Cheetos, looms over us both.

"Sorry," he says. "I didn't mean it like—"

I wave my hands in the air to say there is no need to apologize. "It feels better when people remember her," I say. "This way I know it's not just me alone with her ghost on these sidewalks."

I throw a box of Tampax and a can of Goya on the counter and grab a bag of Flamin' Hot Funyuns to go with it. Carlos looks away like he does for me most days, and I stuff the items in my tote.

"Thanks," I say, and I mean it.

When I walk outside, I stop and listen to my neighborhood. It feels good to remember where I come from. To have a fresh shampoo and my cousin back. I hear everything, every little beat of this place. I sit down on the curb to take it all in. It's like an opera, the screeching of the subway under the earth, and the fire hydrants pouring out water onto the cement, and the babies laughing, and the boys and girls gasping, touching each other's parts around the corner from their parents' apartments. It's so loud and so beautiful, and I am so lost in my own thoughts, sitting here on the curb, that I almost miss it when the casting office calls to tell me that I didn't get the part.

When I don't get what I want, my body moves before my mind does. Before I know it, I'm on the subway like a kid frantically kicking people on the playground. My heart is pounding so hard I think I'll get checked into the hospital. I'm on my way to Manny's apartment and everything feels bigger than it usually does. Like my mind is a fishbowl and I am the fish. On the inside looking out at the big, wide world around me. The subway car goes on for miles and every person who steps into it has eyes that bulge out of their face above their nose.

I haven't said a word to Manny yet about coming over because I think explosive moments like this, especially ones where I will use many swear words, are better left unexpected. I buzz his apartment three times and then another. It's ninety degrees in New York at the end of the summer, and I'm freezing. My teeth are chattering. All the energy in my body has moved up into my throat, and I am ready to let it come out like fire.

Manny asks me who it is, and I say, "Let me in," in a voice that feels more authoritative than I'm used to. He buzzes the door and I swing it open. When I get upstairs, he doesn't seem to be as shocked as I was expecting. He is blinking slowly, like I am the most predictable person he could have ever imagined, and I am immediately embarrassed that I have fulfilled his twisted prophecy.

"You fucked me," I say, sure of myself again.

"In more ways than one," he says back, laughing through the slits in his teeth.

"Be serious! You fucked me!" I say again, while I feel my tears fighting to come out of me.

He moves aside from the doorway like he's inviting me to come in, and I do because I already came all this way and I don't particularly have a craving to be the Black woman screaming in a hallway full of Brooklyn hipsters. The door locks behind me.

"It was Jacey, Xiomara," he says through a breath, pouring water into a glass he once told me he got from Cozumel. "It was always going to be Jacey." Manny puts his thumb and forefinger to the bridge of his nose and closes his eyes while he squeezes.

"Then tell me why," I say. "Tell me why you made me believe it was me. Tell me why you made me do all the things you made me do. Tell me why any of this"—I'm gesturing to his apartment and the space between us—"was worth it at all."

I can see that he is feeling something because he clenches his palms a few times and cracks his neck twice like he always does when he is about to explode.

"Speak!" I shout when he continues to hold it all in. He's red in the face now.

"Stop it, Xiomara!" his voice booms, accusing me of my audacity. "You knew exactly what you were doing. Every minute you spent with me. Every fucking dollar. Wasn't that enough?! You knew who I was. You knew what I was. You knew there was a risk. And you know what, I don't owe you a thing. Nothing. Whether you kept getting on your knees for me or not, it was never going to be you. Never. And you know why? You want to know why?"

I don't think I do. I'm shaking now.

"Because you're not good enough. You never were. You don't have the talent. Your voice? It's a fucking God, but those feet?"—he points to my flappers—"They don't know their right from their left."

I want to tell him that's enough but I can't because my voice is gone.

"We both know you didn't deserve to get this far, so you know what, Xiomara, say thank-you. Say thank you and walk away. Thank me for getting you to where you are now."

"Thank you," I say to him, but my tongue is like a snake hissing at him to come a step closer and get a taste of my venom. Then I am laughing because it's absurd and I am crying because, after all of this, I feel free.

I don't say another word to Manny, but I do show myself out and empty my bag of shoes and leotards and all the other bullshit he's filled my wallet with on his floor. I walk to the subway and my legs are shaking, but I feel lighter. I can see the world clearly again for the first time in months. I hear the mundane melody of ending something that was never meant for me at all. That's it, I'm thinking to myself, there's nothing left. Finally, the hands are off my neck.

When I get home, the moon's already out and I can see the plane lights blinking above JFK like stars in the New York City sky. My eyes are nearly swollen shut and I'm squinting, shaking with the keys in my hand while I fiddle with the lock. My ears are ringing. My body is burrowing in on itself. When Mami comes to the door, she can see it on my face—the torture and the liberation of the day. My shoulders sag and I'm like the hunchback of Notre Dame, dragging my sorry ass through the cathedral.

Once, when we were in high school, Nena stood here like this too, and I was on the other side of the door like Mami is now. She'd just gotten her heart broken, my sister, I mean, for the first time, and I was making a box of Annie's white cheddar mac and cheese.

"She's gonna stay with him," Nena said to me. Her eyes were red like hell. Full of sorrow. An ocean winding and whooshing through her lids. "She said she's decided," she went on, "decided she was done with me and her . . . experiment." The water and the pasta on the stove were boiling over. I held her like she was my own skin, and she cried in my arms. I could really feel the weight of her then. The depths of her shoulders. The soft, supple skin at the base of her neck. I want to hold her muscles in my hands like clay now. Roll them all up on a pottery wheel and put her in an oven. Be surprised and relieved when out she walks of the furnace, alive again. I'm tired of missing my sister. I want someone who knows how it feels to stand here, like me, on this broken side of the door.

"I didn't get the part," I say, and Mami's arms are like mine, wrapped around my body. She's stunned. We sink silently to the floor. The rice and the water on the stove are boiling over.

"Okay, so you try again," she says. Her voice is certain, desperate for me to feel instantly better, and for a moment, before I remember that she might not have space for my pain and her pain too, I resent it, the way that she now believes in me when this is already so fucking over.

"No, Mami," I start. "It's done. Ya se acabo. These kinds of things—these big breaks and easy lives, they're not meant for people like me." I begin to cry. "I mean, look at me! Sitting here in the same apartment I've always been in, doing the same things I've always done, expecting something magic to pop up and sweep me off my feet."

Mami gets quiet, and then I see her jaw harden. "No," she says, tossing my hands out of hers and onto the floor hard enough that they make a sound like bones smacking on cement. She lifts her hips from the ground and scurries to the back of the apartment out of my gray, cloudy view. I sit there in silence, cracking my knuckles and licking my wounds.

When she returns, she's carrying a big woven box almost the size of her body. It's cracked all over and smells like cedar. Inside it, her hands are moving quickly, pulling photo after photo out of this never-ending hole and placing them gently on the floor in front of me.

"Mira," she says, her voice softened. There are a hundred pictures of my family. There, to the left, is a tattered photo of my grandmother—eighteen years old, with a fresh face, heavy curls, and buck teeth. She's on a balcony in Puerto Rico with an orange-painted acoustic guitar in her hands. I laugh immediately because I see it now, her music running all through my veins. To the left, there's a fuzzy Polaroid of Mami and Papi holding Nena's tiny hands, smiling for what must have been the first time ever together. There's Abuelo, making the rubber sole of a shoe at his factory in La Guajaca. And then there are the generic ones, people I don't recognize as my ancestors. Sepia tones and black-

and-white images of people like me, dancing, smiles spread across their faces, making something out of absolutely nothing. Spinning pure gold from a thick and brutal stack of hay.

"We have dreams too," Mami says. She kisses my hands where they've smacked the floor, then places my fingers on the delicate edges of a printout. It's me and Nena, both kids, covered in glitter and fur boas for a living room talent show, a microphone in my hand while she conducts me. "You'll try again," Mami says.

She leaves me there, and for the rest of the night I stare at this photo of me and my sister: my mouth hanging wide to the heavens and Nena's eyes still open.

I barely get a wink of sleep, but in the morning I'm up before the sun, buzzing with something mine again. I put all the photos back in the box and place it in front of Mami's door. On top of it I write a note that says *We have dreams too* with a bubble heart next to it. I know she'll like that, me quoting her, the little heart in the corner, the thought of it all. I keep the photo of me and Nena for myself. For my own kids, my own grandkids even, who will one day want to see who we were before we were wrinkled and dead. I fold it up and put it in my wallet, then walk out the door and start down the street past Broadway toward Audubon.

Doña Carmen's is open early. In the window, I can see the woman, the same one I practically assaulted two weeks ago, while she logs into the computer and stretches the sleep out of her shoulders.

"No, no, no," she's saying before I even walk in, but I'm saying *Wait, wait,* and *I'm sorry* enough that she has no choice but to listen.

"I'm here to sign up for classes," I say and she scoffs. "I mean, for my evaluation."

She shakes her head at me, then calls to the back studio for someone. When the door opens, a short woman with a curly afro and black wrinkled skin appears in front of me.

"It's that crazy bitch I was telling you about," says the front desk lady before she walks off into the studio.

I wave my hand and immediately regret it. I don't think I should get used to answering to "that crazy bitch."

"Um, my name is Xiomara," I say when it's just me alone here with grandma. "I want to sign up for an . . . evaluation."

"Look, we don't swear here," she says.

"I know," I begin to say. "I'm sorry—"

"And we don't throw tantrums," she continues, "and we don't poke our noses up to each other, and we don't, don't, definitely don't bribe our peers into breaking the rules for us."

"Yes," I say. "Yes, I understand and I'm so sorry. I promise it will never happen again. That was just a bad day. It was a bad, bad day, and I think I was, um, I was just having a day."

"One day, okay," she says. "Another one, you're gone. Do you understand?"

"Absolutely," I say. "I just want to get better."

She pulls out some papers from the desk drawer. "Okay, then," she says, and I exhale, relieved. I didn't actually think she'd let me in, at least not without me begging for longer.

"I swear you will not regret this," I say. "Thank you." The bottoms of my feet are tingling.

"Xiomara?" she says before I go, "your sister used to come in here and brag about you. When I heard about your . . . outburst, I told them you'd be back." She winks at me, and when she cracks a smile, I see a gap in her teeth like Santi's. "See you Sunday."

"See you Sunday," I say. I walk all the way home clutching my tote bag and spinning in circles on my toes. My jaw is holding in a hundred tears. My feet are flapping like a penguin's on the simmering city sidewalk.

Mami and I have traveled all the way to the east side of 125th Street this morning to catch a commuter rail to New Rochelle, which Mami says is clean and has filtered air and is nothing like the godforsaken subway. She's scrubbing floors today at a mansion in Manor Park, and I'm interviewing for that music teacher job with Maria's friend Victor Garcia. When I emailed him, he responded in less than five minutes, and it made me laugh, the way she was not kidding at all about having done him that favor.

Before the train pulls into the station above Harlem, I can see the entire city waking up. Right below my toes, there is all of the hood, tugging at their hair and turning on their lights again. Recovering from the shadow of the night.

Mami and I are huddled together here on the yellow edge of the platform, laughing while she pulls me back to make sure I don't fall down onto the train tracks and thanking God that I finally have a respectable job prospect. There's something I want to save about it, the way we are dancing around each other this morning. I take a picture with my mind and hope it stays there.

When the train finally arrives, we shuffle into the car and look for seats. All of them are jammed up with a sea of bodies on their way to make a million dollars at a Connecticut hedge fund. People on the Metro-North are different. Proper in their tone. Polite even when you ask them to please make room for your bag. This is nothing compared to the A train. This is a beginner's guide to public transportation. A suburban pamphlet of the Industrial Revolution.

Mami and I find seats all the way in the last car and she pulls from her bag two thermoses full of hot coffee along with two cheese sand-wiches that were once melty and warm but are now cold and chewy.

"Mmm," I say to her, exaggerating the taste I'm sensing on my tongue. Mami slaps my thigh, and we are giggling again. I'm sur-prised when my head falls on her shoulder while we swallow down the rest of our breakfasts.

At the other end of the train car, I can hear the conductor clicking tickets. It feels like I'm at an amusement park, the way everything here is so cliché, like a movie. They don't tell us in Washington Heights, I guess, that most of the things we think are out of this world already exist in Westchester County.

When the conductor gets to us he's red in the face and excited to see Mami. I can tell because he's been rushing all the other passengers and screaming, "Tickets! Tickets!" but when he gets to us he is sweet as pie and taking his time. He wants to know how Mami's been doing, if she's been taking care of herself, and if she's enjoying the weather. She smiles so big I think her teeth might fall out from all the extra space she's created. I pinch her on the backside and she dodges me with her squirming little legs. When he walks away, Mami's never pulled out a ticket.

The farther we get out of the city, the more white faces I see. At first, it was us and a few other Black people at Harlem. Then it was a boatload more of us at Fordham. But, as we got out to Mount Ver-non, and Pelham, and eventually New Rochelle, where we are now, it was like we no longer even existed. Now, as we wait for a taxi out here in the green of the suburbs, people are looking at us like we are in-truders. We're like the living, breathing poster children for the effects of redlining in the twentieth century. In New Rochelle, I'm like the alien now, observing life unfold on Earth and taking notes to bring back to the mothership.

The school is quiet when I walk in. Exactly the opposite of how I re-member a school being. Everywhere there are big letters spelling out

POST, the name of the charter school. Post Athletics. Post Environmental. Post Debate Club. And my favorite—*The Post Post*. There is a big gym and a field that is perfectly trimmed outside and all the lockers are scrubbed clean like the kids have never heard of graffiti.

The walls are the same color yellow as my middle school's. If this weren't a million miles away from home I would swear that I could still see the spot where they painted over a pair of boobs Nena drew on the wall in the seventh grade. I guess we should have known then that she liked women. A twelve-year-old girl who could only think about what the perfect nipples might look like.

I can hear my feet clacking down the hallway. I'm in an absurdly tight pencil skirt and a checkered black button-up that Mami used to wear to her temp job downtown in the early aughts. I wonder what the kids will think of me when they pass me in the hallway—this old Black lady in kitten heels and a raggedy work shirt vying for the role of their musical theater teacher. I scurry into the office marked PRINCIPAL GARCIA before the bell rings. I can't take the risk of being seen yet by the children. I'm so fragile that the judgment from a twelve-year-old could break the camel's back.

The principal's office is full of colorful drawings and stick-figure sketches of multicolored families plastered on the wall. When he comes out to get me, he's wearing a brown and yellow plaid shirt. His hair is curly on the top of his head and he smells like cinnamon and tobacco. I set my bag down in the chair next to the one he's pointing at me to sit in. In it, I just have a few peppermints, my cell phone, a résumé, which I hand Principal Garcia, and a crumpled-up receipt from Carlos's bodega. He is thrilled, he says, that they finally got enough support to develop a real musical theater curriculum. I nod my head and try to hide the button on my shirt that I've just noticed is hanging for its life by a thread.

"Listen, I want someone and I want someone fast," Principal Garcia says. "But I want someone right too. These are my kids, ya know?"

I nod my head like the little girls in the diner did when I asked them if they were interested in dessert. I'm drooling for this job.

"So . . ."—he pauses and rubs his salt-and-pepper beard—
"I guess my question is . . . why you?" He takes out a pen and paper
as though he's about to take notes on my nonexistent answer. For
some reason, I've completely forgotten that there would be a part in
this process where he asked me questions that I'd have to answer.

"Well, first of all," I say, and Principal Garcia nods. "I love music."

I can see that he's deflated, praying that I'll have more to add to
my response. If I tank this interview, I can already imagine Juan Carlos chasing me down the block with an eviction notice and a red blaz-
ing fiery pitchfork. I want to give the perfect answer, but I haven't had
enough time here to know exactly what that is yet, so I have to give
him what I have: the truth for once. I shift my body in my chair and
let the button on my shirt fall to the ground.

"You know," I say, leaning in, "what I remember most about being
in school is that I was searching for my voice. Relentlessly trying to
find it." I pause. "What I remember about my life, actually, now that
I think about it, is the same. I always seem to be searching. But the
funny part, Victor, is that when I'm singing, I don't have to search at
all. Because when I'm in the music, for whatever reason, I'm not lost
anymore. The sounds and the songs fill me right up. And so now, after
everything that has happened, with my sister dying and my career
being stalled"—I take a breath, and he nods again, this time like he
knows exactly what I mean, so I know Maria has given him the
details—"I want to help people, kids, maybe, find their voice too.
Hopefully, they can do that earlier than I have." He cocks his head
and I keep going. "But also, I think you should know that I'm not the
perfect person. Because these are your kids, like you said, and I want
you to know that I can do a lot of things wrong, but I also think it's
important you know that I don't want to. I desperately want them to
get the things I didn't."

I pause again. I'm surprised at how much I believe in what's coming out of my mouth.

"As for curriculum," I continue, and I almost laugh when I say *curriculum,* as though I'm some tenured professor at NYU, "I want to flip the idea of a musical on its head this year. I want our students to ask big questions about the stories we've typically been spoon-fed. I think we'd study the gender dynamics in *West Side Story,* and the colorism of *In the Heights,* and sure we'd also study *The Sound of Music,* but I'd want us to ask ourselves if and when this kind of radicalized state might happen right here, in New York State. And we'd sing the songs of *Next to Normal,* and talk about mental health, and talk about dead siblings, which I know you know I know a lot about. And then maybe we'd talk about *A Christmas Carol.* Identify what our individual and overarching Scrooges are—write songs about those ugly thoughts—perform them for our community. In music, in musicals specifically, I think we can lose our shame. And now, saying it out loud, I think that's really important. For the kids, I mean. For them to not walk around with this backpack of hidden feelings and moments that they feel like they can never share with the people who love them most. I think that I want for our kids to feel like, I don't know, maybe the worst things won't happen if they open Pandora's box. Maybe they will actually just face their fears and get over them sooner than the rest of us."

The bell rings, and Principal Garcia stands up.

"You'll start next week with the fourth and ninth grades." He says it like he'd already decided before I arrived in the room. "Does eighty work?"

"Eighty what?" I ask, hesitant, wondering how the hell I'll handle a class size that large.

"Eighty thousand," he says. "Eighty thousand dollars for the school year."

"Oh," I say, hoping he doesn't see the way my eyes are spiraling out of my scalp. "Yes. Yes, I should be able to make eighty thousand work, thank you." I take a breath, then add, "With a five-thousand-dollar bonus at Christmas."

"Perfect." Principal Garcia smiles. "No sex, drugs, or rock and roll with the nine-year-olds. And the fourteen-year-olds will act like they're older than you. Otherwise, I'll run your background check and see you Monday."

I pack up my things. My heart is beating so fast that I have to beg it not to go into cardiac arrest before I can enjoy my life. I open the door, half-wood and half-glass, and disappear into a sea of students. I can't tell the difference between me and them now. I fall in perfect line with their footsteps.

Outside, I feel the chill of early autumn make its way up my nose. I decide to wait for Mami at the Metro-North station, and when she finally arrives I'm waving my arms up and down so violently that the white woman next to me crosses the platform. Mami is walking slowly at first and then running until we are jumping together arm in arm on the platform, celebrating my eighty fucking thousand dollars until the train comes to take us back to where we're from.

Before the week starts up, I finally call Santi. His gap-toothed smile has been playing a slow humming reel in the back of my head, and I've been thinking about him in all the blank spaces of my life. I think being cold to him all this time has been my gift and my curse, something that protects me but also something that holds my head underwater until I'm blue in the face and my veins are frozen.

The phone rings twice before I'm sent to voicemail. The butterflies in my belly turn to mammoth moths flapping around inside of me. When I'm real with myself, I have a hard time imagining Santi is the man I've made him out to be—a cheater, a liar, a boy like the rest of them. From this angle, I can see I've made a massive mistake and I wish I'd asked more questions. I hear the beep of the voicemail.

"Hi, Santi," I manage to choke out. "It's Xiomara, returning your call. Or I guess, returning your *calls*. I wanted to say that I'm sorry for being so unrelenting. I was in a really bad place, a lot of pain, you know, with my sister and just a whole bunch of shit, which I know isn't an excuse, but anyway, I, um, I see you've called me . . . a few times . . . and I wanted to make sure that I got back to you, because, you know, tomorrow's not promised like you said, or like I think you said? I don't know honestly, but it sounds like something you would say, and I wanted you to know that I'm thinking about you. A lot. And, um, yeah, I'm thinking about you more than I thought. Maybe we can talk about this over coffee or tea. I'll even pay this time. Not that you need me to. That's not what I mean. So, anyway, I'm so sorry, Santi. Please call me back when—"

The machine cuts me off since I've been rambling for so long. I wish I could play back the message and hear what I sound like, pathetic with my tail tucked between my legs, stringing together the pieces of a half-baked apology. I bury my head into my blanket. It's like I'm the student now, and I would really appreciate it if someone could tell me how to navigate the mess I've made in the hallway.

I make plans at the kitchen table while Mami prepares dinner. With my new job and classes at Doña Carmen's and all the money I'll earn and all the money we owe, there's a lot of new stuff to account for.

I put an Excel grid down in front of Mami. "So this is our budget," I say. The liquid of the beans in the pot jump onto the paper, splattering everywhere. I look at her tightly as she holds it in her hands and moves her glasses from her head down to the tip of her nose. For her, I know this page is full of numbers like dragons, daring for her to cross them so they can blow their fire and eat us alive. "Only a hundred dollars a week for groceries," I say. "That means no more buying too much and leaving it in the fridge until it rots overnight or making enough for the whole building. I'll pay for it all, as you can see here." I point to more numbers, which I've added up and subtracted exactly right from what will be my paycheck. "Your money from cleaning can be just for you—for clothes, or shoes, or whatever porqueria you want to pick up on your walks home from the train."

Mami lightly slaps me on the back of my head with a spoon, but we're not at war anymore, Mami and me, so I don't make a fuss.

Then I pull out another piece of paper, which has another grid full of dates and blocked-out times for the next three months. "Monday through Friday I'm at school," I say. "Here, on the left, you'll see my schedule in red." Red is my favorite color. "It has all the dates and times that I will be out of the house blocked out. Mondays starting at seven a.m. and Tuesdays starting at nine and Wednesdays back at seven but home later because I have beginner classes at Doña Carmen's until eight. Thursdays and Fridays are my chill days, just ten to three. Then class again for an hour on Saturday mornings and Sunday nights." Mami's schedule is in green like the money that I'm about to make. She has way more free time than I do, and I wanted her to see that. I ask her if she can make my lunches in exchange for me cleaning the bathrooms on the weekends. Mami laughs and says that I don't need to clean a thing. That she doesn't like the way I scrub. That it's like medicine for her, the bleach and the sponges and all that good stuff. I had my fingers crossed behind my back the whole time anyway.

Next, I pull out my first little lesson and ask Mami what she thinks. My basic concept is to have the students each write a song about where they come from and perform it for the class. Just as I'm explaining it, Maria walks in.

"Ay, too much," she says, without even hearing the entirety of my idea. "Wayyyy too much. What are you doing, trying to traumatize these kids?"

I delete the whole thing with a thick pink eraser.

Mami takes my papers and moves them to the counter. I see the water and red oil from the achiote spilling through them. When I get up to move them to a safe place, she shoves my shoulders down. Dinner is ready.

Tonight we are eating what we usually do: yellow rice and red beans and chicken in this sauce that I'm sure I'll never know how to re-create. Maria slumps down at the table, and we both yell at Mami to follow. When she does, she puts her hands out for us to hold. I grab one with my left hand, then attach to Maria's with my right. Mami starts praying.

In a past life, I would keep my eyes open, find Nena's gaze across the table, and roll my eyes and mock this silly little thing that the Catholic church has told us we have to do, but today, I shut my eyes tight and I say every word like I mean it.

I don't know if there is a God. I really don't, but I at least hope that Nena can hear me tonight. I hope that she can come down from heaven, or hell, or whatever lesbian lover island that she's chosen to spend eternity on, and see us now—all at this table, making something from the nothing we've been given.

I don't ever go back to Ellen's. I just call Saundra and say that I quit, and she says that I didn't really work there anymore anyway, and I say then she shouldn't be concerned that she'll have to find someone to cover my shift in the morning. She doesn't dignify me with a response. She just hangs up, and then I call Becky.

"I'm so happy for you," she keeps saying, but I know that for her it's bittersweet. I can hear that she is in the locker room alone, buzzing all over about when it will be her turn to hang up her Ellen's apron.

"We'll see each other all the time," I say, but I think she knows I'm lying.

"Yeah," she says to me. "All the time."

When we hang up, I realize that I don't even know Becky's last name. I've just had her saved in my phone all this time as "BECKY Ellen's Diner." I don't know that I'll see her again at all. Inside our friendship lies a version of me that I'm not sure I ever want back. But I'll miss her, I think. The way she always had her shoes tied too tight and cried over things like Rupert, her parents' ugly dead dog.

On Monday, I wake up and my face is so hot that I think I've broken out into hives. I feel the nerves from the top of my head travel down deep into the pits of my spine, wrapping their way around me and clawing into the depths of my belly. It's my first day at school, and I know I can't put on the same half-assed show I did at Alek's or Ellen's. These are kids, I remind myself. They'll see right through me.

Around my body, I button a white shirt that I find in Nena's closet. It's too big and hangs like a curtain because, unlike me, Nena was a woman. Big breasts and tight jeans and long rizos that swayed in the wind like silk. I tuck my shirt into a loose pair of khaki pants that Mami bought me. In the mirror, I'm a stock photo of a middle-school teacher. A generic Google search. I decide that it's refreshing to look a certain expected way for a certain expected occasion. Nothing complicated about it. No one waiting for my wow factor to sweep them off their feet.

As I'm about to walk out the door, Mami pinches the skin between my waist and my hips then hands me her gold rosary beads. "Break a leg," she says in her broken English so it sounds all upside down. I make a cracking sound as if all my bones are fracturing.

The sun has barely risen over Manhattan when I get to the Metro-North. I walk up the stairs to the elevated train and watch my breath escape into a cloud in the air. I wonder where all my particles will go today, and it soothes me to know that Nena's are still somewhere lurking around New York City too. Energy never dies.

The tracks are quieter than I remember, and I'm aware of all the life happening below on the street. I back against the wall and set down all my things. Mami has made me two lunches and a breakfast. Everything all packed up in odd containers that aren't really meant to carry what they contain. An old pasta sauce jar full of sancocho stew. A Ziploc baggie filled to the brim with mashed potatoes. Meat loaf in a Chinese take-out bin.

When the train comes, I pick it all back up and find a seat right away. As soon as I'm on the train, I feel as if I'm the only one who was born in New York City, the only person who actually remembers that the fresh-flower market in Fort Washington used to be a bodegita where I could buy all of Papi's calling cards.

When I arrive at Post, the school is different than I remember. From my vantage point, as I walk up the lengthy hill that comes before it, it is expansive. Sprawling across a campus that seems to be fueled by magic. I'm standing outside, watching the kids trickle in. There are more white faces than I was expecting, and I don't know what to do with a blond kid. I feel all the doubt I threw away this morning find its way back into my bones. I start to pick my cuticles but then stop myself. I read somewhere recently that it's a learned habit, as is all of human behavior, and I don't want to teach my students this kind of anxious tick.

To calm myself, I take extra notice of the kids who are like me. One girl with big glasses and frizzy hair is running into the building with her shoelaces untied. Another is fussing around while her mom puts lotion on her knees in the parking lot. A pair of twins who are big and brooding like their father are yelling at each other in Spanish. One is missing a front tooth. The other is hanging on to his Game Boy, or whatever they call it now, for dear life. They say playing favorites is against the rules if you're a teacher, but fuck the rules; if I'm going to make it here I'm going to have to lean into the kids I like.

I get to the classroom where I'll be teaching music and realize I should have gotten here earlier. I can already hear the hum of the children in the hallway, and everything seems particularly out of place. I move a few things around. There are some instruments, but I don't play them, which means I can't teach them, so I hide them in the closet. I don't want the empty promise of a lingering saxophone hanging over my head all year.

I place a white piece of paper on every desk and a colorful marker next to each sheet. I see a small spider curled up on the radiator, fighting for its life. I squish it with my palm and throw it out in the garbage next to my desk.

Today I'm scheduled to teach the nine-year-olds first. As they trickle in, I realize I'm not sure what to do with my hands, so at first I cross them, then tuck some imaginary hair behind my ear, then get up from my desk and stand close to the door, and then sit down at my desk and intertwine my fingers like I'm one of them, a student. Teach me literally anything, I want to say, I have absolutely no idea what I'm doing.

The twins walk in, and I'm relieved. They fight and play in a cadence that only siblings can be comfortable with. I ask them to sit down, either next to each other or as far away from each other as possible, whichever they prefer, and they try each option out, twice, before moving their desks into one and slapping each other across the face as a game. The bell rings. It's time for me to speak.

"Hi," I say, with a deep understanding that I have to follow it up with another thirty-five minutes of talking. "I'm Miss Sanchez."

A girl, fair-skinned with a gap in her teeth like Santi's, calls out, "MISS or MRS.?" She's sizing me up, all ready to determine my worth.

"Miss," I say to her, matter-of-factly. "Boys have cooties." She giggles, and I give myself a gold star.

Principal Garcia walks into the room and I exhale. He's here for introductions, which he apparently does much better than I do. "Miss Sanchez," he says, "is an incredible musician, who studied vocals in college for four years and is going to teach you all about finding your voice through music."

I nod and take notes in my head. *Finding your voice through music.*

That's what I'm doing here. I want to burn it into my brain so that I don't forget.

We hug when he leaves, which I think is awkward and the kids do too. I can tell because they hide their laughter under their little hands and look at me like I have egg all over my face. When it's just us, me and the kids, I stare at them wide-eyed. Children are fabulous, I decide. Tiny little creatures that have no care in the world. They're free still. The world hasn't gotten its dirty fingerprints all over them just yet.

"Today is going to be simple," I say first. "I'm going to ask you to write down your favorite songs, and then we are going to talk about why those songs hold a special place in your hearts." The kids laugh until they realize I'm serious. "You have five minutes to think about all the songs you've ever heard and then land on the one very special one you want to talk about today."

After two minutes, the girl with the gap raises her hand and I walk over to her. When I land at her desk, her eyes are nearly full of water.

"There are too many songs, and I don't know which one to pick. What if I pick wrong and then I remember my *real* special song and it's too late?" Analysis paralysis. I can already tell the type of adult she'll grow up to be.

"Don't worry," I say, wiping her tears and then worrying that I've touched her more than she wanted me to. "You don't have to pick this one forever. Tomorrow it can change." I want her to learn earlier than I did that just because you say something one day doesn't mean you have to strap it to your shoulders and live with it rotting on your back until the day you are in your grave.

After that, it's quiet except for a girl named Candace, who isn't sure how to spell the name of her song, so I go over and I whisper the letters into her ear. When she writes the words out, her letters are long and wide. Crooked on the page. Perfect.

"Who wants to go first?" I ask when the timer is up. Nobody raises their hand. I fight the urge to say *Don't make me pick* like an obnoxious

substitute would and instead let us all sit in the discomfort of the silence. That's important for them too, I decide.

A small boy at the back of the class raises his hand. His skin is tan
and his accent is thick. His auburn hair sticks out of his Yankees cap,
which I've allowed him to keep on for class because it's still New York,
and what's New York without the Yankees?

"My favorite song is 'Big Poppa.'"

"By Biggie?" I ask, tripping over my words, cursing myself for not
thinking ahead.

He nods his head quickly and asks if I want him to sing it. I tell
him no, that's okay, and that singing is for the next class. I stick to my
plan and I ask him why that song is his special song.

"My dad tells me that my mom used to sing it a lot," he says
matter-of-factly, "before she had me and died."

My cheeks are flushed. I bend down on my knees and grab his
little hands. They are shaking. I think of Santi and his mom, and how
he was this small once when she died, and then how I want to hold his
hand now, suddenly, and feel his long delicate fingers.

"I do that too," I say. "I hold on to the things that the people I love
in heaven used to do."

Then I let him sing all the lyrics. Soon enough we're all throwing
our hands in the air and bleeping out the explicit parts. I hope Principal Garcia doesn't walk in again.

After that, the rest of the class is a breeze. The kids like Selena
Gomez and Taylor Swift and a girl named PinkPantheress. There are
even a few who mention names like Stevie Wonder, Aretha Franklin,
and the Beatles. I love old souls in tiny bodies. I wonder how many
lives they've already lived.

When the bell rings and their permanent teacher comes to pick
them up for math and science and the rest of the day, I don't want to
let them go. I consider locking the doors all at once and telling them
that they can stay the night if they want to. But instead, so I don't get
fired, I high-five them all as they walk out of the room and tell them
that tomorrow we're going to make our very own music. When it's

quiet again in the classroom, I feel completely full to the brim. I know in the depths of me that I need these kids. Maybe even more than they need me.

When I get home, all I want to do is tell Nena what's happened. I want to tell her everything. About the kids and Biggie Smalls and how I think I'm good at something, finally, that doesn't leave me feeling like I'm only worth what the applause says I am.

This is my life now, I come to realize, and I'm starting to think that this is just how it will always be. Salty and sweet when I start new things. A mixed bag of grief and good. I'm starting to think that the hole in my heart will never actually patch back up. That I'll just have to manage the way it leaks so that one day it doesn't stop my soul altogether. I'm starting to think about how I'll be ninety years old one day and say, "I had a sister once when I was younger." And how my grandkids will look at me and nod their heads and say, "It's crazy how you lived more life without her than you did with her." And I will smile and say, "I know, and she was a blessing." But when they leave, I will wish so sorely that she could know them with me, see them there, running out the door to go discover what their unique place in this world will be.

I lose track of the days, so the weekend comes before I can blink my eyes. First it's Saturday, when I lie on the couch all day and eat amarillos from morning to night while Mami tells me that's okay because I deserve to descansar now that I have a job. Then it's Sunday, and Mami wakes me up at the crack of dawn because we are going to the eight a.m. mass.

I kick my feet under the covers so she can hear me without me having to use any words. There's no poetic way of saying it: I just really don't want to go to church today. I don't want to smell the bitter air or taste the potion of the holy water or be forced to eat a stale, thin cracker that is being spoon-fed to me as the body of Christ. I roll over on my stomach and fall asleep again until Mami knocks on the door twice, hard with the knuckle of her middle finger, like she's threatening me with her sound and a cocotazo.

I drag myself out of bed and put on all black like I'm in mourning. When we get to the church, it is exactly what I thought it was going to be. Full of judgment and fake tears and people on their knees praying to a God that never seems to come. It's like a drug, this religion. Always giving us just enough to keep coming back for more. The way I see it, God is like a piranha and we are the rest of the sad fish in the sea, schooling around, waiting until the day we have the honor of being eaten.

When the priest walks in, he is followed by two small boys and a woman in a navy-blue sack behind him. There's also another man carrying a cross, big and silver above his head. And there is smoke, smoke everywhere around me. I wish it would magically transform, like blood to wine, into marijuana and fill my lungs to help me survive this. There are almost too many contradictions for me to point out, and I'm bored with redundancy. Rageful with the way this performance continues to sweep its way across the globe and brainwash people into believing they are only good if they wring out all their bad in a confessional stall.

It's like God can hear me, sitting here swearing every swear I can think of in my head because when Father Mychael, with a *Y*, instructs us to sit for the homily, he says that today he's been thinking about the transformative and destructive power of anger.

"Anger, like fire, possesses a great power, capable of both destruction and transformation," he says. I think of Manny and Jacey and every player I've thought of burying in the past few months. Father Mychael's eyes are burning through me.

Mami nearly begins to clap when he's through, saying "amen" over and over again like she'll get brownie points if she says it enough times. I play over the way he's said *revenge* and *restoration* and *exploitation* and *righteousness* in my head. No matter his words, I don't feel like a sinner as much as a savior. I'm like Jesus, being pinned to the cross by the Catholic church all because I'm a human being with a head of my own.

When it comes time for us to make our way to the front and witness Christ, I tell Mami that I'll stay back and she slaps my side and tells me not to embarrass her. I eat the cracker. I drink the wine. I cut open my guts and levitate the Eucharist out of my system.

When the church clears out, Mami tells me to stay. It's quiet in the pews, just me and Mami and the spirit of the Holy Ghost. She wraps her arms around me and sinks to her knees. I follow her because she's my mother, and no matter how old I get or how far I go, I'm learning that I will always be following her to the ends of the earth.

Mami closes her eyes and I do the same. We kneel there for a long time. So long that my breath starts to become shallow and I begin to see big white pearly gates on the back of my eyelids and a figure like my sister standing in front of them. She's screaming something I can't hear while the camera lens of my mind zooms in to find her. When I get close enough to make her out, though, it's me there, kicking my feet outside of heaven's gates, clanging on the steel doors to let me in. It's like I'm floating again when Nena finally shows herself to me, on the other side of the gates, more beautiful than I've ever seen her. She sits down, glowing in her skin, big curls combed perfectly in every spiral.

"You have to go," she's saying. "It's okay to let me go."

I'm sobbing now, both here at the gate and on Earth in the pews.

"What if I lose you?" I'm saying to her.

"Your hands will never stop bleeding if you keep holding on so tight," she replies. I can see the way my knuckles bulge red around the bars of the gates.

My knees begin to wobble and my ankles start to feel weak. Nena's gone again and I'm back in my body, seeing the blacks of my insides. When Mami and I stand up, I hide myself behind her. She's holding my hand, resolute, walking to the back of the church to see the candles—a zillion tiny prayer lights that'll cost her twenty-five cents a pop to bring to life. When we arrive she inserts a coin and presses the little button to watch the candle burn orange.

"I want to pray for my daughter," she says, eyes to the sky. When I look at her now, I know it's me she's praying for, not my sister.

Principal Garcia was right about the fourteen-year-old girls.
I'm still shaking off the hurt of my weekend when a group of them walk into class on Monday like I'm forcing them to be there. I'm immediately grateful to no longer be in their shoes—all the raccooned eyeliner and the red cheeks and the stuffing my bra with toilet paper is in my rearview mirror.

I stand at the door while most of the students brush past me, walking through me almost like I am a ghost. There's a couple who won't stop holding hands and pecking each other on the lips. It's awkward, the way they force their mouths together like it's the first time over and over again. I want to tell them now how fucked they are. And that I hope, I hope, I hope to dear God that they are not having sex.

The boys in the class are strangers in their own skin, acne filled and red in the face. Some are long and lanky. The rest are short and have not a shot at growing past five-foot-seven. A few act as if they're two years old. A few others seem to be forty. All of them are nonstop. Nonstop nonstop nonstop.

The girls are different. They are quiet. Small. Crushing into themselves with each passing moment. The girls, I think, have already been taught that they are better in silence. I want all of them to break that. I want to open their mouths for them. Let out their air.

"I'm Miss Sanchez," I start like déjà vu when they are all in their seats and settled. "I'm your new musical theater teacher." All their teenage faces are gray now. They are skeptical of me and they wish I'd stop talking. I can tell from the way they text one another under the table and snicker to themselves. In seeing their eyes glazed over like this, I understand I have some ground to break, and so I decide right then to break it.

Instead of standing, I sit in my chair and open my legs wide like I do on the subway at rush hour. I cross my hands together and put them over my head and remember that I haven't shaved in two weeks so my armpit curls are flowing in the wind.

"I'm gonna start this over." I take a deep breath in and out. "I'm Xiomara. You're nearly adults and I'm not even thirty, so I prefer you don't call me 'Miss Sanchez.' You can call me 'X' for short. Or 'Miss X' or just 'Teacher.' Or whatever you want that doesn't start with a *B* and end with an *H.*"

I can see a few of the boys trying to figure out which word I mean while the girls get it immediately and howl with laughter.

"A few things to know about me right away—one, my sister died last year. She's dead." I think about Santi and how it's starting to become my native language now, saying Nena's gone like that. I want to tell him how it just rolled off my tongue like it did for him at Floridita when he told me about his mother.

"Two—I used to be a singer, I used to sing at nightclubs and off-Broadway shows, and in rooms that had very fancy people in them, and I was two seconds, *TWO SECONDS* away from making it big when my sister went into cardiac arrest suddenly and I got handed down all her responsibilities. I didn't sing again for a long time after that, and then even when I did, I was doing it for everybody else and not for me, really. Now I'm doing things I never thought I'd do. Like taking dance classes and getting my ass kicked by fourteen-year-olds who have been en pointe since they were nine." The students are shifting in their seats and tapping on their chairs, unsure whether to revel or reject the discomfort of my overshare.

"Three—in this classroom, I'm not here to teach you anything and I want to be up-front about that. You're not like my fourth-graders, you don't need me to hold your hands. In this classroom, I am here for myself. I want to be a student with you all. I want to discover my voice again, and I want you all to commit to being here for your own individual voices too. Not for me. Not for your friends. Just for yourself. But for that to work, for me to really know that we are in this together, we're gonna need to trust one another. And I'm gonna need to know that you've all bought in to this."

The kids have put their phones away.

"You all have a piece of paper in front of you. Today, I want you to write down one thing that makes you feel alive. Just one thing that brings you back to earth when you feel like you're drowning at the bottom of the ocean. And when we share it, which we'll all do together at once, I want us all to make a big crazy sound that goes with it, move an image in your head to a sound in your voice."

The girls giggle. The boys in the second row make a face like I'm a loser. But then they all disappear into their papers, writing down their life rafts.

When the timer goes off and it's time to share, I count down and it's like an orchestra of banging and screaming and big emotion from a class of people who are used to keeping all their messy shit inside. It's the most gorgeous cacophony of high and low notes, some coming from the chest, some originating in the belly, some from places I didn't even know existed in the human body.

"That's the proof," I say to them when we're done. "We all have a voice." Then, "In this class, I'll expect you to use it."

When the bell rings and class is over, I don't know that I've convinced them that I'm worth their time, but I do know that whatever hardened-up shell has been crusted over me is beginning to loosen up. My hands are tired of holding on, and I think Nena's right, it's time to stop the bleeding.

At lunch, I find the teachers' lounge. It's empty and I'm soaking it in, the quiet I have here. I haven't had a breath all day. Instead, it seems I've been talking and singing and giving speeches to the kids about why they should let their guard down around me, so by lunchtime, I am tired.

The lights are warm in here. There are about six couches all in funky arrangements lining the floor. They're all different colors and fabrics and have little lamps on side tables next to them so that we don't have to turn on the overhead lights and can get a break from the fluorescent lighting of the rest of the building. I think the children should be allowed to come in here for an hour or two, get rid of the cool lighting smacking them over the head every second, making them grumpy and unable to focus.

On the counter, I see a million mugs. None of them match, and it soothes me, the way they look like the inside of Mami's cupboard. Each has a unique logo—one from a diner in Colorado called the Blue Moose, another from Anderson's bookshop down the road; I even see one from Ellen's Stardust Diner in New York City. I can't help but to break out in laughter the way that damned diner is following me like an unsettled ghost.

I spot a Keurig, and though I crave Mami's Bustelo coffee from the greca, I'm in need of caffeine now, so I move toward the machine and look for the K-Cups. When I find them, I insert one into the coffee maker and let it sputter out some coffee-water into a mug. There's no whole milk in the fridge, just alternatives. No sugar in this place either.

I pick a couch farthest away from the door to sit on. I set the warm coffee down on an awkwardly shaped wooden side table and don't use a coaster. My hand reaches into my bag, which Mami's packed for me today with lunch. There's lasagna all smushed up in a container, and a side of alcapurrias that she made fresh last night. She's also thrown in some platano chips and a few pieces of fruit—mango, strawberries, and pineapple sharing juices—and wrapped up the silverware in a paper towel as if they wouldn't have any utensils here at the school. I microwave the lasagna, and while I wait for it to beep, I think about calling Santi again. I page through my contacts to find his name, and when I see it in my phone, my heart starts skipping a beat. I know I'm in trouble now, standing in the teachers' lounge, looking at a sterile name and getting all flustered like this.

I press the call button and hold the phone up over my ear. I'm not sure what I'll say if he answers, but three teachers walk in and I hang up right away. I am flipping over in the bottom of my belly, debating whether I heard a "hello" at the other end of the line before I went ahead and turned the phone off.

None of the teachers in the lounge make eye contact with me. It's like we're students here, in our own little cliques, and I'm the weird girl with the frizzy hair and smelly lunch box. I take my lasagna out of the microwave and spoon it into my mouth. It's not cold but it's not hot either, an awkward middle temperature on my tongue. I can't bear to get up again and face my colleagues, though, so I sink into the couch and finish the whole thing, closing my eyes and imagining how delicious it'd be, actually, if it had just thirty more seconds in the microwave.

After a minute, another teacher walks in. He's tall and doesn't sit with the clique. He doesn't sit with me either, though. I imagine he's the eighth-grade English teacher, the way he forces his glasses up on his face and blows his nose nerdily into a napkin. I imagine in his classroom he'll be forcing the students to study Faulkner and Hemingway and that one passage in *The Catcher in the Rye* in which the main character monologues about girls and how they'll drive you crazy even if they're "not much to look at" or "sort of stupid." I hated that passage the first time I read it. As if women were designed to invoke a feeling out of men.

The door swings open again and it's a hurricane of a woman walking in, like a ball of lightning stuffed into a tiny, beautiful Black body. The room itself seems to shift as she bolts through it, acknowledging the power she carries on her back. She walks past the clique and the eighth-grade English teacher and sets her stuff down right next to me.

"I've been wondering who you are," she says matter-of-factly, like we've made a date to meet here.

I look around to make sure she's talking to me.

"Yeah, I'm talking to you! No other Black girls up in this bitch." The teachers in the clique make a face. "Sorry," she whispers and covers her mouth sarcastically. "I'm Grace," she says, sticking out her hand.

"I'm Xiomara," I say, "but you can call me X."

"Xiomara, damn, what's that? Like Puerto Rican?"

"Yeah, well, Dominican too, but—"

"Same thing," we both say at the same time.

Grace walks to the sink. She's wearing flowy yellow pants that parachute around her hips and a white Aaliyah tee that falls perfectly into her waistline. On it, Aaliyah is wearing sunglasses and a bandanna over her straight locks. I'm wearing my khakis again and a stupid white shirt that crumples at the back of my torso. I've never wanted to burn something off my body more.

Grace returns and looks at my feet on the couch, and I move them so she has room to sit down next to me. Before they even hit the floor, she's sitting on the cushions, staring at me like she expects me to have something more to say.

"So what's your deal?" she asks me, and without protest, I tell her everything I told the ninth-graders this morning.

"Damn, girl," she says, "you didn't have to tell me all of that."

"That's okay," I say completely seriously. "I'm practicing being honest."

"Om," she says, placing her hands in a meditative sign like Buddha. Then she breathes out and says, "So let me give you the lowdown on Post."

I nod my head. Finally, information I can use.

"Basically, you're in high school again. Those people over there"—she points to the three teachers who still haven't looked at me—"they're the old heads. Been here forever. Tenured and pretentious as fuck."

"I figured," I say.

"You get it," she says back. "Everyone has their people. You're mine now whether you like it or not. And, girl, have I been waiting for you. These white people done lost their minds." I raise my eyebrows at the way she says *done lost their minds,* like an ad for what a Black woman should sound like in a movie. "What do you teach?" she asks me.

"Musical theater," I say, wiping the sides of my mouth with my napkin.

"I heard we were getting one of you!" She slaps my arm harder than I'd like her to three times.

"You heard right!" I'm finished with my lasagna now.

"You got a man?" she asks, chewing down on an apple.

"Nope," I say.

"A one-word answer means that you wish you did, though." We laugh. "Who's the nigga?" she asks, and we both laugh again. "Come on, if you're gonna be my work wife, I'm gonna need to know these things."

"His name is Santi," I say finally, before explaining every single interaction we've ever had. As I hear myself talk about the print shop, and our date, and the grocery store, I'm kicking myself about how stupid I've been. Judging myself for the way I'm asking this complete stranger if she thinks I still have a shot.

"No girl, you fucked that up," she says when I'm done. I don't laugh now, but Grace does. Then she shoves me on the shoulder like we've known each other for years. When the bell rings and she starts to stand up, I think of Becky.

"Wait! What's your last name?" I ask before she's out the door.

"Taylor!" she says, starting to escape me.

"Grace Taylor," I say, etching her name into my mind. "And what do you teach here?"

"Eighth-grade English!" she shouts behind her.

My cheeks are heavy from smiling. I don't think the kids are learning about Hemingway after all.

Principal Garcia says that I'm in charge of the school musi-cal now, so on top of my classes, which I'm buying supplies for with my own eighty-thousand-dollar salary, I'm now also staying up all night deciding what exactly I want the children to *say* with our shot at a school musical. Maria says they don't need to *say* anything at all. "They need to sing a low-brow rendition of *Hamilton,* and ya call it a day," she insists, filing her nails while she lies on her back on the floor of Mami's apartment.

But I can't let that happen. I need them to know that musicals have meaning. I know it's pathetic, the way I'm so invested in building these make-believe worlds, but I need them to know that musical the-ater isn't just about breaking into a cheesy song and showing up for your best two-step. Instead, it's about the subversive nature of music and how it makes people listen. How if you put something in a song, you can pretty much get people to say anything you want them to. Maria doesn't buy it, but I didn't ask for her opinion anyway.

After a lot of voting in class and contemplating my decision, I decide to give in to the students and buy the book online for *West Side Story.* This time, though, I tell them, we're flipping the genders. "The Jets and the Sharks are two badass groups of women struggling with the way America pits them against each other. And while we'll keep the boiling racial tension," I say, "we'll expand the theme to include the gentrification of our inner-city communities, like Wash-ington Heights and Spanish Harlem. In that way, the minority com-munities won't be the foreigners."

Along with performing the musical, I tell them, since I've bent my knee to the status quo, they'll each write a three-page paper about the antiquated ways and themes of this story. I want theories and in-depth research on colorism and colonialism, and Puerto Rico's potential path to liberation. And I want thoughts, big thoughts, on why it is exactly that in most productions of this play, Maria is cast as a white-passing Latina damsel while Anita, the fiery supporting actress with an ass that won't quit, is more often filled now with a darker-skinned actor.

When I'm done sharing my vision, I don't think my kids are excited anymore. But I am. I am absolutely electrified.

At auditions, I sit behind a gray folding table and have a stack of papers with all the kids' names written on them. I've had each of them write a statement of intention to go with their audition.

"So much for being a student *with* us," one of the boys says while he slams his head on the table, almost knocking over my coffee.

I hold up a paper and read out loud the statement I've written, about why I'm directing this play and what my intentions are to get it to the best place it can be before our entire school community sees it.

The rest of the afternoon, I'm listening to young squeaky voices attempt to belt like Ariana Grande. I try not to laugh when a girl the size of a mouse stands up on stage and misses every note and riff in the song she's chosen. When she's done, which I've been waiting for, she takes a bow and starts clapping for herself.

"I nailed that," I hear her say to her friends behind the curtain.

The next two girls who come on stage sweep me off my feet. First, it's Gloria, a sophomore who can fill the entire room with her falsetto, and then Charlotte, who brings me to tears when she sings a Whitney Houston song a cappella. At the end of both auditions, I'm on my feet busting my hands together.

With the guys, it's a little harder, because they are all going through puberty and their voices crack when they sing "I Feel Pretty." I start to think that maybe switching the gender roles wasn't as good of an idea as I would have hoped.

There is Simon, though, who is so small I can barely see him, but who can salsa like he was Albert Torres in a past life. I sigh a big breath of relief before I write a star down next to his name and pen exclamation points next to the rest of the kids I thought had potential.

"You know this isn't *actually* Broadway, right?" Grace says to me when everyone's gone and I've spread the paper with all the students' names out on the floor of the stage, marking each with a unique role and slipping their assignments back into the binder I've created.

"Ha. If this were Broadway, half these kids would be crying down Eighth Avenue right now," I say, laughing.

"Savage," Grace says back to me.

We sit there on the floor of the auditorium together and decide on our cast. Gloria will play Tony and Charlotte will play Bernardo. Maria will be played by a woman, too, I decide. Nena would like that. Anita will be played by Simon. He will get to pick a new name for the character unless he doesn't want to, and I make a note that he and I will have to sit and talk through the dynamics of what his filling this role means. The rest of the parts I might as well just eeny-meeny-miny-moe. Grace has the good idea to draw the names out of a hat, and we do that, while I play the instrumentals of the show behind me and belt the play from start to finish.

Grace doesn't compliment me once for my voice, but she does lie down on her back to hear me with her eyes closed. When I get up and start dancing, she immediately says she'll act as the main choreographer for the show. I'm wiping the sweat off my forehead, out of breath and cackling, finally, about the beauty of my two left feet.

When we post the cast list, I walk into the bathroom and see a few of the girls crying. They run into the stalls and yell at me to get the fuck out. To them, I'm Manny or, worse, that casting girl Justice, who might as well have been picking names out of a hat when she called me.

I want to ask them if they're okay, but they're yelling too loud, and so I spin around and leave them in their echo chamber to curse my name. When I tell Grace at lunchtime about the girls in the bathroom and how bad I feel that they didn't get what they wanted, she nods her head ferociously and says, "A little disappointment never killed nobody," but I think she's wrong because it nearly killed me.

"You can't skip freshman year," she goes on. "You can't get to the gold without studying your craft first."

"Yeah, I guess you're right," I say, eating my leftover black beans.

I think I missed that adversity lesson when I was growing up, though. That part that Grace is talking about where you have to sit flat and stale in your failure never made its way to me. Nena always gulped it all up so I never had to feel it.

Maybe this is my freshman year. Doña Carmen's dance classes and this school and Grace too. Maybe the memories of Manny's hallway and the way I couldn't fix my burning hamstrings at the audition playing over in my head are just there as a reminder that I was barreling down the graduation stage, grabbing for a diploma when I hadn't yet sat through all of the curriculum.

Tonight, the teachers have decided to all go out for after-school drinks at the Cellar Bar. "It's a shady place in Larchmont they like to go to," Grace says while she leans over a sofa in the lounge and sucks on a lollipop like she's a teenager. I'm starting to get used to it, the way Grace talks about the rest of the staff like she's not one of them. "It's close enough to the Metro-North so it's not a hassle, but far enough away from the school so we won't bump into any parents."

"Let's go," I say when I hear her start to contemplate it. "I could use a night without my mother." I immediately feel guilty for talking about Mami this way. It's like a demon that's come back to life without my permission.

"Okayyyy," Grace says while she snaps her fingers. "Miss Sanchez wanna get lit!"

I shake my head and hide my smile.

After school, we meet in the parking lot. It's nearly November now, and the air is officially freezing. I've started to deviate from my khakis and white shirt, so today I'm wearing a long black dress and a turtleneck underneath it. Even with all the layers, my teeth are still chattering.

"I'll drive," Grace says like she has a choice.

"Great, because I don't have a car," I say, pulling at the old handle of her silver Buick. Inside the car, there are coffee and salt stains everywhere, like she's had this car since the day she fell onto the earth.

"Sorry," she's saying, throwing old receipts and sweaters and paper towels into the back seat. "I share this car with my sister, and she's a fucking mess." I imagine that's something Nena would have said about me to Celeste while they were sneaking around in our bedroom.

"No worries," I say, as I sit and feel peanut butter staining the silk of my skirt.

The entire car ride over, she plays The Weeknd and screams the lyrics. They're disturbing, when you really listen to them, the way he talks about dying and living and floating between the two.

When we pull into the parking lot, we see the clique climbing out of their cars and a few other teachers trickling in. "Don't say hi," Grace says, slamming her door, and so I skirt around them and dodge their eyes, which aren't eager to meet mine anyway.

Inside, the place is small and dark and smells like Bud Light. There are Christmas lights strung all over the walls, posters of old rock bands hanging under them, and a turntable below the disco ball that is blaring "These Boots Are Made for Walkin" on repeat. Grace beelines for the bar.

"Hey, Harry," she says.

"You're back . . . again," he says like he's sick of her.

"Oh, stop, you know you love me." I can see in his eyes that he does, actually, love her more than she'll allow for. He starts pouring tequila before she can ask for it, and she gestures *two* with her left hand, so he grabs another glass and pours one for me.

"Never seen you before," he says to me as he hands me the glass.

"Never seen you either," I reply. "I'm Xiomara."

"Harry," he says, taking my hand and shaking it hard. The three of us shoot our tequila back.

"Harry was voted BEST bartender in *Westchester Magazine* last year," Grace says, leaning over the bar and grabbing his cheeks in between her fingers before he shoos her away.

Later, when Grace goes to the bathroom, I talk to a few of the other teachers. They are boring and want to know what my credentials are. I'm drunk, so I lie and say that I went to Harvard for a master's in education.

"What year?" Jean, the ninth-grade social studies teacher, asks like she went there herself.

"Two thousand seventeen," I say, shaking my head up and down while I try to do the math in my head.

"Affirmative action, am I right?" the gruff redheaded gym teacher says while he slurps down a warm Natty Ice. It's becoming easy for me to understand why Grace hates them all so much now.

By the time karaoke starts at nearly midnight, I'm ready to go home. Grace and Harry have done what I presume they always do and snuck into a corner to whisper feelings into each other's ears that they'll deny in the morning. Without them to keep me company, I'm stuck reaching over the counter to refill my cup myself while I twiddle with my thumbs and wait for the next Metro-North train to take me back to my apartment.

When it's close enough for me to hear its horn across the street, I kiss Grace twice on the cheek and tell Harry that I completely agree with *Westchester Magazine*. Then I run across the street and nearly get hit by a taxi in the parking lot. I knock hard on the hood of the car twice and stick up my middle finger. You can't take the New York City out of me.

On the train, everyone's all coupled up. It's late, that time of night when people are rushing home to get under the covers together. The seat next to me is empty, and I'm surprised when I long for Santi's hands to hold. Gut punched in my realization that when I get into my twin-size bed tonight, he won't be there waiting in a beat-up pair of boxers, rubbing his eyes awake and asking me how the rest of the teachers were.

Maria tells me I need a grand gesture. "I don't know what to do," I'm crying over the kitchen sink. It feels good, the way the water falls out my body, like it's been building up for centuries and clogging up my pores. Maria is running a wet towel over my forehead like I have cholera and this is the sixteenth century or something. I rip it out her hands and tell her to stop.

"Bueno," she says to me, banging on the kitchen sink and slamming the faucet closed. Maria doesn't like when I'm aggressive with her; in her head, it only works the other way around.

"Sorry," I say. "I just never imagined I'd be so fucked up over this. Rory and I fucked for like six years and I went off him cold turkey, never looked back. Santi and I barely kissed and I can't get this feeling out my stomach. It's like I've been hit head-on by the A train and lost all my ability to walk or talk."

Maria's expression softens again. She's a sucker for a good "I'm sorry."

"That's love, amigita," she says. "One day you're walking down the street completely fine and the next you're flattened out like a rat stuck on the subway tracks." Her hand is on my face all wet, and the faucet's on again.

We are three and a half weeks into rehearsal now, and it's "time to start thinking about marketing," Gloria, who is cast as Tony, tells me. She is, apparently, also the student council president and the editor in chief of the yearbook, so she's "had practice engaging with the community on these things."

She waits for me to thank her for the advice, but I refuse to and instead look down blankly at her tiny shoulders and overdrawn eyeliner.

"Since you haven't brought it up," she says, pulling out a folder from under her armpit, "I've had the art club make a flyer." She holds up a thick piece of paper and stares at me with resentment like we're part of a group project and I'm the dead limb not pulling my weight but still getting an *A*.

When I look down, my eyes are surprised with color. Blue and yellow vivid images that have been hand drawn by someone I can only imagine is the earth's next Picasso. There are sketches of a white dress and a Puerto Rican flag and an intricate New York City skyline sprawling across the page under big bubble letters that spell WEST SIDE (SORT OF) STORY. That's what we've renamed the play after one night of rehearsal delirium when we ate chocolate cake on the floor and decided once and for all that all our crazy changes make this play only "sort of" *West Side Story*.

"We need about three hundred printed by the morning, and Mrs. James says we can't use the library's ink for all that." Gloria says it like she wants to bury the librarian alive. "I didn't want to ask for your help because I'm usually completely self-sufficient, but now, since she's being such a bitch, I have to."

"Yes," I say like I'm the student while I grab the flyer out of her hand so hard it almost rips. "I'll have three hundred of these to you by the morning." It's a Wednesday and I know Santi's working. The shop closes at 5:00 and it's nearly 3:30, so before Gloria can thank me, I'm sprinting to the Metro-North, screaming, "And watch your mouth, Gloria!" behind me while I run like my life depends on it toward the commuter rail. I think Maria would be disappointed in me if she found out that *this* was my grand gesture, but seeing as Santi hasn't returned any of my calls in weeks, it feels like my only option.

When I get off at Grand Central, the subway down to Union Square takes longer than I remember. It's almost foreign to me now, this route to Alek's, like retracing the steps to a language I once knew before I learned my own native tongue.

I can't remember the last time I saw Santi. Or, I should say, I remember exactly the last time I saw Santi, and I just can't remember why I made the decisions then that I did. I can't remember why I acted so tough, like nothing he did or said could hurt me when in fact everything he did and everything he said pierced the very flesh out of my soul.

I smooth my shirt about eighteen times before I walk into the shop and let the bells ring hard behind me. I look down and up and down, searching for a sign of life, until Santi walks out of the back room and drops a big stack of papers, white with blue lines running horizontally across them, on the ground in front of his feet. I don't give him a chance to ignore me before I speak.

"Santi," I say with a soft voice like he should be happy to see me. I'm all wound up. I figure the first thing that comes out of my mouth should be simple and uncomplicated. Not something that can be analyzed for interpretation.

"Hey, Xiomara," he says to me like I've broken his heart but doesn't want me to know it. I let his voice settle in the room for nearly sixty seconds. "Now you say something," he follows up, and I feel bad for making him do any of the heavy lifting.

"Right, listen. So, is Alek here?"

"No, he's not." His voice is shaking and I can see that I've already pierced him. "Sorry to disappoint you." He knows. About the back room and Alek and me. I bet Alek told him some kind of twisted fucking story.

"No, Santi, no, that's not why I came here," I say forcefully, following him to the back room because he's turned on his heels so quickly.

"You don't work here anymore," he says. I can't tell if it's a statement or a question. He's put up his hands like he doesn't want me to come any closer.

"I know," I say, gripping the flyer in my hand so tight I feel my knuckles start to pop.

"So you can't be back here."

"I know," I say again. I think I've lost all the rest of my language.

"Say something other than 'I know,' Xiomara." He's put his hands on his head like I'm giving him a headache.

"I know." I take a breath before he can manage to growl at me any more. "I actually wanted to say I'm sorry."

"You wanted to say 'I'm sorry'?" He's mocking me. "Sorry for what, Xiomara?" He's taping boxes, and I think this is a test.

"For writing you off," I say right away "For not asking more questions. For going completely ghost. For being a bad friend, I think, to—"

"You're not my friend," he cuts me off. "We both know that. You're not my friend." He says it twice to make sure I can hear him. "Friends don't do whatever it is you're saying you did to me." It hurts, the way he says that. Like I've done so much to hurt him by doing so little.

"I need a few copies," I say, handing him the flyer before he can be done with me altogether. If I need something from the shop, I don't think he can actually kick me out. I'm a customer, and the customer is always right.

Santi punches in his code and turns the computer toward me, telling me to scan the flyer for myself. I load the tray and correct the settings on the computer to make 350 color copies. The machine starts right up, scanning and printing like it's all of a sudden in a rush to get me out of there by Santi's orders.

"I know I'm not your friend," I say. There I go again. Saying *I know* when I don't know anything at all. "I know I should have been completely different. And that you tried with me. That one day on the train platform, and at Floridita before my audition, and after Ellen's maybe too, but I missed it, and"—I raise my voice desperately over the loud banging of the copy machine—"I know it was nothing, okay, I know whatever we were, it was nothing, but I'm sorry. And you deserved better. And I'm sorry."

"It wasn't nothing to me, Xiomara," he says after a long while, "but it's okay. I know how it goes with girls like you."

Girls like me. I wonder what he means by that. Girls who eat themselves alive before spitting themselves back up and feasting on their very bones like a vulture?

"Okay, but what about your girlfriend? Because when Alek told me—"

Santi doesn't let me finish. I know in every bit of my body already that there's been a horrible game of telephone.

"My girlfriend?" he spits out at me.

"Yeah, you know, your sick girlfriend." I'm desperate for this part of the story to be true, to take the onus off of me a little bit.

Santi stops and shakes his head a hundred times until I can see the blood start to boil from his chest up into his face. "You have no idea what you're talking about." His voice is low and he's angry. "My girlfriend?!" He's rushing to the front of the shop to get away from me before he turns around and looks at me like I'm garbage. "I went home for one week, and Alek says some stupid shit about a girlfriend and you decide that's it? That's all there is to it?! I don't deserve a conversation?!"

"But I called and—" I stop talking, but my question is still burning.

"No girlfriend, Xiomara. Never a girlfriend. In case you were still wondering, which from your sour face, I know you are. It was the fif-teenth anniversary of my mom's death, and I felt like the world was caving in on me that weekend. Like it was going to trample me to the ground, and so I told Alek I had to go home to take care of a sick friend, but really that sick friend was me. I was running out of air, but you couldn't see it. You could never see it because you were too busy looking at yourself in the mirror. And then when I tried to tell you, it was like you had no room for me. No room at all to do what I've done for you a hundred times and give you the benefit of the doubt."

I'm not good at being wrong, and the printer is done spitting out my pages.

"I fixed it," Santi says. "The printer. So you can take your copies and leave."

"Okay," I say, swallowing down the salt of my tears. "I'll go." But I wish I could stick my hand in the back of the Xerox and tear the whole thing down to shreds to buy myself more time. "I'm really sorry again, Santi. I really am. I wish I could have seen you then, the way you needed me to, the way I see you now."

He doesn't have anything left for me.

"I'm working at a private school now," I say to him before leaving. "I know you're probably thinking I shouldn't be working around kids and stuff, but it's actually incredibly therapeutic. And I think I'm okay at it too. You should come see our musical." I hand him a flyer, still warm from the hot ink of the printer. "I think you'd like it."

"I'll think about it," he says and takes the paper from my hand. His thumb presses so hard into it that I think it will finally meet its fate and rip in two. I want him to be careful—with me, I mean. And with the flyer too.

On the subway ride home, I call Maria.

"He'll come," she says, but I'm really not so sure that's true.

It's payday today, and I have finally saved up enough in my bank account to pay this month's rent and utilities plus all the backlog we owe Juan Carlos, *and* get a new vacuum that Mami's been wanting for her cleaning service. I keep telling her that she doesn't need to do that anymore, sweep floors and pick up rich kids' crumbs, but she swears that she likes it. Something to remind her to keep moving.

I wait for Juan Carlos on the corner where I usually duck for cover. It's cold enough that I feel it behind my ears, and I'm getting impatient by the time I see him, huffing and puffing down the block like he's all ready to be through with me.

"Mira, here's your fucking money," I say in my best Maria impression, waving an envelope in the air. Juan Carlos barely stops walking when he grabs it from my hands.

"Same time next month," he grumbles, bolting down the sidewalk. His footsteps are louder than the sirens in the city.

"Men like that will never be satisfied," Mami says to me later. "Now that he knows we have it, he'll come back wanting more."

Cassie writes me a long letter and sends it in the mail. I open it while I'm cleaning out the refrigerator and read the whole thing almost in one breath.

Dear X,

The other day on the news I saw a Black woman get shot and killed by the police and thought of you. Seventeen bullets! I'm disgusted, really, by this country and the people who live in it. I know we're not talking right now, but I know you feel this way too and I wondered if you needed someone to talk to. Have you seen it? The video?

(I wonder which video she means, the one from this week or last.)

If not, that's okay, it's not your responsibility to see them, it's mine. I've watched it enough times for the both of us. That and the war are so crazy. Can you imagine? The way people are bombing each other across the world like that? We're so lucky that we're here and have our free-doms. Anyway, I figured writing this on paper was better so you didn't feel any pressure to respond via text. I think it's important that you have a voice in how we move forward in our friendship, and as I think about it, I'm realizing that I've cannibalized a lot of that. This letter is my commitment to do better and be a force for change. I hope you'll give me another chance and join me. The world needs more friendships that look like ours—complicated and messy. Not just Black and white (no pun intended).

The truth is that when you left, at first I was happy, being rid of you and your dragging-me-down attitude. It was really hard, those last few months seeing you dig your own grave like that. But then one morning I started to miss you too. Seeing your face and having someone else stirring in the apartment—that was nice, and I know you're probably settled, but this is just to say that if you ever need it, my door is always open.

In solidarity and power,

Cassandra (Cassie)

P.S. Matt and I didn't work out, in case you are surprised (which I know you're not, because I saw the way he looked at you too).

I laugh and toss the letter in the garbage with the rest of the stinky leftovers on the kitchen counter.

The night of the school play, everyone is there except Santi. Principal Garcia and Maria and Mami are all in their best outfits. Even Carlos from the bodega has a front-row seat. But no sign of Santi. *He'll come,* I hear Maria's voice in my head reassuring me.

Even without him here, though, I'm beaming. Sure, I'm checking the door every other blink, but I also think somewhere in the mix of it all I'd forgotten how much I love this—opening night and the promise of a play's potential. Every part of my body is turned on, kicking, like I have a duck swimming in my stomach, or a leap frog jumping around in there.

In the hallway, Gloria and I are trying to stick extra flyers onto the cement wall, but they are too heavy for the tape to hold steady.

"See, I told you this is not the paper I wanted," she says.

"Well, this is the paper you've got," I say.

She grabs the flyers out of my hand and I tell her to watch herself unless she wants me to recast her role five minutes before curtain. I imagine she'll repeat all of this to her parents later tonight so I might as well start packing my classroom because I'm sure I'll be fired by the morning. You can't say anything to these kids nowadays. They'll stage a protest and throw a fit. I laugh because I realize I'm getting older, standing here taping flyers to a wall and thinking such grandfatherly thoughts.

I'm ushering the ensemble into a single-file line when I remember Santi again. There's still no sign of him, and it's getting closer to places. Grace is hammering in on the choreography with the kids. "I'll kill you if you fuck this up," I hear her say to one of them, and I think she should start packing her classroom too.

Simon, who is playing Anita, is whisper-screaming at me to make sure there are no wrinkles in his dress while I tie the red bow to perfection behind him. I tug it nice and tight so that he loses his breath a little bit, and he says thank-you, and that he likes the way it makes his waist look when it's tighter.

When the lights start to flicker we do our preshow ritual, which involves us whispering a little chant several times (*"Post is good, Post is great, it's Post that we appreciate"*) while we snap our fingers and gradually get louder until we are screaming at the top of our lungs and jumping up and down and clapping for one another.

When we're through, I squeeze all their hands. I squeeze Gloria's twice, and I tell her that she is already a star in my eyes, no matter what happens on that stage. I don't know where that comes from when I'm saying it, but I think it's what I'd have wanted to hear if I was in her shoes. Someone I trust to tell me that I am valuable even if I am not perfect.

I feel my feet guide me toward the audience, and I stand and look for a sign of Santi until the lights flicker again and I have to make my way to my seat. My throat is sore when I realize he isn't coming. Like there's a pit stuck in it that I have to swallow down without it scraping out my insides. I open my bag and pull out a tiny flask in which I've packed myself a Washington Heights margarita—Capri-Sun and Casamigos. It's innocent, the way I am sipping on a bit of tequila before a suburban school musical. I bend my knees to get into my seat and move the program off the folding chair before I feel a breath behind me and a hand on my shoulder.

"Can I get a little bit?"

It's Santi. He showed up. I try to hide my smile, but I can't because it's taking over my entire face. I hand him the flask and he takes a swig. He sticks out his tongue like he's disgusted.

"You're a bad teacher," he says, then takes another big sip. I slap his arm and clear the program off the seat next to me.

"You saved me a seat?" he says like he wants me to admit I was waiting for him.

"Oh, no, this was just a coincidence," I say casually, but then I lose my cool and add, "I'm really so happy you came."

Santi and I watch the show together. *West Side (sort of) Story*. He squeezes my arm during the balcony scene, and a magnetic current runs up my spine, so I fold all the way into him. My nose is on his shoulder. His skin is cool and soft. Maria is in her seat two rows behind me, and I can feel her gaze like a laser burning through the back of our heads, watching our every move like a hawk.

The finale is flawless, so when the lights go down, I'm lit up. The entire audience jumps to their feet. Santi is shouting, whistling through his fingers while I stand on my chair and scream, "Ow ow!" I want the whole world to stop so that I never have to move on from this moment. I want to be finding my balance here on this plastic chair with Santi next to me and those kids on stage for the rest of eternity.

When the curtain falls to the floor and the kids' toes are finally covered up, I ask Santi if he'll wait for me and I fly backstage. We are all screaming again. Gloria is hugging me and crying.

"You were everything," I'm saying to her over and over, "absolutely everything."

She pulls me over to meet her mother, who won't stop thanking me and hands me her business card. It's white and blue and thick and reads:

Liza Frank

Theatrical Agent

William Morris Endeavor

"Gloria tells me you're quite the talent yourself," she says, petting her daughter's hair. "Call me when you've come down from this."

She's out the door before I get the chance to tell her I'm taking a break from meetings. But I slip the card into my pocket and feel it burning there for the rest of the night.

When everyone is gone and I am all shouted out, it's just me, Mami, Maria, and Santi in the auditorium. Mami and Maria pace around us like piranhas while Santi and I look at each other out the sides of our eyes.

"I'll take Tía home," Maria says matter-of-factly, like she knows the favor she's doing for me. I nod my head casually while Maria grabs their things and ushers Mami out of the room. I can hear that she's asking when I'll come home until the doors shut tight behind them.

"A bunch of us were planning on going to a diner," I say to Santi when it's just the two of us. I can see the kids out the window, rushing into their cars to get there first. Grace is looking for me out in the parking lot.

"What's with you and diners?" he says, and we laugh about the way I used to belt show tunes on the countertop at Ellen's. It's funny to think that was me not so long ago and now I'm a completely different species.

"No singing servers in suburbia, unfortunately," I say, "but it's like a theater school tradition or something."

"Is that an invitation?" he asks.

"I think so," I say, picking up the rest of the programs and pacing around the tension between us. I move slowly because I don't want this to end. The aimless footsteps and the way the air smells like only the two of us.

"Sign me up," he says before he swings the door open. I curtsy and we walk out into the hallway together.

"Anita stole the show," Santi says at the diner to break the silence. It's me and Grace and Harry all sitting at one table while the kids make fart jokes behind us.

"She always does," Grace says, smushing french fries into her mouth and chewing like she has no manners. Harry's looking at her like she's God's gift to the Earth and attempting to spoon chocolate ice cream into her mouth.

"It's a thing!" he says, trying to convince her. "Fries first so it's salty, ice cream next so it's sweet. Salty then sweet." There's a pause. "Just like you." He boops her nose.

Grace makes a face and says *ha ha* in a droll tone.

The men get up to go to the counter and order us "adult drinks." Harry keeps calling it that and Grace keeps slapping him, saying he's making it sound like we are sipping on porn juice or something, which is disgusting and I can't really imagine.

"He's fucking hot," Grace says to me about Santi when they're gone.

"I know." I'm calm, but I'm holding off from screeching. I take the card Liza gave me out of my pocket and slip it across the table.

"Gloria's mom," I say.

Grace looks at the card and then up at me and then down at the card again. "That little bitch was good for something after all!" she says, and we are both giggling, banging on the table, and opening our mouths like we can't believe it. We stop when the boys get back with our tequilas.

"So how do you guys know each other?" Harry asks, pointing back and forth between me and Santi.

I go to respond, but Santi doesn't let me.

"We're just on the same life path," he says, like all the things that happened before this moment don't really matter anymore. I like that. Being on the same life path as Santi.

"Poetic." Harry shrugs and rubs on Grace's leg under the table. They're gone less than a minute later, making out before we've lost sight of them from the window.

"Hi," Santi says when it's just us at the table.

"Hi," I say in return.

"You look different now," he says, staring at me with his head in his left hand.

"Different how?" I ask, pinning a curl of my hair behind my ear.

"Different like . . . here, I guess."

"I'm always here!" I say, tossing the napkin across the table and onto his lap.

"You're never here," he says, tossing it back.

We both laugh.

"I'm so sorry, Santi," I say. "I'm glad you came tonight." Then I stop talking because I want to keep it simple.

"Me too," Santi says, then grabs my hand and nods his head slowly. We're both forgiven. Santi hums "America," and I hum it along with him. The waiter comes and Santi picks up the whole check, even Harry and Grace's unaccounted-for drinks. On the way out I wave to the students and they make big eyes at me like I'm breaking the rules. I stick out my tongue and then spin back and forth, pretending to fluff out my dress like Maria in the musical.

Outside, Santi and I are laughing for no reason. Saying things that make no sense. I'm finding quiet moments and then filling them with melody and speech because when I'm around Santi, it's like I'm singing.

"This is me," he says finally, pointing to an old navy-blue Pontiac.

"I took the train," I say, and he offers to give me a ride to the station.

The entire ride over I watch the way the lights glow on his skin like in a movie. I'm pinching myself, leaning close to him so I can smell the way he is tonight, young and fresh and full of things I desire.

When we arrive, Santi runs out of his driver's seat to open the passenger door for me. A loose playbill falls out of my bag as my feet swing out of the car, and I kneel down to pick it up and so does he. Our hands touch on the ground, and I go to say I'm sorry, but before I can his lips are on mine, kissing me long and wet and like there's nothing else in the world that matters. Just his lips and my lips. Our breaths, the only two breaths left in the whole world. I didn't know that it could feel like this with a man, soft and sure and steady. All the wait was worth it to find out this way. Our hands are like magnets, pulling toward each other while we kiss and clasping so the electricity pulses through our bodies. When we're through, Santi walks me to the platform. My lips are trembling and my body is tired from craving him.

"I'll see you soon?" he says while my face disappears into his shoulder. The train is pulling into the station.

I nod and take a whiff of his body once more. It smells exactly the way I want it to.

He grabs my shoulders lightly. "Don't you go ghosting me again, Xiomara Sanchez."

I'm laughing and I'm crying and I don't know why. It's like he can see right through me and I like it, the way his eyes let the light get into me. I think my devil is dying. When I get home, I have butterflies in my stomach. Birds chirping in my ears even though it's the dead of night.

We let the kids out for Christmas break, and I have my meeting with Liza back in Manhattan, so I am running, rushing my kids out of the classroom and into the cars with their parents for the rest of December.

Grace is screaming at me in the parking lot, asking where I'm going, but all I can say is, "My train leaves at three!" before I'm in a taxicab speeding to the station. I make it right on time and tip the driver with the last of the ones I have in my pocket from Ellen's.

When I'm inside the train, watching the suburbs pass by, I feel Nena like a gust of wind next to me. Our whole lives flash before my eyes in between the trees and the cars of New Rochelle. There's the day with the Skip-Its and the bubble baths. There are the twin beds and the purple turtlenecks and the bolitas in our hair smacking the sides of our ears. There's the relaxer stinging our skulls, and of course the fights and the long nights and the talking and screaming at each other and the crying. There's the laughing, the sneaking out, and the learning. Every glorious moment I had with my precious sister, displayed like a painting on the canvas of this train car.

For a moment, I forget where I'm going and sit in the beauty of a locomotive, the way it's neither here nor there yet. The way I don't know what's coming next for me. The way it reminds me that nothing will last forever, even when it feels like my stop is a hundred light-years away.

I look around and am in awe now of the way that on this train I'm not Xiomara from the Heights or Xiomara with the dead sister, or the bad sex habit, or the devil inside her veins. I'm just Xiomara, an anonymous passenger zooming somewhere I can't quite say yet.

Acknowledgments

I couldn't have written this novel without Sabrina Taitz, my stunning agent and even sweeter friend. Now, as I type this, I can just hear her crunching her seaweed chips and cheering me on. Sabrina: When no one else saw me, you did. Thank you is not nearly impactful enough to say how grateful I truly am to you. Never lose your thunder. So smart. Ready to fly.

I'd also like to thank, from the deepest part of my heart, Nicole Counts, my extraordinary editor who I've been admiring from afar and now get to be in awe of up close. The first time I talked to Nicole, I hung up the phone and cried and wrote in my little diary that I wanted the WHOLE world to talk about this book the way that Nicole Counts does. She is fierce in her reading and in her nature. Nicole, this book would be nowhere without your careful eye, steady hand, and heart full of questions. Thank you. Here's to many more.

Thank you especially to my family: Guerreroville, Mom, Papi, Alexis, Luis, and my sweet Izzy. You guys are the center of absolutely everything for me. My biggest cheerleaders, my best friends in the world. I love you each more than you'll ever know, more than is ever possible to imagine. Your handprints are all over these pages. I hope you can see that, feel that. This book is yours, too.

I'd also be remiss not to mention my absolutely perfect grandmother, Abuelita Dolores, who helped me to fall in love with reading and life, as well as my cousins, every single one of them and especially the Reynosos, who grew up with me as second siblings and taught me that family really does make the best friends. I love you guys. I really do. So, so much.

Thank you to Valdair Lopes, who never pulled me back into bed at five a.m. when I so desperately needed to get to these pages. It's extraordinary to see you and a gift to be seen by you.

Thank you to Ellie Lynch, whose creative spirit and larger-than-life friendship gets me through every day—big and small. There's no me without you.

I'd also like to thank Allison Podolsky, who is my best musical-theater girly, high school honey, and forever friend. What a life we've had together. So much more dancing to do.

Thank you to Jennifer Rudolph Walsh, for pulling out the big astrology book in her office that day. There are some people who come into your life and change it forever, just by being themselves, just by reflecting who you might be able to become back to yourself. Jennifer is a person like that. The lessons I've learned, the love that I've felt knows no bounds. I'm lucky to be in your school for girls. Lucky to call you a godmother. Thank you for lighting the way.

I'd also like to thank Mark Anthony Green for the goooood laughs but especially for that one night at Crossroads Kitchen when I couldn't stop crying. You've inspired me so much as an artist and a friend. It's a pleasure to know you.

And of course: Thank you to Mara Brock Akil who gave me time and space at the Writers' Colony to find my voice. One-to-one change. It's what we always talk about.

Thank you to Jenifer Lewis, for taking a wild chance on me and teaching me that I can, actually, write a book. What a lucky woman I am to be in your world.

Phil Sun and Maya Rodrigo: Thank you for allowing me the space for the big questions and risk taking that have allowed me to become what I am becoming. Your support has opened so many doors for me, and I'll hold our time together so close in my heart, always.

There were so many people who worked on this book, and without whom it could never have been finished. The WME books team deserves my deepest gratitude. Thank you to Jay Mandel and Tracy Fisher for your constant and loud support. Thank you to Alicia Everett, Pat Polite, and Ty Anania: You each pushed this forward in such an essential way. And Nicole Weinroth, thank you for your excitement and energy. I am overjoyed to be on this team together. And DUH a big thank-you to Cashen Conroy, who is the mastermind behind it all. Cashen, you're an absolute star. Call on me for anything, always. Thank you. Truly.

And wow—my One World team. You put this book on your back to make it what it is today. What a seamless experience you have made this for me. Lulu Martinez and Tiffani Ren, thank you for your brilliant ideas and constant excitement for my color-coded emails. My brain feels good when we talk. Carla Bruce-Eddings and Rachel Parker: Thank you for all the work you put into *My Train Leaves at Three*, for indulging my Excel sheets, and for making me feel so supported, so held. And of course Oma Beharry, who keeps ALL of us in check and does so much, always. I can't wait to see your growth; the sky is the limit.

I'd also like to thank my production editor Andy Lefkowitz (I REALLY loved getting those notes in the margins from you!!!), my managing editor Rebecca Berlant, production manager Mark Maguire, designer Susan Turner, copy editor Mark McCauslin, and proofreaders Alissa Fitzgerald, Karina Jha, and Brianna Lopez.

Xiomara's story has the blood and bones of every woman I know inside of it. While I was writing this, I often thought of my late grandmothers Carmen and Marcela who I still have so many questions for, who I will continue to try to understand, who I will carry with me always. I also, and of course, thought of my uncle, Harold, who was taken from us too soon but who I feel is so alive here. I hope you can feel his heart beating beneath the pages.

And to you, whoever you are, reading this. What a privilege it is to know each other now that you've seen and read every fiber of my soul. There are loads of books in this world. You're part of me now that you've picked this one up and spent your time to read it.

About the Author

NATALIE GUERRERO is a Dominican and Puerto Rican writer based in Los Angeles. Her writing has been featured in publications such as *Electric Literature, Byline, Goop,* and *Blavity. My Train Leaves at Three* is her first novel.